All rights reserved.

Cover design © 2016 by Mayhem Cover Creations

No part of this book may be reproduced in any form or by any electronic or mechanical means, including information storage and retrieval systems, without written permission from the author, except for the use of brief quotations in a book review.

This book is a work of fiction. Names, characters, places, and incidents are either the product of the author's imagination or are used fictitiously, and any resemblance to actual persons, living or dead, events, or locales is entirely coincidental.

The following story contains mature themes, strong language and sexual situations. It is intended for mature readers.

All characters are 18+ years of age and non-blood related, and all sexual acts are consensual.

Table of Contents

Revenge	4
Chapter 1	6
Chapter 2	20
Chapter 3	27
Chapter 4	37
Chapter 5	45
Chapter 6	53
Chapter 7	62
Chapter 8	69
Chapter 9	77
Chapter 10	86
Chapter 11	101
Chapter 12	109
Chapter 13	116
Chapter 14	123
Chapter 15	137
Chapter 16	148
Chapter 17	157
Chapter 18	170
Chapter 19	177
Chapter 20	183
Chapter 21	189
Chapter 22	194
Chapter 23	199

Chapter 24 216
Chapter 25 224
Chapter 26 241
Chapter 27 247
Chapter 28 255
Chapter 29 261
Chapter 30 268
Chapter 31 272
Chapter 32 279
Epilogue 284

Revenge

By Lauren Landish

<u>Katrina</u>

Revenge never tasted so sweet...

The DeLaCoeur family destroyed mine, and ever since I was a little girl, I vowed I would have my revenge.

Now the time has come, and I've waited my whole life for this. The heir to the family fortune is first on my list. Jackson. It should be easy—he's just a billionaire playboy that's used to women falling at his knees. I'll play along, I'll seduce him, and I'll humiliate him. But the second his warm lips burn into my neck, I fear that I might wind up sleeping with the enemy...

<u>Jackson</u>

She pulled my c*ck out in front of the paparazzi... now it's war.

Katrina Grammercy is after me for a crime I didn't commit. She wants to ruin my reputation—make me pay for my father's sins.

But she doesn't know who she's f*cking with. In this game, I make the rules. She'll be just like the rest—one taste of me, and she's done.

She wants revenge?

I'll give her revenge, by owning her sweet, tight little ass.

**Revenge is a full-length romance with an HEA, no cheating, and no cliffhanger!

**Revenge is Book 1.
Retaliation, Book 2.
Retribution, Book 3.

Chapter 1
Kat

Red. He likes red. I chose this dress carefully, making sure to pick one that would be both classy and slutty at the same time. The fabric is skintight, and I can't wear anything underneath except for a G-string. I can't even wear a bra, and he'll notice for sure. Jackson always notices a woman's breasts. Mine aren't the biggest, but that's okay. He has a thing for nipples, and I've been told mine are perfect.

Next come the silk thigh highs. The dress has a slit that goes almost all the way up my right leg, revealing a lot of thigh. He'll notice the lace top, and the fact that I'm wearing something other than pantyhose will draw his attention. I put less care into selecting the heels I'll be wearing. We'll be in a car for most of what I have planned for him, so they're what I'd consider reasonable. They're just meant to draw attention to my calves, so they're only three inch heels. I like my calves. They're pure muscle, and extremely defined from all the training I do.

Now is the hard part, the wig. I don't want Jackson recognizing who I am at first, so securing my naturally brown hair underneath this platinum blonde wig is vital. I want this hair to look like it really belongs to me. It's why I spent nearly as much money on the wig as I did on the dress, and I've practiced multiple times with the spirit gum to make sure it all looks natural. My eyes... well, blue eyes go with blonde hair all the time, but the false eyelashes I'm wearing can partially hide my eye color for a while. A little bit of makeup will help soften my jawline. I've increased my food intake over the past few days, trying to add a little bit of body fat—at least enough that you can't see my jaw muscles flexing when I chew. I don't give a shit, since I like my body the way it is, but Jackson likes women with a little more meat on their bones. I'm glad at least I keep my hair short, not quite butch short, but it's still considered short for a woman. I don't have time to deal with that shit... I've got other issues to deal with besides worrying about my looks.

Okay. Dress, stockings, shoes by the door, hair... check. As for makeup, I'm going with sultry and dark eye makeup to help my eyes look larger, more doe-eyed. I made sure to spend extra time on my eyeliner, because when I make my big reveal, I want Jackson to know exactly who I am as he stares into my eyes. And I know he remembers my eyes. The lipstick I'm wearing matches my dress, and makes my lips look plump and pouty. Everything I'm wearing practically screams, 'Fuck me, Jackson DeLaCoeur!'.

I look at myself critically in the mirror. The woman staring back at me isn't Katrina Grammercy, the twenty-two-year-old orphan whose parents were ripped from her by a car bomb a decade ago. She isn't the Katrina Grammercy who did nothing but sob for weeks, living in a haze for months. That woman never heard the rumors, never had to learn that her best friend's father, Peter DeLaCoeur, had orchestrated the whole thing. I stare at my reflection, and I don't see any traces of the woman who swore vengeance on the DeLaCoeurs, the woman who no longer goes by Katrina, just Kat.

Instead, all I see is exactly what I want Jackson to see. He might have been my best friend ten years ago, but a lot can happen in ten years. The Jack DeLaCoeur I knew is gone. Jackson has followed in his criminal father's footsteps—partying, fucking, and ruining people's lives. While Jackson may not have had anything to do with my parents' death, this is the only way to put my plan in motion. Besides, I'm leaving him alive. That's better than what his father did to my parents.

Thinking about the bombing, the way the fireball rolled across the concrete ceiling and stained the parking garage by the convention center, singeing my hair even though I was fifty feet away, the smell of everything burning... knowing my parents were trapped inside, and I couldn't do anything but watch helplessly...

I shake my head. I can't let the blackness overtake me, not right now. I can't afford it. Before it sinks its eagle claws into my brain again, I go over to my dresser to retrieve a small plastic bottle. This isn't on any medical directory in the world, but this special concoction my herbalist connection makes for me works wonders. It's got GABA, a little THC extract, and some Chinese shit I can't even pronounce. Unscrewing the top of the bottle, I shake out four capsules. They look like rabbit food—little pellets of grass trimmings and yellow pollen sitting in my hand. I down them with a glass of water, then grimace. They taste like rabbit food, too. I lie down on my bed, the cheap springs creaking in complaint despite the fact I only weigh one hundred and twenty-five pounds. The bed's a piece of shit, but it's all the bed I need.

I made sure to leave myself enough time for this next part, and I close my eyes, starting my meditations.

There is no peace. Peace is a lie.

Freedom is a lie.

Happiness, love, and the future... are lies.

The rage is the truth. Rage gives me power.

Anger gives my power focus.

I have my target.

Rage... Power... Anger... Focus.

DeLaCoeurs... Vengeance is mine.

It takes me fifteen minutes exactly to run through my meditations until I'm calm and my pills kick in. I sit up and double-check my outfit, noting that everything's still in place. Good. My training is still strong. I am still strong.

I go to my dresser again and pick up my work phone. It's a cheap prepaid burner, and I make sure to switch out the SIM cards every four days on a rotating basis. I take a deep breath, then punch in the number to reach Domino. That's not his real name of course, but he lets me call him that. He understands my need for secrecy, as well as the meaning behind the nickname I've given him. Once I tip him over, the domino effect starts.

"Domino? Yeah... yeah, it's me, Mercy. You still want those pics of Jackson DeLaCoeur, right? Come on, Domino. You know once you break a scandal on the Big Easy's biggest playboy, you'll have a ton of website hits, and that's just the minimum. You know you can even sell some print copies if you work the angle right... Yeah, okay, I'm not gonna tell you how to do your fucking job, but I'll do mine. So you gonna be there, or not? If not, I can always call up Vicki at the Picayune. No? You know if you aren't there, I'm gonna come after you next... okay. That's right, Riverwalk, the event tonight. Don't sweat it, he'll be there. You'll get your money's worth and then some."

I hang up with Domino and place a second call, this time to Vicki. She's probably going to be there anyway, but it doesn't hurt to make sure that she's cued in. Domino's going to be expecting it anyway, and I'll let them jockey for the best position for the pics themselves. They're both vultures, but at least they're useful vultures.

I swap out the SIM card on my burner and slide it into my tiny clutch along with a few other essentials. I also make sure to grab a pair of sunglasses for my getaway. Putting on my shoes, I check myself one more time in the mirror, then nod. "I hope you're ready, Jackson. Because tonight... I start to get my vengeance."

* * *

Jackson

She's moaning, her caramel-kissed skin dotted with sweat in the muggy New Orleans afternoon heat, begging me to fuck her, fuck her harder... give it to her the way she needs it.

"Oh Jacky, oh God baby, you're going to make me... Jackkkkkyyy..."

Her pussy tightens around my cock, and she's not faking

it. I can tell that for sure. I've been pounding her like a machine for I don't know how many minutes, and she's barely coherent at this point. It's easier now to detect the syrupy accent of her native Acadian Creole, but I'm already bored with her. She might be beautiful, and she might be a student at Tulane, but this girl just isn't a good fuck. Besides, I hate being called Jacky. Jack—I guess that's okay, even though that's what I went by as a kid. Jackson's better. But never Jacky.

I speed up a little more, closing my eyes and letting my fantasies push me over the edge so I can come. All glove, of course. I wouldn't give her the gift of my come even if I believed her story about being on the pill. I can't take that chance.

She collapses on the bed next to her friend. The other girl's been passed out for a good ten minutes by my estimate—I played with her for a while, but she didn't have my stamina. They never do. I pull out and slide the condom off before taking it to the bathroom. I make sure to rinse it out in the sink before I flush it down the toilet. I'm not taking any risks. I don't need some gold digger saying I knocked her up or any stupid shit like that.

I splash some cool water on my face and look in the mirror. My last shave's still holding up, so I'm not looking too bad. I can probably get by with just rinsing off quickly before I need to get ready for the charity event. But not here. This bathroom fucking sucks.

I go back into the bedroom and see both of the girls sprawled out across the bed, completely passed out. Earlier I'd considered taking one of them with me to be my arm candy for tonight's event, but looking at them now... that's a hard nope. I grab the bed sheet from the floor and cover them up. When they wake up, the house staff will see to them and show them out.

I leave the spare bedroom, walking down the hallway toward my room when I hear a disgusted cough behind me. "For fuck's sake, *niichan*, can you at least put on a robe after you get done?"

I turn around and see my half-sister Andrea behind me. Her almond-shaped eyes betray her mother's Japanese heritage, although her eyes are the characteristic DeLaCoeur sapphire blue. "Why, Andi? It's not like you haven't seen it before." I smirk.

"So? That doesn't mean that I *want* to see it," she says crossly. Andrea hates it when I call her Andi. She wrinkles her nose. "Besides, it's not that big."

"Bullshit," I brag, looking down. "I know your exes, Andrea. And none of them have what I've got."

"What's that, an ego bigger than your dick?" she retorts. "Seriously Jackson, you can swing that meat around me all you want, but I'm not interested. Even if you weren't my half-brother, I would never be interested."

"Riiight," I reply, turning around to head for my room and giving her a nice view of my ass along the way. I'm not seriously interested in Andrea. Even if we weren't related, her personality really turns me off. We've butted heads for far too long. Still, it's fun to needle her every once in a while.

I shower in my own bathroom quickly before I start to get ready. Running my hand along my jaw and feeling the stubble there, I decide to shave a bit after all. A quick trim with my electric razor, some aftershave, and I'm good to go.

I go back out into my bedroom and start to get dressed. I throw on a pair of boxer briefs and decide on a moisture-wicking undershirt since the humidity here in New Orleans is no joke. After buttoning up a white dress shirt, I'm ready for my tux now. It's a Gucci with a shawl collar, but in a lighter fabric appropriate for the climate. I'm skipping a cummerbund today. I don't need that fussy bullshit. Plus, it's just more that some lucky girl will have to take off later tonight. I take the time to put on a silk bow tie though. That's definitely classier than some damn cummerbund.

I check my shoes and head out after slipping my billfold into my jacket pocket. I go downstairs and ring for Mike, my chauffeur. "Yo Mike, I'm ready."

"And the young ladies, sir?" Mike's from Boston, so there's a hint of Southie in his speech, but he's actually been trained in England. It sounds impressive, but what it really means is that he has all the stuffiness you'd expect from a driver born and bred in London. He's worked for my family since I was in elementary school though, so I don't know why he won't just unclench his asshole around me already. "Are they not coming with us?" he asks politely.

"Oh, they came all right, but they're not joining me this evening," I reply. "Back to the Watering Hole."

Mike frowns slightly, and I already know what he's going to say even before he opens his mouth. "Sir, I understand that you want some female... companionship for the evening, but do you really think it is wise to be picking up easy women from the Watering Hole? Think of your reputation, and that of your family's."

I glare at Mike. My eyes have a tendency to change color when I'm pissed, and right now I'm sure they're an icy blue instead of the sexy sapphire I'm known for. "That'll be enough on that from you, Mike. You work for my family, and your job is to drive me around, not tell me what's wise and what isn't. I'm going back to the Watering Hole, then you're going to drive me to the charity event, and that's all there is to it. If you have a fucking problem with that, you can talk to Pops or Nathan."

Mike presses his lips into a thin line, but he just nods before walking to the limo and opening the door for me. "And will Miss Andrea be joining you tonight, sir?" he asks dispassionately.

"She's taking a pass on this one," I inform him as I get in. He shuts the door, and I watch him through the nearly opaque windows as he gets into the driver's seat. I wait until he's inside the limo, and then I deliberately engage the divider. I don't want to talk to him, and I sure as fuck don't need him telling me what to do. I sit back, trying to cool off a little. My family's reputation? What the fuck does Mike know about my family's reputation? On the surface, I'm sure we look great. We go to events like the one tonight, handing out charitable donations and glad-handing every motherfucker with a cause plus the sob story to go along with it.

But that's just our public face. It's all just an act. My father, Peter DeLaCoeur, has another side, a side I don't like. It's a side that... I don't want to deal with it right now. I never want to deal with it, but especially not now while I'm trying to have some fun. "Fuck this," I say to myself. It's a party, and what's a party without the party favors?

I reach over to the little cubbyhole built into the wall of the limo, and pop the cover, taking out the contents within. Pops has his own favorites, specifically Colombian in nature, and I've had to be careful not to mix his shit with what I like. No way am I getting hooked on fucking coke.

But Special K and X? Ground up and sucked through a Benjamin into the nose, it'll brighten up any day. Best of all, it doesn't create physical dependency. I want it, but I don't *need* it. It's a small difference, but one that's important to me.

I get four bumps prepped, but I'm saving them for when I pick up some honeys. I leave them on the black glass topper I prefer for party time as Mike pulls around to the Watering Hole. It's not an actual business, it's just what we call this place near UNO where girls who are looking to party all hang out. Some of the girls are pros, or close enough to it. But a lot of them are just sluts, college girls, or girls from the city looking to walk on the wild side a bit.

The car stops and I get out. The sun's just starting to go down in the distance, but I don't have time to admire it even though this is my favorite time of day in New Orleans. There's still enough light to see the girls, and I catch sight of a new face that has my jaw on the floor. She's rocking shorter heels than what I'm used to seeing on the girls out here, but she looks like she's close to my height in them. Maybe even level with my height, and I'm six-foot-two. And her body... holy damn. Looking at that ass... my cock's twitching already, and I don't even know her name.

She's got a hot body, but a heavenly face. It gives her that sort of fallen angel look I've always had a thing for. She has long hair, but what really catches my eye is the color. It's the same shade as mine, a blonde color that's so light it's nearly white. It really makes her stand out from the typical brunettes I see here in New Orleans and gives her an almost exotic look.

"Well hello," I say as I approach. Some other girls, regulars that I've partied with before come over too, but I only have eyes for the new girl. I'm trying hard not to adjust my cock in my pants already. Jesus, even her eyes are sexy. They're a pale light blue, unlike any other eyes I've ever seen before, except for one pair a decade ago. "I'm Jackson."

"I'm Kitty," the girl says, giving me a naughty smile. "Nice car," she says admiringly.

"It is," I reply confidently. "Think you might want to take a ride, join me for a party?"

Kitty looks over the limo, giving me a measured look, then nods. "Okay, big boy. My, are you into weightlifting or something? You're built like a comic book character. Sure your name isn't Bruce Wayne?"

"Nope, just Jackson," I reply, smiling. Chick knows her comic books, or at least her comic book movies. I can get with that. "How much?"

"I'm just looking for a good time," Kitty says. "If you're feeling generous though, I bet some of these other girls would love to join us. What sort of party is it, anyway?"

"Black tie. You're dressed perfectly for it," I say as I look over the other choices. "Okay, you... you... and you."

The five of us get into the limo, and Mike pulls away. I pull out some cash and lay it on the seat beside me. All the girls except for Kitty are all over it immediately. Whatever... at least I know Kitty meant it when she said she was just looking for a good time.

She's practically eye fucking me as she leans back on the side seat. She turns a little, and it really showcases both her long legs and her tits. Damn do they look delicious. "So, Jack... did you say a black tie party? And is there going to be any fun at this party?" I know what she's getting at, and I grin. So maybe she doesn't want money, but she's definitely looking to score.

"We can have some fun beforehand, a little... preview if you like," I say, gesturing to the black glass. "A little K-X mix if you're into that."

"I think I'll wait a little bit. I know K can hit quick," she says as she slides over next to me. Her hand's resting on my thigh, and she's pushing that hard body of hers against my arm. My cock's already fully hard for her. I can see the other girls getting mad as they scowl, but there's plenty of me to go around. Before I can say something though, Kitty touches my face, and I swear it sends a jolt of electricity straight to my cock as I stare into her eyes. "Hey, lover... I'm over here," she says.

"Well, if he's gonna fuck her, at least we can have some party favors," one of the other girls says scornfully. She reaches for the black mirror, but Kitty takes her finger off my face, and suddenly I'm free of her spell. My full attention is on the other three girls, and I'm pissed off.

"Stop. Mike! Pull over!"

Mike stops the car, and like I said, I'm pissed, staring at these wastes of my fucking time. "Take the money and get out," I growl, throwing the cash at them. "Easy dough, right?"

The girls grumble, but they've partied with me before,

and they know I'm not playing around. They take the money and get out, and I notice we're near the Superdome. Mike knows that after I stop by the Watering Hole, I always need a little time to decide what comes next.

The last one slams the door in a huff, but I don't give a fuck. Kitty's already straddling my lap. Her dress rides up as she begins massaging my shoulders and chest while she kisses my neck. I don't know what's so different about her, but my body's on fire. I've never been this hot before so quickly. She's got me trembling, ready to pop already, and as she grinds on my lap, I can't help the whimpers coming out of my mouth.

"Shh baby, we're going to have a lot of fun," she reassures me as she shoots me that fallen angel's smile again. She reaches the waistband of my pants and cocks her head when she sees I'm wearing suspenders. Well no shit, I'm wearing a tux, and you don't wear a belt with a tux. "I like it. Very fucking sexy," she says as she gives me a seductive smile.

"You're fucking sexy," I reply, reaching down to stroke her hair. I'm only dimly aware of Mike saying something up front, but whatever it is, it doesn't matter. All that matters is this sex goddess in front of me and the way her fingers are unzipping my pants.

"Mmm, you're so big," she whispers. I'm trembling again as she wraps her fingers around my cock and pulls it out. I'm rock hard, and Kitty licks her lips as she leans in closer... closer...

Suddenly, she pulls back as she jabs me in the chest below my right pec, and I find myself paralyzed. I can only watch as she opens the door to a crowd of paparazzi. My cock's still hanging out for the whole world to see, and countless flashes are going off. I can hear gasps of surprise, but also mocking laughter as Kitty sits back. She gives me an evil grin as she pulls what I'm just now realizing is a wig off her head. "Well, well, Jackson... nice to see you again," she says, but the tone of her voice indicates otherwise.

I blink as my body slowly regains the ability to move, and the face in front of me drops into focus. The blue eyes that I haven't seen in ten years, the angular jawline, and hair so dark it's almost black, but it's shorter than it was before... I can't believe it, but it's true.

"Katrina?" I whisper, which is the most I seem to be able to do.

"It's Kat," she says as she pulls some sunglasses out of her tiny purse. She puts them on before getting out of the limo, leaving the blonde wig behind. "And you just got scratched. That's for my parents. Have fun, Jackson."

Chapter 2
Jackson

"Are you fucking kidding me?" Pops asks as he slams the tablet he's holding down onto the desk. He probably just broke the fucking thing, but I don't think anyone really cares right now.

"Why do you care? It's not like I had your nose candy out," I shoot back. He's really pissing me off. Seriously, I just went through the worst night of my life. It was only because of Mike's fast reflexes that I wasn't arrested. Mike got me out of there after Katrina...no, after Kat got out of the limo. Once he realized something was up, he hauled ass for the Pontchartrain Expressway. By the time the photos went to print and anyone looking at the drugs in the photo instead of my cock could even ask questions, the limo had been taken care of. At this point, I doubt even the FBI could find a damn thing.

"Coke, K-X, whatever it was...it doesn't matter, Jackson! The pictures are all over the Internet, and you even made the goddamn Picayune, for fuck's sake!" He makes a sound of disgust.

Yeah, I know all of that. In fact, I've already gotten five texts from as far away as London about the pics. At least the ones in the print newspapers were censored with a black box over my dick. The pics available online show everything, and of course everyone's focusing on the ones taken from angles that make me look damn near dinky-dicked.

"No shit, Pops. By the way, Ellie in London says hi."

What Ellie actually said was *I thought the cucumber in the pants thing was just in Spinal Tap*, but I knew what she was getting at. Pops, however, doesn't think any of this is funny.

"You want to make jokes at a time like this, you little shit?" he asks as he rounds the desk to get in my face. I'm ready and on my feet in an instant. He might have a temper, and he's got a violent streak that makes me look like fucking Gandhi in comparison, but I'm no slouch either. I've got an inch on him, a lot less body fat, and twenty-eight years less mileage on my body. Pops knows this, and while his hands are clenched into fists so tight that I can see his knuckles turning white, he manages to hold himself back. I take a step back before either of us do something stupid.

I sit back down. "Okay Pops, you're right. Just... fuck, that was Katrina. Or Kat, as she's calling herself now. What the fuck did she mean when she said that was for her parents? What the hell do we have to do with Katrina Grammercy's parents?"

Pops shakes his head, and I know he's not going to answer me. I learned a long time ago that some things were off-limits. The problem is, I need to know. When it comes to his dealings with crooked cops, or the groups that run the Ninth Ward, or any of his other criminal enterprises, he's right. I shouldn't be asking questions, and I shouldn't concern myself with any of it. But this is Katrina... she was my best friend when we were kids. And less than twelve hours ago, she gave me half a handjob right before setting me up for global humiliation. No, this time, I need to know.

"Pops...Dad, I need to know this time."

Pops shakes his head again and acts like he barely heard

me. "Mike's already been informed, but you're not allowed to use the limo anymore. I can't have him associated with your bullshit any longer. These are matters best left to others, Jackson. I'll let you handle them someday when you're ready, if you ever are. In the meantime, I need you to go tell your mother that I need to discuss something with her after I speak with Nathan. Tell her to come see me here in my office."

Nathan. I can't help but shiver at the mere mention of that cold bastard's name. Officially, he's our head of family security. Unofficially, Nathan Black is my dad's enforcer, or worse. I don't know for sure, but I don't think I want to know for sure. Nathan has this perpetual look of surprise on his face due to a long scar that winds up and across his left eye, pulling it up slightly. On anyone else, it'd be amusing, but there's nothing amusing about him.

"Fine," I say and step out into the hallway. Nathan's already waiting. In the dark linen suit he's wearing, he looks like an undertaker coming to collect his next body. He greets me with a slight nod as I come out of Pops' office, but his expression is as unreadable as ever.

"Mr. Jackson," Nathan says in that quiet, icy voice of his. Jesus, if the Grim Reaper needs a voice, I know who he can call.

"Nathan. Pops wants to speak with you," I respond.

Nathan's fifty years old, but he could pass for forty, or maybe even younger. Up close it's easy to see the fine network of crow's feet around his eyes, but it's also easy to see how his eyes are completely flat, devoid of any emotion. They're a green shade the color of swamps, and they remind me of gators. Maybe it's because Nathan's clearly a predator, just like them.

"Very good. Later, perhaps we can speak on how to avoid further... incidents?" he says.

"Perhaps," I reply, trying not to stammer. Nathan scares the shit outta me, plain and simple. I've got at least thirty pounds of lean muscle on the man, but I have a feeling that if he wanted to, he could drop me without even blinking. "I need to get going."

Nathan nods and goes into Pops' office, closing the door behind him. I know I should run along, even if the request to fetch Mom is bullshit. I shouldn't be hanging around. But... it's Katrina, and the look in Pops' eyes...

I know this is stupid, but I can't help myself. It's been years since I've done this, but I should be able to eavesdrop through the lock on the door. The mansion is an old antebellum plantation house, and it took a small fucking fortune to repair the place after Hurricane Katrina. *No relation to Kat*, I think to myself. Still, the interior doors are mostly original, and this one happens to date from the original Civil War days. I press my ear against the office door.

"Mr. DeLaCoeur, how can I assist you today?" That's Nathan, professional as always.

"That bitch...the one who set up Jackson. I want her taken care of."

"Sir, no offense, but haven't we done enough to this girl? You know, ten years ago?"

"I don't give a fuck!" Pops hollers, slamming his hands on what sounds like his desk. "That bitch dropped a lot of trouble in our laps, Nathan. I want her found and eliminated, got me?"

There's a long silence on the other side of the door, and I can imagine Nathan coldly processing my father's words. Before he can answer, I hear someone coming down the hallway and I beat a hasty retreat, going to look for Mom. As I do, my head whirls. Sure, I've always known that Pops is involved in some bad business, even if I don't like to think about it. Seriously, who the hell has the police chief at his house one night, and then well-known gangsters there the next, unless he's also involved in some shit?

But I never knew for sure how much shit he's been involved with. Of course, I've lied to myself over the years. Denial is a powerful drug. And I guess maybe my coping mechanisms weren't the best, what with the parties and the sluts, and the drugs and the alcohol... but at least I've managed to keep my own hands clean.

Now I know for sure about my father, and I can't get it out of my head. What the fuck do I do? On one hand, Kat made me look like some high school dweeb who was whacking off in the back of a rented limo or paying some hooker to lose his virginity. But she was angry, and it wasn't the sort of anger I've seen before. It wasn't hot anger—it was the cold, obsessive type. Whatever she thinks my family did...she's been angry for a very long time. And it's the sort of anger that makes me think there's a genuine reason for her to be pissed off.

And then there's the way she made me feel. What the hell was that? A few touches, a few kisses, and I was ready to pop. Where the hell did she learn that? Was it because my body knew it was Katrina even if my brain didn't recognize her at first? Or does she know something that most women don't? I mean, I'd just busted a nut less than two hours before, and she had me trembling on the edge in minutes. I didn't even touch her skin other than feeling those lips on my neck...

I look down, realizing that I'm sporting wood again, and adjust myself. Not what I need. What I need to be doing is looking for Mom. I find her in her bedroom, looking at herself in the mirror. She and Pops have separate rooms now. Great, just great. Mirror, mirror, on the wall, who's the craziest one of all?

"Hey, Mom?"

"Jackson, do you think I'm starting to sag around my neckline?" Mom asks as a way of greeting. Well, no Mom, I think you've got more plastic in you than your average Barbie doll, and that you can't even squint because you've more or less killed off your eye muscles with Botox. In fact, you barely look like a woman anymore.

Instead of saying that though, I ignore her question. She doesn't want my answer anyway. "Pops was saying he'd like to talk with you in a few. He's talking with Nathan now."

"Yay," Mom says sarcastically, her nose twitching. I'm surprised it can still do that. The amount of putty and plastic in there is probably what you'd see with repairing a minor fender bender on a car. "What's he want now, to discuss your little faux pas last night?"

So she's been sober enough to pick up the news. "Fuck all if I know. He just said to get you," I say with a shrug.

Mom's eyes glance over to me, and I can see that she doesn't have them in. Or more precisely, she doesn't have in her colored contacts that she normally wears, the ones that give her the DeLaCoeur blue. Instead, I can see her normal muddy hazel eyes, and to be honest, it's refreshing. Hey Mom, nice to fucking see you for once. How long has it been? "You don't take that tone with me, Jackson Garfield DeLaCoeur. I am your mother," she says coldly.

"As much as you wish you weren't," I snap back, pushed to the limit. Seriously, when you grow up listening to your mother bitch at least once a week how giving birth to you ruined her figure, you kinda feel unwanted, you know? "I mean, I'm sorry I made your tits sag, but they're holding up... reasonably well. At least they stick out past your stomach."

Okay, so I'm being a dick with the backhanded compliment, but she deserves it. Mom didn't even say anything to me on my last birthday. Probably because my birthday always reminds her that no matter how much Hennessy she sucks down, or no matter how much work she has done...fifty's just around the corner.

At the mention of her stomach, Mom touches her abdomen, checking that she's still flat there. I give her a little smirk. "I'll go see what Andrea's up to. You should go check on Pops soon, he might be wondering where you are." I leave without waiting for her to reply.

Instead of finding Andrea though, I head back to my room, my head still trying to make sense of the look in Pops' eyes, and what he said to Nathan. What the hell am I supposed to do?

Chapter 3
Kat

Success! Oh, it was fucking sweet, too! The look on his face, the flash of the bulbs... and best of all, not a single soul knew who I was.

Don't get cocky, Katrina. Your work is just beginning.

I nod at the words from long ago and take off my dress. I strip everything off before sticking it all into a plastic bag for later disposal. It's going to suck throwing a thousand-dollar outfit into an incinerator, especially since that's more than I make in a month sometimes, but it's necessary. Peter DeLaCoeur's going to send his men after me, I know it. I can ghost, but only if I leave as few clues behind as I can.

I go back over to my dresser and open it up, grabbing my favorite black *gi* pants, and the sports bra I prefer for exercise. I get dressed quickly, then turn and walk across the big, empty space of this old warehouse until I reach the post in the middle of the floor. In exchange for teaching kids' martial arts classes twice a week, the owner of the boxing gym downstairs lets me crash here. Right now I'm buzzing on adrenaline, and I need to refocus.

The post is steel, but I've wrapped it in old, bald tires that provide just enough padding for me to use it as my own personal training dummy. My sparring gloves are an old castoff pair I rescued from the garbage downstairs, but they serve their purpose well enough, which is to prevent scrapes on my hands. I take them off their hook, and pull them on, sneering at the tires. Except they aren't tires any longer. They're Peter DeLaCoeur's fat, piggish face.

My first punch lands hard, but it jars my body. The first punch always has that effect. I can punch far above my weight, but my first punch always knocks me a little off balance. Still, it doesn't take long for my body to adjust. It's trained to compensate for the shocks, turning them into energy I roll with and use to power the next strike. Kicks come next, then knees, and elbows...this is just a light workout for me. I can't practice my deadlier techniques on this simple training dummy, but it's a good way to relieve some of my stress.

With a scream, I throw an overhand elbow that would dislocate a man's jaw before falling to the floor, covered in sweat and gasping for breath. That's good enough for tonight. I'll get a real workout in tomorrow.

I peel off the gloves, hanging them up on their hook again and go over to the mat on the far side of the room. I've removed the lights, and darkness reigns. By pure muscle memory, I find the lighter and light a single tea candle, setting it in front of me and assuming the *seiza* kneeling position that I learned long ago. I send my mind into the flickering light of the candle, and what comes up are my memories.

"You are filled with anger," Virginia says, two days after I've come to her home. It's the third foster home I've been placed with, the other two having sent me back after what the social workers called 'inappropriate behavior'.

"No shit, lady," I snap back at her, twisting my hair around my finger. "You'd be too if you got treated like last week's Big Mac."

"Perhaps I would," Virginia says. She's lean, and according to the file the social worker showed me before she dropped me off at the house, she's former military. She looks it too, with muscles outlined against her chocolate-brown skin, and eyes that look like they've seen some shit. "But I wouldn't be helping those people who treat me that way by acting like an inconsiderate baby."

"Excuse me, bitch?" I snap, sitting up. "I ain't no goddamn baby."

"First of all, it's 'I am not a baby'. Second of all, in this house, you will not *curse me, nor any other person who is my guest. What you do outside I cannot control, but you will show respect to me and my house."*

"Or else what? You send me back to the orphanage? Return to sender, address unknown?"

Virginia gives me a little smile, which pisses me off for some reason. "Well, you can't be all bad, you at least have some knowledge of Elvis. As for what will happen... no, I will not send you back, for two reasons. First off, because I don't fail, and sending you back means that I fail. But more importantly, because I won't let you fail, and sending you back will guarantee you that you will end up a failure in life. You're not going to get another foster home, not with three strikes against you. Even if you are a pretty little white girl, the only place you'll end up is some pervert's house. And while I may not live in the best home in New Orleans, that's by choice, and you will not fail on my watch."

"I ain't no failure!" I scream, getting to my feet. "You take that back!"

"Make me," Virginia says softly, shifting her right foot back. "If you can."

I charge her, my right hand already cocking back in a punch that comes from the depths of my rage, but instead of hitting her, I'm redirected.

She sends me spinning through the air and crashing to the hardwood floor of the dining room. Virginia keeps a hold of my wrist and twists, and I howl, tears of anger and pain already flowing as she turns me over onto my stomach. She wrenches my hand around and up until I feel my little finger touching between my shoulder blades and her knee on my spine near my waist.

"Your anger makes you strong, Katrina. But you must learn to control it. Now tell me, before I have reason to dislocate your shoulder, why are you so angry?"

I cry, trying to look up to see her, but I can't, no matter how hard I kick or fight. Finally, I howl, letting the truth out. "My parents! They got blowed up!"

Virginia eases off her arm lock slightly but keeps a strong grip on my wrist. "Tell me what happened."

I close my eyes and struggle against the memories, but they come flooding out anyway, carrying me away. "Mama and Papa, we were at the Fair Grounds. We'd gone for the horse show... I'd begged them to take me after that movie, and after the hurricane. Mama said that she'd dropped her phone, and I told her I'd go get it. I run back and see it on the ground near the door to the elevator, and turn around. The car... the car blew up! The fire... it's so hot... MAMA! PAPA! DON'T LEAVE ME!"

I'm sobbing, and Virginia releases my arm to pull me up into an embrace. She lets me sob and scream my horror, anger, and everything into her chest. When the tears finally stop, Virginia lifts me to my knees and looks into my eyes. "This is very, very important, Katrina. What do you want to do with this rage?"

I sniff and wipe at my nose, looking into Virginia's sand-colored eyes. "I want to kill whoever killed Mama and Papa."

I know I shouldn't say it. The social workers tell me that it's wrong to feel this way, that I'm supposed to live and let live like Pastor Gibb who comes by the orphanage says we should do...but I'm no Jesus. I want something darker.

But Virginia doesn't flinch, and instead she nods, brushing a lock of hair out of my eyes. "Good. You're being honest, which is a good thing. Then I make you a promise. Your training will not be easy. You may not survive your vengeance. But I swear to you, as someone who's been there... you will not fail."

I open my eyes to see the candle's burned itself out. I smile, feeling refreshed. Using meditation to supplement sleep wasn't something that Virginia taught me, but I can't deny that I learned a lot from her. She was the first in a long line of instructors, of teachers who gave me the skills that have finally brought me to this point.

I shift positions, rolling onto my back because I know my feet are going to be asleep still after kneeling for what's most likely been an hour or more. As blood flow slowly returns to my toes, I feel a pain that gradually subsides into the familiar pins and needles sensation that's always a part of this process. My feet are still tingling when I hear the door to my loft unlock. I sit up immediately—only a few people have a key to my place, but still I'm wary. It pays to be careful, and pays more to be paranoid.

The door opens, and the soft lighting above my door shows me it's Darcy. She's another one of my mentors, but more importantly, she's my best friend. She's thirty-two years old, but Virginia introduced us six years ago, on my sixteenth birthday. Meeting Darcy was my birthday gift from Virginia, and in the long run has been the best gift I've ever gotten. "Darce, I'm over here."

"Damn girl, I know you want to cut down on your electricity bill, but you could run this entire setup right now with two nine-volts and a hamster wheel," Darcy says, making her way through the dim space. "What, short on money again?"

"You know that's not the problem," I tell her, although there have been times in the past when I barely had two dimes to rub together and another payday nowhere in sight. "The skills you taught me provide better than that."

An anarchic, idealistic hacktivist, it took Darcy a long time to come around to my point of view on things, and agreeing to teach me more than the basics of computer science. Not that my education was ever traditional, but nowadays, under the hacker handle Coup De Grace, I'm able to earn enough to put food in my stomach and keep the lights on.

"Yeah, of course I know," Darcy says, her boots clomping on the floor. She and I share somewhat similar viewpoints on fashion, and that's one of the things we bonded over first. Well, that and a hatred of all things Microsloth. "Jeff saw the pics a half hour ago. I dropped Henry off with his grandmother and hightailed it over here, telling her a client had a computer issue. She doesn't quite understand my work, so it's cool like that."

"You didn't need to rush over here. I'm fine," I say, getting to my feet. My little toes are still tingling, but it's not too bad. "Have you seen them?"

"Sho'nuff. Didn't think he'd be so... short. Thick, but short." She holds the tips of her index fingers close together, indicating his length.

I laugh and get up. I know she's talking shit because she

knows my hatred of the family. He damn sure wasn't *short*. "Actually, he's bigger than the average man. I'd say a solid eight or nine, although I didn't have my ruler with me. I'm guessing the jacket hid some, and the angle of the photo hid some more. They get any of me?"

"They got your body and hair, but the photos released so far don't show your face. Don't matter, though, since you're off-grid so much. But from what I did see...you were lookin' good, girl."

Darcy's comment about me being off-grid is true. Katrina Grammercy has no driver's license, no photo IDs, no voter registration card, not even a library card. Everything is handled through 'Net identities and anonymous numbered accounts, or face to face with no paper trail. Cuts down on my income... but money isn't what I need. And it's definitely not what motivates me.

"Well, regardless, you and I both know that Peter DeLaCoeur's going to be coming for me. I just need enough time to take him the rest of the way down," I say.

"And your friend? I know he's a womanizing asshole, Kat, but he was your best friend when you were kids. You take Papa DLC down, you take down Jacky-boy, too."

I sigh and shake my head. It surprised me, but it actually hurt when I saw the look in Jackson's eyes. Once he realized who I was, there was a distinct look of betrayal I saw before I got out of the car. "You know there's no other way, Darce. I can't attack the DeLaCoeurs head on. Hell, I can't even hack their systems. Peter runs his business the old-fashioned way, with a lot of offline backups, and he only keeps paper trails on the stuff that's legit. From what I can tell, his memory's the only thing that keeps track of his illegal dealings. I need to pull the king out of his fortress, or else I'm dead before I get anywhere near him."

"You could be dead either way," Darcy reminds me. "And that, to me at least, is a greater loss than not getting your revenge."

This is one of the few areas where we still disagree, but we're at peace with the situation. By that I mean I'm at peace with Darcy continually trying to get me to have a more positive outlook on life, and she's at peace with wasting her time trying to achieve that. "Not revenge, Darce. Vengeance. There's a difference," I say.

"So you've told me for the past six years. But you know I disagree."

We walk toward my sitting area, if you can call it that. My sitting area is mostly two old, patched-up wooden chairs from the boxing gym. The accompanying "table" is nothing more than a board of plywood sitting on top of two old computer towers. Since Darcy's here, I turn on the light, which is a solar-powered LED lantern that recharges during the day from the small amount of sunlight that comes in through the only window that isn't boarded up in the warehouse. "Darcy, if you really disagreed with me that much, you'd tell Jeff. If he busted a hacker like me, he'd get a promotion for sure. At the very least, it'd get him off patrols and a detective's shield."

"And betray my best friend?" Darcy asks, shaking her head. "No honey, me and Jeff, we got ourselves an understanding. He don't ask about what I do besides put together custom computers for people, and I've backed off my online stuff for the most part. He helps me sometimes too though, when our purposes align."

I chuckle. "Backed off? Since Henry's been born, I barely see you on the boards anymore. Let alone see your traces around the systems."

Darcy smirks and shrugs. "Ah, it's all good. I keep up-to-date, and besides, I make more money building kits for Tulane kids than I ever did trying to change the world one server at a time. And you know, if you really need my help, well, BlakDhal1A can always make a comeback."

"You still worry about me though," I say with a smile. "Why?"

"You know why, Kat. I already buried my family one time, when Katrina came through. I don't wanna bury you, too."

"If by setting one's heart right every morning and evening, one is able to live as though his body were already dead, he gains freedom in the Way," I quote to Darcy, smiling softly. "The *Hagakure.*"

"I hate that fucking book," she counters, then sighs. "All right Kitty-Kat, you my sister. You wanna run headlong to your doom... I'll be there to make sure you at least get a proper funeral. We'll have jazz and everything."

I stand up, and Darcy follows. We hug at the door, and I give Darcy a bit of a smile. "Don't sweat it, Darce. Give my regards to Jeff and Henry. Someday I'd like to meet them in person."

"I'd like that, too. Good night, Kat."

"Goodnight, Darcy."

Chapter 4
Jackson

I find Nathan in his workshop, where he's patiently cleaning each spring and screw of his Colt. While the military may have shifted to the Beretta 9mm, Nathan's old school, and shoots American, using the Colt 1911 as his preferred carry piece. Until today, I was able to lie enough to myself that the chromed cannon was used only for practice and defense. Dangling from the coat rack next to his workbench is a single hanger that has both his suit jacket and dress shirt. There's not a single wrinkle or crease in the whole works, and I can also make out that his tie has been draped around the hanger with equal care. He's sitting on a barstool in front of a drafting table in just his suit pants and a wife beater undershirt, intensely focused on his weaponry.

"Hello, Nathan." His workshop is an odd comparison in contrasts. Along one wall is his gun cabinet—containing not only pistols, but larger guns and weapons. No surprise there, since you'd expect that from someone who works in private security. But across the room is a wooden rack that's devoted entirely to tea. The rack is five feet wide by two feet tall, and the entire thing is filled with canisters of loose leaf teas plus an electric hot water dispenser. I didn't even know they made that many different types of tea, and he's got them all organized by type, flavor, and country of origin. In the corner next to the tea area is his fish tank, which contains a dozen different tropical fish all swimming peacefully. I guess it's great he has hobbies beyond being a scary motherfucker, but it's just... weird, I guess.

"Hello, Mr. Jackson. Is there something I can do for you?" Nathan takes a small toothbrush from a cleaning kit and begins scrubbing the trigger area of the pistol. Periodically he pauses to dip the brush into a small bowl with some nastyass smelling solvent before resuming brushing away.

"I came to talk with you about the errand Pops is sending you on. I trust we can keep this conversation between us?"

It's a risk, but one I have to take. Nathan's always been loyal to Pops, and I know that even approaching the man I could be risking a lot of anger. But this is Katrina... I can't sit back this time.

Nathan, however, scrubs at his trigger assembly a little bit longer, saying nothing before setting the whole thing down. "What did you hear?" he says coolly.

"That he wants Katrina Grammercy... dealt with. And something about ten years ago. What the hell does that mean?"

Nathan shakes his head, refusing to answer. Instead, he picks up the barrel of his pistol and something that looks like a round, giant Q-tip. I think it's called a bore swab? Anyway, he starts using it to wipe out the barrel a few times before he responds. "He did ask me to deal with Katrina. Do you have an issue with that?"

I blink in surprise. I wasn't expecting him to answer me, let alone admit to anything. "You're goddamned right I have an issue with it, Nathan! I mean, I've assumed for a while you had... skills, but to use them just because someone made me look like an ass?"

"Actually, she made you look like a dick," Nathan jokes softly, and I stop. I've known Nathan for most of my life, and I think this is the first time I've ever heard him make a joke. I didn't know the man even had a sense of humor. I just assumed it had been shot off in the same war where he'd gotten that wicked-looking scar.

"I... Damn, Nathan, I didn't know you could make jokes. Not a bad one at that," I say with a small laugh. "But seriously, though, it's just some pictures on the Internet. That's no reason to have a young woman... oh fuck it, let's talk like men. It's no reason to have someone killed!"

Nathan goes still for a moment, and I worry that I've crossed a line or something. He pulls the bore swab out of the barrel of the gun, setting everything aside before turning to face me. "And what would you know about good reasons to kill someone, hmm? Before I started working for Peter DeLaCoeur, I was in the Special Forces. I've killed people for a lot less," he says softly.

"That was in the military. It's different."

"Is it? Jackson, when I was at Campbell, we were sent to Somalia right after the end of the first Gulf War. This would have been right around the time you were getting your first teeth. It's not on the official list of deployments, but we were sent up to try and pacify a country that was embroiled in a civil war that's still going on today. The 75th Rangers might get the glory and the blame for that Charlie Foxtrot, but we were there, too." He pauses, and shakes his head before continuing.

"The problem was that we couldn't find anyone worth turning the country over to. Each warlord was just as depraved and morally bankrupt as the next. It wasn't even a matter of having to choose between the lesser of two evils, it was more like deciding by randomly tossing a dart at a list of names. I saw things... I *did* things that made human life very, very cheap. I saw plenty of people killed, and for a lot less than some embarrassing photos."

"It still isn't right, Nathan. Whatever happened twenty years ago... that was then, this is now. And what the hell's this about Katrina's parents?"

Nathan starts reassembling his pistol, slowly making sure each piece is perfectly aligned before he makes tiny adjustments with a miniature screwdriver set. "Samuel and Theresa Grammercy were killed when their car exploded in a parking garage near the Fair Grounds ten years ago. Katrina survived because she was fifty feet away, partially shielded by a concrete pillar that protected her from the worst of the bomb blast."

"A bomb ordered by my father," I say bluntly. "You can say it; I want the truth."

"It may have been ordered by Peter, yes," Nathan says quietly. "It may very well have been."

"And is it possible that maybe you were involved in planting that bomb?" I ask. Nathan slides the barrel of his Colt back into the sliding upper part and checks the action.

"If you're asking me if I have experience with explosives, the answer is yes. Special Forces trained me in those and a lot more. But I didn't kill Samuel and Theresa. I didn't really like Samuel, but he was a family man, and someone who was doing a little bit of good in this town. I certainly would not have blown them up in front of their daughter. Besides, weren't you two close back then?"

"We were good friends," I admit. "I met her when I was six, I think? We were in the same class through most of elementary school."

"Did you have feelings for her? She was blossoming into a young woman right about the time her parents died, and you were... well, if my memory is correct, that was about the time you started showing an interest in women."

It's my turn to remain silent as I think back on the past. Had I been interested in Katrina? I remember thinking she was cool, and not yucky like I thought most girls were back then. And she was really cute, in a way that... oh, fuck this, I can't tell Nathan all this. I can't even be honest with myself. "She and I... she was a special friend, which makes what happened in the limo not just embarrassing, but painful, Nathan. Regardless, I don't want her killed over it. It's not right, dammit!"

Nathan finishes putting his Colt back together and jacks the slide, checking the action. It slides back with a deadly hiss. Everything is perfectly clean and steely efficient before it catches in the open position. "You keep saying that word, 'right'. Tell me again, Jackson. What do you know about right and wrong?"

I square my shoulders and look Nathan in the eye. I don't know where I'm getting the guts for this, but I suspect it has something to do with Katrina. "I know enough to say that's it's wrong to order a young woman to her death over some embarrassing pictures. Especially when she might have a valid reason to hate your guts."

Nathan flicks his wrist, and the slide on his pistol snaps back. He checks the sights quickly before setting his Colt down on the table and giving me... a smile? "Come, have some tea with me. I just acquired some charcoal-roasted Taiwanese Li Shan oolong that was grown on the southern slopes of Mount Ali. We can discuss your sudden interest in ethics as the tea steeps."

I'm not a huge fan of tea, not even sweet tea, despite living in the South. Whatever fancyass tea Nathan's talking about is sure to be wasted on me, but fuck it, if it helps, it helps. I cross the workshop with him and take a seat while he draws water from the expensive-looking water heater and pours it into a pot. "The key to making good tea is to make sure you don't burn it," Nathan explains. "That's where most people mess it up. Making tea isn't like making soup; you don't need to boil it. The tannins and flavonoids in tea are much more fragile than the ones in coffee even. So they require a slightly lower temperature, and a lot more patience. Instead of using boiling water, the ideal water temperature is between 180 and 190 degrees. I always keep my water at 182, to allow for the slight cooling that occurs with transfer to the pot. But if you go over 200 degrees, you might as well be dropping in some of those cheap Lipton teabags," Nathan says disdainfully.

Nathan selects a canister from his rack and unscrews the top. I can see that the inside is lined with plastic, or maybe it's glass. Nathan notices me looking at the canister. "The glass prevents any oxidation that would result if the tea came in direct contact with the metal, and the metal keeps all light out. I could go with plastic, but I've noticed a decrease in flavor when the tea comes packaged in plastic."

"Jesus man, how much does all this cost?" I ask, amazed. Seriously, this is some over-the-top-shit.

"The tea you'll be trying with me cost me a thousand dollars for the pound I was able to get my hands on. I have more expensive ones. This one though was a very good find for me, as it's been years since I was able to find this particular blend. I do hope it's as good as the last time."

Nathan carefully scoops out some tea using a wooden spoon before placing the leaves into a ball-like thing with holes in it for water to flow through before he seals the thing and drops it into the pot. "Let's wait four minutes for the tea to steep, and then we can pour. Despite how particular I am when it comes to brewing tea, I just drink it from plain old coffee mugs. Give me a moment to grab some."

"Really Nathan, you don't have to. I appreciate the gesture, though. I just never knew there was so much... complexity to tea."

"Teas are like people in the sense that they're often very complex, and never quite what you expect until you try them. Now tell me, Jackson, why should I ignore your father's orders and spare Katrina Grammercy? Do you even have a reason beyond saying it isn't right?"

"Because it's like you said... haven't we done enough to this girl?" I ask, attempting to make him see reason. Why won't this guy listen to me? "Please Nathan, I'm asking you directly. Spare her."

"And what will you do if I agree to spare her?" he asks, retrieving two mugs from a cupboard next to a small sink I hadn't noticed earlier. "Extract your own measure of revenge?"

"No... yes... fuck, I don't know. I want to start by talking to her. Nathan, I never knew why she disappeared from my life.

I just went to school one day and the teacher said that Katrina had transferred schools. I wasn't into reading the news back then, I just rolled with it. But it hurt, and what she did last night hurt, too. I need to know. I need to look her in the eyes when I ask her why she did it."

Nathan considers me for a long moment, then nods. "All right. Perhaps I've grown weary of death myself in my old age. When a man reaches fifty, the Reaper's a lot closer of a friend than you like to admit when you're twenty-two. Or hell, maybe I'm just trying to balance some old debts. I'll find Katrina, but I won't eliminate her. I'll report her whereabouts to you instead. If Peter asks... well, I doubt any woman who was able to put together the PSYOP that was done on you last night is going to be easy to find. It wouldn't be the first time someone's twisted Peter DeLaCoeur's tail and ran like a jackrabbit afterward."

"Thank you, Nathan," I say quietly. Nathan nods and sets a mug in front of me. He picks up his teapot and swirls it three times, then gives me a small half-smile.

"You're welcome. Care for some tea?"

Chapter 5
Kat

"You know, the Ghetto Goth look kinda went out fifteen years ago," Darcy says as we exchange hugs outside Cafe Du Monde. They've got great beignets, which Darcy only got used to eating after she got married. I sometimes tease that marrying a cop has changed her in more ways than one, but it's all good. I love her for who she is. "You know, right about when Aaliyah passed?" she says.

"She's more from your time, not mine, even if you and Virginia gave me an appreciation for Baby Girl. Besides, if I went with just a sports bra, people'd stare, even here in New Orleans," I reply, looking down at my outfit. I'm wearing a pair of lightweight black BDU pants, a slate gray sports bra, and a navy blue shirt I've left unbuttoned and untucked so my skin can breathe in this humidity. Black sunglasses and a pair of black lightweight mid top boots round out my look, although I'm not wearing a hat today. It's a little cloudy, so I don't need it. "You know how it is," I say.

"Yeah, I know," Darcy says, looking for all the world like any other average thirty-two-year-old mother in jeans and a tank top. "I mean, I think this little bit of color on my shirt here might be peas, but it might be pee. I'm not too sure."

I laugh softly and sit back, sipping my coffee. Darcy insists on covering the costs for our little trips out into the world, what she calls my "social training," since it's the only way she can convince me to leave the loft except for my mission or work. "You always did have a good sense of color. So, what's up?"

Darcy, who is also one of only five people in the world with my permanent phone number, reaches into her purse and pulls out a thumb drive. "Thought you might like this. My friends finished the translations for you."

"No shit?" I say with a grin, sitting forward and taking the drive from her outstretched hand. "Took them long enough."

"Hey, the Osaka police are behind on digitizing their files, and this literally took some... clandestine activities that you're probably more trained for than I am," Darcy replies. "Some of the people involved... well, let's just say that finding anti-government anarchists in Japan is a lot harder than finding them here in the States or in Europe."

"At least ones who have the skills I need," I reply with a chuckle, thinking about some of the Japanese hackers I know online. They're definitely a... unique group. "So did you take a look?"

Darcy nods, watching as our waitress brings her a plate with two beignets dusted with powdered sugar. "You know Kat, you can indulge in these every once in a while. You don't need to live on health food all the time."

"Performance food," I correct her, looking wistfully at the fried and glistening puffs of dough. "Maybe when this is over, I'll take you up on that offer for the second one. Till then, give it to Jeff with my compliments."

Darcy rolls her eyes and takes a big bite of the treat.

Some of the powdered sugar puffs up as she lifts it to her face and settles on her chocolate-colored skin. But a bit goes up her nose, and it makes Darcy sneeze. She sets the beignet down and wipes at her face with a napkin, getting most of it. "There's a reason us black folk don't usually eat this way," she grumbles. "You white girls got it lucky."

"Right... meanwhile, black don't crack," I return, falling into some of the old racial jokes that I learned in Virginia's house. She never let the difference in our races be a factor between us, but she also didn't let us ignore them either. "So what's it say?"

"Aiko Mori was born in 1972 in Chikuhoku village in Nagano Prefecture, Japan," Darcy says. Her memory for this kind of thing is nearly flawless, and I'm one hundred percent sure all the details she's reciting are correct, despite the fact she isn't reading them off a file or anything. "In 1992, once she was legally considered an adult in Japan, she moved to the United States to pursue a career as a pastry chef, apparently a very popular career choice for Japanese girls." She pauses to take a bite from her beignet before continuing.

"Her parents had a little bit of money since her father was the president of a construction company that had some government contracts in the village, so they granted her wish to study at the New Orleans School of Cooking. Aiko wanted to learn how to make French and Creole desserts in particular. Soon after coming here, she met Peter DeLaCoeur and started having an affair with him since he was already married to Margaret, as you know. No one's sure of the exact length of the affair, but it continued for a while, even after Jackson's birth, since his half-sister Andrea DeLaCoeur was born two years after Jackson.

"What happened to Aiko?" I ask quietly, but I suspect I already know the answer to the question.

"After Andrea's birth, she was registered as Peter's biological daughter, which is a rarity given his indiscretions. This fact will be relevant eventually in the story. Aiko returned to Japan and took Andrea with her. Her parents had moved to Osaka while Aiko had been away. Apparently her father's business had improved, and he was now working out of the larger city or something—my friends didn't dig too deep into that. But what they did find was evidence that Aiko was shamed by her parents for having a *haafu* daughter out of wedlock, and that the *gaijin* was obviously playing her." Darcy pauses and finishes her beignet, but this time she manages to avoid getting powdered sugar up her nose.

"Aiko refuted those claims of course, saying they were in love, but when she called him and asked him to talk with her parents, he laughed at her and told her she was lucky he'd at least acknowledged Andrea as his own daughter. That's Mrs. Mori's words, by the way. So Aiko, distraught over the rejection from her lover..."

Darcy's voice fails, and I'm touched. She might be an anarchist, a hacktivist, and more than willing to try and take down the rich and powerful who she blames for her family's death in Hurricane Katrina, but she's also never lost that sense of optimism about the world that's been ripped out of me. Still, I need to know. "How'd she do it?"

"Jumped off her parents' apartment building," Darcy

finally gets out. "She left a note behind saying that she apologized for being such a bad daughter and horrible mother."

It's my turn to blink, the grief-stricken look on Darcy's face touching even my heart. "What happened next?"

"Her parents tried to keep Andrea, but Peter DeLaCoeur had her kidnapped and returned to the United States. Since he was legally on record as her biological father, the American courts sided with him. The Japanese courts sided with the Moris, but it didn't help them since Japan hadn't signed the Hague Abduction Convention yet. Andrea's been raised in her father's house ever since."

I shake my head, shocked. "And why aren't we releasing this right away?"

"You know why," Darcy says. She pulls a paper bag out from her purse and wraps the beignet inside before placing it all back in her purse for later. She always saves her second beignet for Jeff. "Come on, walk with me."

We get up and make our way through the French Quarter. It's only mid-morning, so it's nowhere near as busy as it'll get tonight. The St. Louis Cathedral is relatively quiet at the moment, which feels out of place here in the portion of the city best known for sin. "Remember the first rules I taught you about tunneling into a system?" Darcy asks as we stroll through Jackson Square, keeping toward the trees that line the outer edges of the park. "Come, I know it's been a few years, but I know you haven't forgotten that."

"Of course not. Once you have a crack, ease it open slowly."

"Exactly. You hit a system with a big hit all at once, that's what gets noticed and tracked. You get caught, and you end up doing time in some women's prison in Kansas. But if you work the crack open slowly, carefully, you end up with a tunnel that can go unnoticed for years until you're ready to bring down the system totally, or you exploit for as long as you want."

"I've already been waiting for ten years, Darcy. I don't have time for the whole Shawshank Redemption route."

Darcy shakes her head. "You haven't had a crack for ten years, you had a target. It took you pulling one dumbass stunt to even start to get a crack, honeychile. Now is not the time to hit them with everything. You do that, and all the bad guys surrounding the DeLaCoeurs are going to condense around him, protecting them because they're going to be afraid you're coming after them next. You gotta poison the well slowly, isolate him, and then you'll have your chance to actually strike."

I sigh and run my right hand through my hair. "This is such bullshit, Darcy. I was right there. Hell, he couldn't even move after I hit his trigger points. If I'd given him one more shot, Jackson would be dead. I didn't, and now you're telling me to wait some more?"

"Jackson ain't your target. Peter is. Don't become what you hate just to get your... vengeance."

I stop since we're nearly at the cathedral, and I close my eyes. I'm not praying though. There's no redemption for me, and I seek no forgiveness for what I want to do. I'm just trying to gather my thoughts. "Okay, okay, we'll do it your way. Andrea first, then the other affairs, then the nastier stuff. I'll talk to Domino soon."

"Good. By the way, check that flash drive, I've got

something else for you."

"Oh?" I ask, patting the little bulge in my pocket. "What?"

"Something that'll keep food in your belly, and maybe put some newer pants on your skinny ass," Darcy says with a chuckle. "Totally legit, too. I built the system myself, and now the clients want to see if Coup De Grace can crack it."

I arch an eyebrow. "You built it?"

"I built it. Hardware too, not that I'm telling you what I used. System's up right now with dummy data files. You get in there and leave behind your signature, you get ten grand."

"And if I don't?" I ask. With Darcy's projects and offers, there's always a catch.

"I get twenty, and you get twenty percent, so I clear sixteen and you clear four. Difference of six grand for you."

I chuckle and look up at the sky, then at the cathedral. The clouds are getting heavier, so I suspect by the time I get back to the loft, it'll be raining. Good, I need a reason to stay indoors now. "Fine. You know it's not going be that hard though, Darcy. You taught me everything you know."

"Almost, Kat. Remember, you hack great, but I'm a great hacker."

"We'll see. You giving me a deadline?"

Darcy nods. "One week. Just enough time for you to get the first bit out to Domino, then prep the next little needle for Peter. One last thing though... have you thought about the collateral damage? Andrea's even more innocent of this than Jackson. You could hurt the girl."

I nod. "I've thought about it ever since we heard the

rumors. But if she doesn't know, then she deserves to know. Besides, judging by everything I've researched on her... she's grown into one tough woman. I remember her as a little girl, she was tough then, too. You know she's the only one of us all that actually went to college? She's working on her MBA right now, and she's still only twenty."

"Sounds like you admire her."

I shrug. "I'm driven, not blinded. Not all the DeLaCoeurs are scum."

"Yeah well, while you're being not blinded, keep your eyes especially open. Jeff heard that the Black Man is looking for you."

I can't help it, but I shiver. Nathan Black is not someone I want on my tail, but I knew he and I might have to throw down at some point when I started this. "I figured. I know it must burn your ass that he's known as the Black Man."

Darcy chuckles and shrugs. "Can't help it, it is his last name. Seriously, that's one badass son of a bitch, you keep yourself safe. He might even be able to take you in a fight."

I nod and adjust my sunglasses. "He might. But *bushido* is realized in the presence of death."

"Goddamn samurai."

Chapter 6
Jackson

A week. I've been holed up in the mansion for a week, and it's driving me up a fucking wall. There's only so many laps I can swim in the pool, so many workouts I can do in the gym in the garage, so many movies I can watch before I go apeshit.

Not that Pops cares. He's instructed the staff, and Nathan in particular, not to let me off the property, regardless of how I want to go about it. I'm not even allowed to walk out of here if I were feeling up to it. Mike won't even talk to me any longer. When I went to Pops to ask him about it, he just reiterated that Mike is no longer to answer to me, and works for only Pops now. Fucking ass.

So I find myself in the one room of the mansion I rarely visit, the library. Image is important to my family, so even though nobody other than Andrea's even ever actually been to college, we still have an impressive-looking library. The library contains mostly books bound in leather, but there are still some regular hardcovers and even some paperbacks. I start looking at the titles, idly wondering if anyone's actually taken them off the shelves and read them, or if the maid just comes by twice a week to dust them.

"You should try *The Count of Monte Cristo*. It's about someone seeking revenge for being wronged," someone says behind me, and I turn to see Andrea sitting in one of the leather lounge chairs. Either she came in nearly silently, or maybe I'm just more distracted than I thought. Probably a bit of both, since she's capable of sneaking around like a ninja when she wants. She's dressed in her normal daytime clothes. For Andrea that means she's wearing her take on a power suit, wearing hip-hugging pants with a matching vest and blouse, plus four-inch heels. When you see the whole thing paired with her long, black hair cascading down her back, it gives her a really severe appearance. Andi's finishing up her MBA and probably can already take down a lot of young executives in the brains department. "It seems appropriate for what's going on in your life," she remarks casually.

"Our lives," I retort, moving over to sit down next to her. I'm wearing a tank top and shorts. When you see our outfits side by side, I look even more casual by comparison, but it's not like I need to get dressed up just to sit around the house. Hell, the staff should just consider themselves lucky I even took a shower before my workout today. "She embarrassed the whole family."

Andrea scowls, making her look older than her twenty years. I've pointed that out to her before, but it just makes her scowl more when I do. "No, she embarrassed you. She pissed off Peter and put herself in danger as a result. But she hasn't done anything to me."

"Whatever. If she takes down this family, which is what it seems like she wants to do, you can say *sayonara* to your gravy train, too."

Her scowl disappears, replaced by the sarcastic grin that is the second most common expression she normally wears. "I don't need a gravy train, *niichan*. I'm going to break free on my own someday. I've got things to do as well."

I nod, half-frowning to myself. Andrea's always had this strange little driven side to her personality. I've never really been able to see all of it, but she hints at it sometimes. "If you say so, Andrea. But then why haven't you broken free yet?"

"Just wait. I'm biding my time, that's all. Patience can be a virtue."

I shake my head and get up to walk toward the door, having had more than enough of this conversation. "Yeah, well, my patience is at an end. I need to do something to take my mind off this bullshit, have a little fun."

Andrea shakes her head, snorting. "What's her name going to be?"

"Their names, Andrea. Their names."

* * *

Tiffany is an old hook-up of mine. We've played all sorts of games together, but what she loves to do best with me is costume play. I swear this bitch has a closet reserved solely for the outfits she wears when she's fucking me. So far I've seen various costumes, company uniforms, and other clothes specifically for fucking, but she's almost never repeated any of the pieces with me. Most of them allow for easy access between the legs.

Today she's Doctor Tiffany, although I doubt a real doctor would wear a skirt this short and still expect to be taken seriously. Or not get slapped with a malpractice suit with this much cleavage showing. "Hello, Jackson. What seems to be the trouble today?" she asks in a breathy voice.

I smirk. She's a terrible actress, but I didn't invite her

over to read Shakespeare. I lean back on my bed and give a fake cough. "Oh Doctor, you know how it is. My throat's sore and my body aches all over. And I think my balls are turning blue."

"Aww, you poor, poor man," Tiffany says, giving me a naughty smile. I know a lot of men who'd already be creaming their jeans at that smile alone. She knows how to work what she's got, and she's got a body like Carmen Electra in her prime. "It sounds like I might need some help for this exam. Nurse?"

The door to my walk-in closet swings open, and Allison comes out. She's my other little playmate. She and Tiffany are pretty much night and day in appearance, but they're good friends, and sometimes more than just good friends. Allie is short where Tiffany is tall, and skinny where Tiffany is stacked, but she still has a sex drive that borders on the nymphomaniac level. And despite only having little A cup tits, she's got an ass that you just want to pour some maple syrup over and lick out for hours. Just like Tiffany, she's wearing a costume, but no nurse I've ever seen has ever worn thigh high stockings that stop an inch below the hem of her uniform.

"Yes, Doctor?" she asks, prancing her way across the floor. Allie loves playing up her youthfulness, and always tries to come across as an innocent young thing, even when she's riding my cock like a pro rodeo cowgirl. "How can I help you?"

"This patient, Mr. Jackson... he's not feeling good at all. He says his throat hurts, and his body aches."

"Oh no, Doctor, what should I do?" Allie asks in her little girl voice, taking a seat on the bed. Tiffany climbs onto the bed next to Allie as she speaks.

"I thought you might want to start by checking his

tonsils while I measure his temperature," she says. Allie's lips find mine and we kiss, her long tongue already sweeping my mouth.

"Mmm, I think I need more exploration," Allie whispers when she breaks our kiss, biting her lip. "What do you think, Jackson?"

I should be into this. I should be hard as a fucking rock. I've got two hot and horny nymphos in my bed, ready to do just about anything I want. Hell, I should be tearing off Allie's nurse uniform right now and feasting on those tiny but yummy tits of hers. She's able to come just from nipple play. I should be looking forward to Tiffany riding my mouth while Allie turns my cock into a pogo stick.

I should be... but I'm not. Tiffany runs her hand over my cock, and while there's a little twitch, that's it. "What's wrong, baby?" she asks, sliding up higher on the bed. Allie notices the look in my eye and sits up as well. "Talk to us, Jackson. Sure, we have a lot of fun fucking, but you've been an okay guy to talk with, too."

I sigh and sit up, scooting back. "I don't know... maybe it's just stress. I thought that a little playtime between the three of us might help ease my mind."

Tiffany nods. She's a nympho, but she's also an accountant, and I hear she's a talented one at that. She just likes playing the dumb slut for fun when we get together. Allie's actually a bimbo, but she's got a decent heart, too. "I gotcha, baby. Wanna talk about it instead?"

I shake my head. "Nah... it's nothing you girls need to worry about. Listen, I'm gonna go catch a swim or something.

Feel free to stay as long as you want, play if you want. I know I got you two all heated up and there's no payoff."

Allie looks over at Tiffany, and I can see the look in her eyes. She's still ready to go, and while playtime with just the two of them might not have been her first choice, she'll still take it. She looks like she wants to push me on the issue, but she also knows I'm nobody to be trifled with. "Well, okay... but if you're feeling up for it later, maybe we can still have a little fun?" she asks. "We don't even have to have the costumes."

I reach out and stroke her cheek and nod. She's cute. "Maybe, baby. But don't get your hopes up too much."

I get off the bed, making sure my shorts are okay before glancing back. Tiffany's already got Allie pinned to the mattress and is kissing her, the two of them quickly getting into it. Any other night I'd be up for at least watching, but I'm just not interested right now. I leave the spare bedroom and go out into the hallway, making sure to close the door behind me.

The problem's clear. I can't get Kat off my mind. Not only am I pissed at her still, but the way she touched me, the way she looked, the way her dress clung to her body... great, now my cock twitches and wakes up again.

"Face it, you dumb fuck, you want her," I whisper, sighing. I go out onto the back patio that overlooks the garden, which leads to the rest of the old plantation lands. Ten acres is all that's left of one of the biggest indigo plantations of the pre-American days that once covered an area larger than the French Quarter, but it's a beautiful ten acres. I lean against the hundred-year-old red brick wall that lines the patio, and look out into the sky. After days of cloudiness and some rain, the weather finally broke just around sunset today, and now I can look up to see a mostly full moon shining down on the property, stars glittering around it. "Ten years."

It's the part that's bothered me the most this past week. Nathan's question of if I had feelings for Katrina continues to dance around in my head, because the honest truth is... I probably did. There's never been a lot of love in my family, and even Andrea I can't call anything other than a close acquaintance. Mom... ha. Pops has always treated me like an annoying little insect to be paid off more than anything else. At least I've lived comfortably this entire time, I guess. Hell, more than comfortably.

But Katrina... from the first time we hung out together, we just clicked. Her father had brought her by on one of his visits to see Pops. We liked the same games and even had the same hobbies. When I went through a phase where I was into building plastic car models, she was right there with me. She'd help me cut out all the parts from the tree and sand the edges, making sure each piece fit perfectly. Her hands were steadier than mine, so she'd always paint the individual pieces before the two of us would work together on the final assembly. Going to the same school meant that we got a decent amount of facetime together, but we were pretty much inseparable even outside class. Riding bikes, doing homework... all of it. She got me through my times tables, and I helped her with learning how to swim in our pool.

I'd almost grown out of the plastic model phase when she dropped out of my life, and yeah, it left a hole inside me. Now she's back... and she's pissed. Considering what Nathan told me, I can understand. I don't like Pops either. In fact, the only person in my family I even respect is Andrea. But Pops... fine. He's scum. But how am I supposed to break away? Andrea talks about it, but the only step she's taken toward it is getting her MBA. I've never even thought about college, and my only skill is knowing how to party. That's good for about fifty cents above minimum wage if it weren't for Pops' money.

I shake my head and go inside, leaving the door to the garden open. I head back toward the guest bedrooms, when a cough behind me catches my attention.

"Nathan," I say after I turn. "Didn't think you'd still be dressed in your suit."

Nathan looks down at his black linen suit and brushes a bit of lint off his lapel. "I didn't think I'd find you... dressed," he replies. Nathan looks pointedly at the door where I'd just been with the two girls, then shrugs.

"Wasn't feeling it tonight. What can I help you with?"

Nathan reaches into his jacket pocket and pulls out a slip of paper. "An address. You were looking for it. She lives in a warehouse over on Market Street."

I look down at the numbers written on the paper. "And you haven't told Pops?"

Nathan shakes his head. "Not until you find your answers. I told you, Jackson, I've got some debts to balance out. Or maybe in my mind I just keep seeing the little girl that Katrina Grammercy was when I first met her. I've done a lot of nasty things in my day, Jackson... but I don't touch kids."

I nod and fold the paper up, putting it in the pocket of my shorts. "I see. Thank you, Nathan. And sometime... perhaps we can have a cup of tea again."

Nathan, who's already turned to go back down the hallway, stops and looks back. "I'd like that. Have a good night, Jackson."

Chapter 7
Kat

I'm inverted, my feet pointing straight in the air as I lower myself on the two steel bars which let my head dip lower until my hands are next to my ears before pushing up, locking out. Seven. Three more and I can kick back down and let my shoulders rest a little bit.

I lower myself, sweat dripping off my nose to soak into the wooden floor below me, and push again. Eight.

I focus on the pain, tasting the metallic tang on my tongue and savoring the electric fire that runs up from my elbows to my spine. Soon enough, I may not feel anything at all except the eternal satisfaction of vengeance before Peter's men tear me apart. Nine.

One more. I can do this. My elbows are shaking, but I can make it. Don't cheat yourself, there's nothing that can bring defeat faster than cheating yourself... now PUSH! I push, and in my mind I see the fire rolling across the concrete ceiling of the parking garage, hungry and reaching for me after it's already taken my parents' lives. It's coming, ten years later now to claim me, but claim me it will...

Ten. I kick over and land on my feet, shaking out my arms. I don't need my pills yet, in fact since the night with Jackson I've only had to take them once. Still, the image of the explosion is hot in my brain, and I have to do something constructive before the anger morphs into depression. I know the pattern, but I'm going to fight it this time.

I grab the sandbag next to my handstand bars and lift it, whipping the forty-five-pound bag up and onto my shoulders. I start crossing the floor of my loft with long, lunging strides. Each one brings me nearly to the floor before I force myself to rise and take the next long step.

I'm on my second trip back across the loft when my computer beeps from the corner. Darcy's little setup on the shipping company she wants me to crack is tougher than I thought it'd be, and I wonder if she's calling me on time. I still have thirty-six hours left on the deadline that she gave me though, even if my tools are still barely chipping away at the firewall, still searching for that elusive crack. I know one has to be there, so it's just a matter of patience, processing power, and tools.

I set my sandbag down and see that I have an IRC chat window up on my screen. Only Darcy and a few others have my IRC handle, although it's not that hard to figure out if you know my hacker name. I mean, CDGrace and Coup De Grace aren't really all that different, after all.

But I don't know this IRC handle at all. Blue Sakura... intriguing. Maybe it's one of Darcy's Japanese contacts?

CDG- Hello.

BS- You're a hard woman to find.

CDG- I prefer my privacy. Who are you?

BS- An ally.

CDG- An ally? In what? I can count my allies on one hand.

BS- An ally who agrees with your vendetta against Peter DeLaCoeur.

I'm tempted to close the window now and reset my router. It'll cost me Darcy's contract, and six thousand dollars because of it, but this person knows who I am. I'm reaching for the power button when Blue Sakura pops up again.

BS- Please don't shut me off. I'm really not trying to expose you or hurt you. I messaged you to warn you.

I pause, my finger hovering over my power button, and go back to my keyboard.

CDG- About?

BS- Nathan Black has found out where you live. He's passed along that information. You need to get out of there.

CDG- If they want to come here, they can. Makes my job easier. Little messier, but a lot easier.

BS- Please watch your back, in any case. You deserve closure.

CDG- What do you know about closure?

BS- You're not the only one who's lost a parent because of Peter DeLaCoeur. Be careful.

The IRC window says that Blue Sakura has left the room, and I consider what just happened. Blue Sakura, huh? Makes sense... Andrea. That you found me at all online tells me that you've got some skills yourself. I run a backtrace on her IP and see that she's also using at least one signal relay, as the address says that Blue Sakura is currently on the Ross Ice Shelf, Antarctica. Doubtful at best.

I could use my tools to continue running the backtrace, but I don't need to. It'd be easier just to get Andrea's phone number if I really want or need to contact her again. I've had access to that particular database for years. Instead, I go back to my workout, not letting myself get distracted. I've still got three hundred pushups to do, and then I'll go into my form training. Without a lot of partners, I have to keep my skills up as best I can, and that means lots and lots of mental imagery while I drill on poor substitutes for real people.

I wonder if Andrea can be a resource? There are so many things I can't verify yet, the things that can really take my campaign against Peter DeLaCoeur from just harassment to putting him behind bars. Not that I want it to stop there, but it's a start. The dirty cops, the mob connections, the bodies dropped off in the swamps or somewhere in the Mississippi... if I can verify those, I can really put the pressure on him. Maybe not enough to get him into a court of law, but certainly enough that his allies would move to distance themselves. Without their support, the walls he's carefully built over the years would surely start to crumble. If I can take down enough of those walls, maybe I can get him out of his fortress.

As I start my first set of fifty pushups, I think about the juiciest case I'd like to connect Peter to. He's no longer in office, but Dutch Landry is from one of the two biggest political families in this city. The Landrys and the Morrels have traded the mayor's office back and forth in five of the last six administrations. His son is currently on the city council and has a good shot of running for mayor himself in three years.

But Dutch... Dutch Landry was the type of mayor loved by the press, and hated by the underclass. Virginia and Darcy showed me the evidence firsthand, but hell, I grew up seeing it often enough in Virginia's foster care. I saw the drugs, the street crime that was only checked when the police rolled through in paramilitary fashion. I saw classmates show up with wounds from both police and gang bullets, and I know that a lot of the guns were bought through Dutch Landry's connections. The drugs for sure came in with his authorization. Of course, someone had to arrange transport for all of that, and wouldn't you know, Peter DeLaCoeur knew some friends among the longshoremen who were willing to look the other way as the shipments flooded the Port of New Orleans.

It's how Peter's stayed in business so long. He doesn't directly touch anything. Instead, he makes introductions, facilitates communication between interested parties, and collects his middleman's percentage regardless. He's the ultimate in one-stop criminal shopping. You want it, he knows a guy.

He's completely crooked, but there's no hard evidence. His business dealings are done face to face with cash on the table most of the time, and the IRS thinks he gets his money through renting residential properties in the Lower Ninth Ward. Hell, in their estimation the man's a saint, owning so many Section 8 properties. He's not looking out for anyone but himself, though—he filters his money through those houses.

Say you have a house that you're renting for a thousand dollars a month. Sometimes housing assistance provides full credit for rentals, and sometimes they only provide partial credit. Peter DeLaCoeur only rents to those with partial credit. The government gives him between three hundred and five hundred a month... and the rest of the thousand comes out of his illegal business. He makes friends with the IRS and HUD, who think his fifty houses are all rented out to families in need. Meanwhile, the families think he's renting to them cheap on the down low.

He's just using those same poor families as a cover, since

the funds he's filtering are in fact coming from the same drugs and guns that are killing the neighborhoods he owns. He makes even more profit from the Section 8 money. I have to admit, it's a smooth scam, but it's just one of half a dozen that he runs.

If I could just prove it... maybe Andrea can help with that. It'd damage him more than just exposing an embarrassing affair. I don't know. In the meantime, I keep doing my pushups, even though my chest and shoulders are screaming at me at this point.

Someone knocks on my door and I pull my right leg up, bounding to my feet. I approach the door slowly, since it's one of only two entrances to my loft. The other entrance is the old freight elevator that connects to the boxing gym downstairs. Unlike the door, I can control the elevator entrance fully.

Next to the door is one of my home defense weapons. After all the years of martial arts training, you'd think that I'd have something exotic like sai or a wakizashi sword. Maybe a hundred years ago, but what I have instead is a Glock 18. They're highly illegal since they're fully automatic, but since I don't officially exist as far as the law's concerned, I'm not worried about illegally owning this gun. If I need to, I can fire all fifteen rounds through the door in less than a second, and whoever's unlucky enough to be on the other side is going to get turned into Swiss cheese.

I pick up the Glock and flick the fire selector switch from safe to semi-auto, and look through my peephole. I really should invest in a higher tech security system, but it hasn't been a priority.

Whoever it is knocks again as I open the cover on my

peephole, and my fingers go numb when I see who it is. I'm only dimly aware that I drop the cover on the peephole. Jackson?

"Open the door please, Kat. I'm alone, and we need to talk."

"What are you doing here, Jackson?" I yell through the door. "Don't try and knock the thing down either, it's steel core."

Actually, my door isn't steel core, it's just a plain hollow metal door, but that's beside the point. If Jackson is alone, then just what the hell is he doing here?

"Please Kat, open the door," Jackson repeats. "It's just me... I want to talk, that's all. Come on Kat, it's been ten years. If our friendship meant anything to you... I just want to talk."

Against my better judgment, I lower my Glock for a moment and unlock the door, stepping back before raising my gun again. "It's open."

Chapter 8
Jackson

The first thing I see when I open the door to Kat's loft is the pistol pointed at my chest. Her hands are completely steady, and she keeps the gun solidly trained on me as I approach her. I don't know what type of pistol it is, except that it's not the same as Nathan's 1911, and that the whole damn thing is black.

Next, I see Kat, sweat glistening on her skin as she stares at me with killer's eyes. She's wearing a dark gray sports bra and what looks like martial arts pants, plus a pair of black Nike Frees, and that's it. Her eyes flicker over my body for a moment before she jerks her head to the side, and I get the message. I go deeper inside her loft while she checks to make sure that I was telling the truth about being alone. She reaches out and jerks her door shut, throwing the bar lock that's at the top as soon as the door's closed.

"How'd you find me?" she asks, spinning around. She's still got the gun pointed at my chest, and to be honest, it's pissing me off.

"Think you can lower the fucking hand cannon first?" I ask, keeping my hands out. "Seriously, I know you're pissed at my family, but I'm unarmed and alone. And the longer you keep that thing pointed at me, the more you're pissing me off."

Kat considers it for a moment, then lowers her gun slowly, flicking a switch on the side and tucking it into the back of her pants. She smirks, and for a moment I see my old friend in her eyes. "Fine. Would you like a drink of water, Jackson?"

"Uhhh... sure," I mutter, caught off guard again. Seriously, she was just pointing a gun at me five seconds ago, and now she's asking if I want a drink. "Actually, beer if you've got it."

"I never touch alcohol except to treat wounds," Kat says tersely as she passes by me. I reach out to grab her shoulders to get her to stop, but before I can even touch her she's grabbed my wrist and flipped me over her hip like I weigh nothing, sending me crashing to the floor. She twists my hand and my left arm is in immense pain, and twisted in ways I didn't think arms were supposed to go. Her gun's suddenly in her hand again, and the momentary friendliness in her eyes has completely vanished, replaced by the look of a stone-cold killer. "And I have a thing about personal space. As in... don't try and breach mine."

"Goddammit Kat, I'm not your enemy!" I hiss. She steps back and puts her pistol down on a small table. I glance at it, then see her eyes. The message is clear. I reach for it, and regardless of what I might say, I'm leaving this room in a body bag.

Instead, I roll away and get to my feet, shaking my wrist. "Where the fuck did you learn that?"

"Tamura-*sensei*," Kat says simply. "I learned from him after my foster mother got done teaching me what she knew. He taught me aikijujutsu."

I look around and really look at the loft that Kat's living in. To be honest, calling it Spartan would be an insult to the Spartans. Her bed looks like it's some kind of reject from a military surplus store with only a thin mattress on top of the cheap metal frame. My eyes drift over to a cheap Formica dresser that looks like it doubles as one of her tables, then to a couple of wooden folding chairs. Her kitchen... well, I've seen office break rooms better equipped. A hotplate, a mini fridge, a cheap sink with a single cupboard above it... I don't even see a shower, although most of the loft is dimly lit, so I guess it could be on the far side of this huge space. "Love the decoration style. What do you call it? Goodwill Chic? Haute Homeless?"

"I call it functional," she replies, coming around and pulling two jelly jars down from the cupboard and running the water until it's obviously cool to her touch before she fills them both up. "Vengeance isn't a well-paying job."

"Yeah, about that," I say, sitting down in the folding chair that looks slightly stronger than the other. I notice that she's got a computer in the corner on a table that looks strong, if a little cheap. Like one of those all-plastic office desks you can get at Wal-Mart for about thirty bucks. The computer, though... damn. I don't know a lot about computers, but any computer that's running an actual antifreeze-based cooling system and pump has to be some serious shit.

"You use that thing to help set up your little stunt on me?" I ask, taking a sip. The water's not the greatest I've ever tasted, since it's unfiltered city water, but at least it's cool. "That shit'll give you cancer."

"Not worried about cancer," Kat says, taking a seat in the other chair. I get a better look at her, and my cock twitches in my slacks again. Jesus, she's fucking sexy when she's angry. Her eyes are sparkling with an inner fire, and the way her body's put together, she's built like a cat, all feminine curves and deadly sleekness.

"You... Katrina, what the hell were you doing, pulling that stunt in the limo? I mean, in the past few days, I've learned a lot about why you might want to be pissed at Pops, but why'd you have to do that to me?"

"You think what you've been through the past few days is hard?" Kat spits, angry again. "You didn't have to go through what I did! Try three foster homes in six months! You try finding out that your best friend's father ordered the car bomb that blew up your parents! You try watching as your parents are turned into a fucking fireball!"

She's on her feet, yelling at me, her chest heaving and her forearms bunched. I'm kinda glad she left her glass on the floor by her feet. I think she might be able to crush that jar in her fist the way her muscles are flexing. My cock twitches again, but I tell it to shut the fuck up. I'm pissed off too, and I'm on my feet before I know it. "That doesn't mean you go and humiliate me! Hell, I barely talked Nathan out of killing you and giving me your address instead!"

"Killing me? I don't fucking care if I die," Kat responds, stepping back and turning around. "If I can take down your father, I don't care if my next home is six feet under. After what I've been through the past ten years, death would be a vacation."

Her words chill me to the bone, and my anger dissolves, at least temporarily. Instead, I back up, away from the chair. "Kat... Katrina. Whatever you want to be called right now. Tell me what you know."

She turns back around, and I see a hint of humanity in her face, and not just the enraged warrior I'd been looking at most of the time since I walked in the door. "You really want to know?"

I nod and sit down on the wood floor. "Yeah, I do. If it makes you feel better about it, you can get your gun and keep it on me. For the first time in my life, I want to know the truth."

After a moment, Kat nods and comes over close to me before sitting down. The way she sits hikes up one of the legs of her martial arts pants, and her calf is just a foot away from my hand. It's defined, and perfect, and oh my holy God so sexy. I start to reach out, but stop. Kat notices, and gives me a little nod of appreciation for my restraint. "So what do you want to know?"

"Why didn't you reach out to me before? All I knew was that you'd left school, and that one day you just dropped off the face of the earth. I didn't even know your parents were dead until months later."

"Probably had your head buried in that '67 Corvette model we were working on," Kat says with a little smile. "We'd what, gotten the engine block completed together?"

"And the tires," I added. "We'd just finished the hubs the day before you disappeared. I never did finish that kit. I did a little of the framework, but after you left school... I just never wanted to finish it. It wasn't any fun anymore. I think it got thrown away maybe six months later or so."

"Shame, it was a nice kit," Kat muses, then sighs. "But you asked what I went through. Well, at first I was pretty fucked up, it's the only way to describe it. The first foster home... to be honest, I don't remember much of it. I was going through a lot of shit back then, but I do remember them trying to hit me. I hit back and ended up right back in the orphanage with a broken arm. The second home, well, they were nice, but way too old, and they didn't know how to deal with my anger. You see by then I'd started to hear the rumors, a lot of the older kids at the orphanage were running in gangs pretty much, and word on the street was my parents were killed by a car bomb, and it was your father who ordered it. I wasn't sure though for a few years after that, but I had a name. Still, I was too angry, and took advantage of them. I lasted a month with them before they sent me back after I slapped the woman. Then they sent me to Virginia... she was my first real teacher."

"And what did she teach you?"

"Quite a few things. Krav Maga at first, then later on, she hooked me up with people who could supplement my education. I spent more time on my real education than I did on my high school education, not that it mattered. When I was sixteen I took my GED and said farewell to public education. Actually scored a ninety-nine percentage overall. I spent the next five years doing my real training."

"Ten years... well, I guess nine if you account for the time before you met this Virginia... all to do what?" I ask, caught up in her face. My body remembers the feeling of her in my arms, the way she caressed my body, the feeling that shot through me. "And what did you do to me in the limo?"

Kat chuckles and gives me a sexy look, her eyes... I'm being seduced, and I can't resist it, even though I'm pissed. "Liked that, did ya? Little trick I picked up from one of the best escorts in the city. She says she picked up the Touch from living in China as a little girl, but I don't care if she got it in Detroit.

The woman makes half a million a year, most of her clients never even get her dress off, and she's more in demand than ever even though she's over forty."

"And what you hit me with under the pec? That shit bruised like a motherfucker for about three days," I ask, rubbing at the spot unconsciously.

"I bet it did. Probably connected to the other ones too, but I got that from aikijujutsu. I have some more... ones I'm planning on using on your father if he gives me a chance."

At the mention of Pops, I'm finally able to tear my eyes away from Kat again and regain some semblance of my anger. "Taking him down... I get that. You're right. From what I can figure out, he ordered the car bomb that killed your parents. Why, I still don't know. Doesn't really matter, but Kat... we were friends. You were my best friend even, for fuck's sake!"

"I was," Kat admits. "But the person I was best friends with was a sweet, maybe slightly spoiled, but overall good kid. Not a douchebag with a set of steroid muscles and a black mirror full of K-X, handing out party favors in the back of a limo."

I'm on my feet in an instant, staring at Kat and pointing at her. "You're not the only one who's been trying to cope! And for your information, this body has *never* seen a steroid. Lots of hours in the gym, probably just as many as you put in from what you're looking like, but I've never put a single pill in my mouth or needle in my butt."

"And the K-X?"

I shake my head, knowing we're not going to get any further right now. "We all have ways of coping, Katrina. You know, next time you decide to do something against me, or Andrea or the rest of my family... think about that. We've all had to cope in some way or another. And not all of us are deserving of being destroyed."

I walk to the front door and pull the handle on the lock. Turning around, I see Kat still sitting on the floor, looking sexy and untouchable at the same time. "I hope that you can understand why I'm doing what I'm doing."

I open the door, temporarily blinded by the bright sunlight outside. "I do," I say. "But I'd still prefer if you didn't get yourself killed because of it. Or me either. Watch yourself, Katrina."

The afternoon sunlight is hot and bright, and I'm finally able to adjust my cock in my pants as I head down the stairs on the side of the old warehouse. I get into my car, the first time I've been allowed in it since the incident, and once inside, I throw my head back, sighing. She's dedicated, she's deadly, she's a fanatic that's on a level that makes those jihadist assholes look like a bunch of pushovers... but she's also beautiful and sexy, and part of me wants to go up there and tell her right now that whatever she needs, she has my help.

But I can't. Not yet. I'm too pissed off, and I don't want to fight with her. Instead, I turn the key on my engine. I'm about to drive back to the plantation, and try and do some serious thinking, when the door to Kat's loft bangs open, and she comes running down the stairs.

What is it now?

Chapter 9
Kat

I really don't know why I'm running down the stairs. The question that I have in mind isn't all that important. Besides, I can't trust Jackson to answer me truthfully anyway, if he even knows the answer. Still, for some reason I'm pounding down the stairway, my Glock tucked into the back of my pants.

"Jackson! Jackson!" I yell, hitting the blacktop. The parking lot of the gym is cracked and worn, and alternates between dusty and soaked depending on the recent weather, so my feet raise little puffs of dirt as I cross the few yards still separating us.

I'm glad when he shuts off his engine and rolls down the window, although he's visibly annoyed. "What, Kat? Wanna arm lock me again? Tell me I'm a piece of shit?"

I stop, frozen more by the pain in his voice than by his words themselves. "I... I need to know if Nathan Black is coming for me," I finally say. "Are you going to send him to see me?"

Jackson looks out the front windshield for a moment, then slams his hand against the steering wheel of his Audi. "You really think I'd do that? You think I'd just come by, ask a few questions, then send Nathan after you? I'm not my father, Kat. I'm not like him at all."

"You might want to reconsider that," I tell him. "From what I saw in the limo, you're going down the same path he has."

Jackson's eyes are blazing in fury when he looks back at me, and his teeth are bared. "Goddammit Kat, I told you, we all have ways..."

"Yeah, yeah, ways to cope. I'm just saying, you might want to check yours, ask yourself if they're making you the person you want to be... or not," I say, gentler than before. "But fine. What about your father? Will Nathan tell him about me?"

"I don't know... I don't think so. But Kat, I do know this about my father... this isn't over with Pops. He's not going to let it drop."

I smirk and tilt my head. "I hadn't planned on that at all. Hell, Jackson, what I did to you is just round one. I've got all sorts of shit planned."

"Then it certainly won't be over," Jackson says, calming. He looks at me for a moment, his eyes uncertain. There's something in them, and I kinda understand, I think. It's the same uncertainty that's haunted my dreams for the past week. It's the same feeling that I have right now, looking at Jackson. Douchebag, yes. Spoiled rich kid, yes. But he's still Jackson, and we were friends.

"I know it won't. But, *'even if it seems certain that you will lose, retaliate',*" I tell him, knowing he won't get the reference. It doesn't matter, I understand it.

I'm surprised, however, when Jackson chuckles and shakes his head. *"'But in the end, the details of a matter are important. The right and wrong of one's way of doing things are found in trivial matters.'"*

I blink, absolutely shocked. Jackson shrugs. "You're not

the only one who's read that book. I went through a phase of trying to find a philosophical backing to my bodybuilding. Katrina, my father probably deserves every bit of retaliation, hatred, and punishment that's in your heart. Just... make sure you're doing the small things right. As for Nathan... I won't send him. If he's coming, I'll try and warn you at least."

He starts his engine again and I watch as he drives away, and I'm still speechless. Finally, I shake my head, smirking. "Who the hell would have thought that?"

I walk up my stairs and lock my door behind me, going over to my computer. The processors are still pounding away at Darcy's system, although I think they're developing a crack that I can exploit. I pull my chair over and sit down, looking at the readouts. Okay, so there's a hole. Maybe.

"Yes!" I hiss quietly, seeing the target system open to me. I browse around quickly, knowing it's just a fake mainframe until Darcy gets her reports back, but I still poke around a little, seeing if she left any Easter eggs for me to find. Nothing all that interesting really, so I go into the home directory, create a file folder called CDG and drop in a JPEG of a misericorde dagger. I back out, and shut down both my connection to Darcy's target system and my Internet connection. It's a precaution, but since Andrea already found me, I don't want to make it easier to trace my online footprint.

That done, I type up a quick report for Darcy telling her exactly what hole I found, the crack I used to exploit it, and what recommendations I'd use to shore up the hole. The biggest problem, as Darcy knows, is that no system, no matter how strongly put together, is ever secure forever. Darcy uses a lot of the best tools to reduce the chances of a hacker getting in, but nobody can protect against everything.

Just as I'm finishing my report, my personal phone rings, and I see that it's Darcy. "Hey Darce, guess you found my little present?"

There's disappointment in her voice, but at the same time, pride. She really wanted to stump me, but she's proud that I've actually grown beyond her teaching and become, as she put it, a great hacker. "I did. Where'd you get in?"

"You used some old code, I found a loophole. I might have cracked it a bit faster, but I had a visitor."

"You? A visitor? You becoming a social butterfly on me?" Darcy asks, laughing. "Next thing you know, you're going to be asking for my earring collection."

I lean back in my chair, chuckling. "Hey, I'm not the one with seventy-two pairs of earrings I can't wear anymore because my son got too grabby. Besides, you look better without all that junk stretching out those earlobes anyway. And I bet Jeff appreciates being able to nibble on your ears without possibly getting something caught in his teeth."

Darcy purrs, and I can't help but feel a little jealous. A husband, a child, a dog even... she's got a pretty ideal situation. "He does like doing that, that man and his... well, never mind me. Who was your visitor?"

"Jackson actually," I say, clicking save on my file and putting it on the same thumb drive she gave me the initial information on. "Seems your prediction was right, Peter sent Nathan Black after me. But Jackson sort of deflected Nathan, somehow."

"Wanna talk in person about it? I can come by this evening."

I think about it, then nod. "Yeah. You sure Jeff and Henry won't be upset?"

"Nah girl, tonight's Daddy Night before Jeff goes on night shift for the next month. The two of them are going to stay up and watch the game, so they won't mind, and Jeff and I will have our time after Henry goes down. When you want me to stop by?"

"How about seven? I've got class downstairs from five thirty to six thirty."

"Cool. So do those parents know just how badass you are?"

I chuckle and think about my class. "They have no clue at all."

* * *

"Front kick series three... ready, go!"

I'm actually wearing a karate *gi* right now, even though nothing I've ever studied was called karate at the time, but after I kicked the ass of the third person who came in trying to call my teaching skills into question, nobody says a thing.

The fifteen little kids, ranging from ages six to ten in the class, from white belt up to what I'm calling a purple belt, all strike the right pose as they bear down, throwing their rear leg thrusting kicks before following with a straight jab, a strong side elbow smash, and finally pretending to grab their opponent and kneeing their 'head' with a loud shout. One of the boys, a new kid named Dylan who's only been in class a few months, shouts louder than normal, and I notice that he's sporting a black eye.

He's a thin kid, the sort that just puts off an effeminate air, mostly because of the fineness of his features. He's a cute kid, and I know that in about seven or eight years he's going to have a look that's going to turn teenage girls weak in the knees, but for now he's probably getting picked on.

"Okay, grab shields, I want you to pair off and practice that sequence and the reverse. Dylan. Up front with me."

The other fourteen pair off pretty quickly, but Dylan's dragging a bit as he comes up. Still, he assumes the proper posture that I taught the kids for using when speaking to me, and his eyes are clear, even though it's more obvious than ever he's sporting a shiner, and what looks like the remains of a fat lip. "Yes, Teacher?"

I don't use foreign languages in my classes, even though some parents expect it. "You put a little extra into your combination today. Nice. But what's with the eye?"

Dylan shifts side to side, and I kneel, looking the seven-year-old in the eye. "Who did it, Dylan?"

"Bradley," Dylan says quietly. "He's in my class."

I nod, even though I have no idea who Bradley is. "What happened?"

"He made fun of me," Dylan says heatedly. "He made the other kids laugh at me."

I nod, then lower my voice. "And did you start it?"

He goes red, but nods. Dylan's a good kid. He doesn't lie to me. "Yes, Teacher. I know you said not to, but I tried to kick him."

"Tried? Then I take it you lost the fight?"

Dylan nods, and he's turning redder now. "Yes. I'm

sorry."

"Losing a fight is part of life. I've gotten my a... my butt kicked plenty of times," I tell him gently. "But I have a more important question. What was your goal, to hurt Bradley?"

"No. I wanted the other kids to stop laughing at me."

I figured as much. Dylan's a good kid, not a bully, and doesn't have a natural killer instinct. He hasn't had enough pain in his life yet to develop one either. "And did you accomplish your goal?"

"No. They laughed at me more after Bradley beat me up."

I nod and lean in. "Then perhaps you need to change tactics. Focus on your goal, and not on the immediate target in front of you. Now go join Patience and Callie on the end, work as a three-person group."

My own words to Dylan keep coming back to trouble me as I finish up class and go upstairs, and I'm still troubled when Darcy comes by. "Hey, Darce."

"Hey... got your cash for you," she says, handing over a paper bag while I pass her the thumb drive with my report. That's how we work, cash and carry only. It's one of the ways I've ghosted the system for so long. "So how was Jackson?"

"Arm locked," I say with a laugh before becoming more serious. "And pissed about what I did to him."

"I figured as much. Still, says something about him that he called off his daddy's dog in order to come talk to you. He must not be as much of a bastard as his old man."

"Maybe." I lock the door and Darcy and I walk over to my relaxation area, where she takes one of my chairs while I sit on the floor. "I'll be honest with you, Darcy... maybe I shouldn't have started my campaign this way."

"Maybe you shouldn't have," Darcy agrees. "Actually, I remember telling you as much when you first told me your plan. Hey, I just gotta know. Some of the photos aren't very flattering, but the others..."

I laugh and shake my head. "Jackson's just fine downstairs. Actually, he's pretty fine just about everywhere. He definitely takes care of himself. Did you know he's read the *Hagakure*, too?"

"Sounds like you see more to him than just the party boy you thought he was." Darcy has always been one to have great insight, and it's one of the reasons she's one of my mentors. "You going sweet on him?"

"Jackson? No way, he's still a douchebag," I protest immediately. "But still... he said some things that are making me reconsider my original plan. I need to focus on my real target, Darcy. Slash and burn tactics that damage the family as a whole can alienate potential allies."

"I thought you said you don't see any allies within the DeLaCoeurs," Darcy comments. "In fact, I think your last analysis on them was 'a total nest of vipers and poison that would kill a bayou gator if it ever ate one'. Or was that someone else I remember?"

"No, that was me. But... well, maybe I was a bit off on that. Peter... he's still a dead man. But Jackson, maybe Andrea... maybe I need to rethink things."

Darcy sits quietly for a moment, then hums. "Does that mean you're going to ask Domino to hold off on tomorrow's bomb?"

I shake my head. "No chance in hell. First off, I know Domino well enough to know that once he's got information, he's going to run with it no matter what. But also, the info I gave him is aimed solely at Peter, I didn't want to blow open Andrea's past just yet. I was gonna save that one for a bigger move. This one... it's just to irk him some, get him a bit more uncomfortable."

"And if Peter decides that he's a lot more interested in Nathan Black finding you because of it?"

"Then I guess Nathan and I will have to have a meeting of the warriors. I know his training, Darcy. The advantage I have is... he doesn't know mine. *'If you know the enemy and know yourself, you need not fear the result of a hundred battles.'*"

"*Hagakure* again?" Darcy asks, and I shake my head.

"Sun Tzu. *The Art of War.*"

"You have such wonderful reading tastes," Darcy quips, then chuckles. "What else is on your reading list?"

"*Computer Hacking for Dummies.*"

Darcy blows me a raspberry before laughing. "So you do have a sense of humor still. Even if it is total wiseass."

Chapter 10
Jackson

I wake up early today, filled with a sense of purpose and drive that I haven't had in a really long time. The sun isn't even up yet, and I'm already dressed and heading through the mansion to the converted garage where the gym is set up. I switch on the lights and look over the one area of my life where I'm the undisputed master... or at least I thought I was, until Katrina put me on my ass in about two seconds yesterday.

I'm no pushover. I've had more than my fair share of throw downs, and my forty-eight-inch chest isn't just bodybuilding muscle. I've trained too, mostly in BJJ and MMA, getting into scraps and knuckling up with some bad fuckers. It was one of my adrenaline rushes for a while, going down to some of the worse neighborhoods, or under the bridges near the Pontchartrain Expressway where they do the bum fights, and throwing down.

But while I took some licks in those underground fights, I never had my ass handed to me as quickly or as effectively as what Kat did to me. Sure, she caught me off guard, but that won't happen again. I promise myself that as I grab my workout notebook from the shelf and look at the page in my journal, seeing that today's a chest and triceps day. Good, I can use the heavy work to get myself calmed down again.

I start with an empty bar on the fifteen-degree incline press, just getting the blood flowing into my chest and shoulders and grooving the movement again.

I haven't done these in a month, and my first set with 275 feels a little heavier than normal, probably since I'm not used to lifting this early in the day, but I get through it okay, and note that on my upper set I might need to drop a rep.

I slide the next set of two and a half pound plates on each side when the door to the gym opens and Andrea walks in, stopping when she sees me. "Whoa. What the hell are you doing up at six thirty in the morning?"

"Oh, come on Andi, you've seen me awake plenty of times at six thirty," I say as she shrugs and comes in, stripping off her outer t-shirt to just her sports bra and running shorts. The gym has more than just weightlifting equipment, and she gets on the StairMaster, draping her shirt over the bar above the console.

"Of course I've seen you awake at six thirty. But usually when you're stumbling in the house still half-drunk after a party," she says. "Not in here, and certainly not lifting."

"Gotta do what I gotta do," I say, setting up under the bar. The gym isn't air-conditioned, although I can turn on a high-velocity fan if it gets too bad, but that's on purpose. I don't have any pussy pads on the squat bars, and I don't need no pussy air conditioning, either. "Enjoyed getting out of the house yesterday, and think it might be time for me to get out some more again today. Besides, maybe if I act like I've got my shit right, Pops will get off my ass."

"Well, good luck with that," Andrea says, starting up her workout. "You really think Peter will give you a little more slack with that leash he's got on you?"

"Maybe not the full amount, but he's gotta let me out sometime," I say. "Might be a month before I'm going to be safe to go by the Watering Hole again."

"You'll just have to content yourself with your previous playmates," Andrea says. I ignore her, though, doing my next set at 280 before moving up in five-pound increments, finishing with 315 by the time I've hit my target for today. I set the bar back down, and I see that Andrea's still grinding away on the StairMaster, her head down, sweat dripping from her chin to drop to the moving beltway stairs.

"How long you going for today?" I ask, figuring she can't last much longer. I'm surprised when she looks up, and she doesn't look tired at all.

"Still got another half hour on here. Today's all endurance. Besides, this thing gives me some killer calves and a nice ass, too. At least as much as us Japanese girls get," she says self-deprecatingly.

At the mention of calves, I think of Kat, the way her legs looked yesterday in those martial arts pants, and my cock twitches again. I grumble, turning away from Andrea quickly before she gets any ideas. I go to my next exercise, weighted dips alternated with bodyweight pullups, ten and ten before I rest, six sets. I finish up, then climb onto the StairMaster next to Andrea for a quick fifteen minutes.

Andrea finishes soon after I climb on, and pats at her face with her t-shirt. "So did you go see her?"

I blink and glance over, but there's no deception or slyness in Andrea's face. I've suspected for a long time she hates Pops nearly as much as Kat does. I can understand, when her entire presence in the house has been to basically serve as a giant 'Fuck You' to Mom. That's not the sort of thing anyone wants growing up.

"Yeah," I say after a moment. "She's... motivated."

"Seems to have rubbed off on you," Andrea says as she steps off the machine and gets to the floor. "You sure it's safe?"

"No... but then again, when do I ever do the safe thing?" I ask, to which Andrea doesn't smile, doesn't smirk, nothing. "What?"

"Someday, Jackson... someday I hope you really learn what not doing the safe thing means," Andrea says mysteriously after a moment, then pulls her t-shirt back on. "In any case, have a good rest of your workout, I've got class."

Andrea leaves, and I finish up the rest of my quick cardio, just letting my mind drift. I figure I'll get a swim in later, but maybe today instead of a swim I'll pull out my old gloves and throw down a few rounds with the heavy bag in the corner. It's not quite the same as actual training, but it'll help in starting to get me back in fight mode. I won't be caught by surprise again.

I go inside and drop off my shaker cup of post-workout protein mix in the sink for the maid to wash and run upstairs to take a lengthy shower. I even make sure to condition my hair. I've been lazy with it since I've been cooped up around the house, but it's time to get back to normal.

I dry off and put on my first set of clothes for the day, some Burberry pants and a button-down Ralph Lauren shirt. I grab my Steve Madden loafers, and I'm all set for the morning.

As I walk down the hall toward the stairs, Andrea's door opens and she comes out, also dressed for success in her typical power suit look, although I see she's skipping the heels for something a little more comfortable. I guess doing close to an hour on the StairMaster does have side effects after all. "Well, you are dressed today. Back to your regular duds, I see."

"Not totally regular," I note, showing her the Maddens. I normally reserve these for when I go out and go around the house in training shoes instead. "What do you think?"

"I think you need to keep them polished better," Andrea replies. "But they're fine. What's the occasion?"

"Like I said, I was thinking of going out today," I reply. I stop at the top of the stairs. "Andrea... would you mind if I borrowed some of your business books? I mean... oh fuck it, never mind."

"Whoa, whoa, *niichan*, stop," Andrea says, putting her hand on my shoulder. "Slow down, what's all this?"

"Just... I had a dream last night, and with what you said... I was thinking that maybe I can start learning about more than bodybuilding and partying," I say. "And I was thinking that maybe I could learn a little bit about investing and stocks, or real estate, or something like that." I shake my head, and shrug before giving her a grin. "You know, something actually useful in real life."

Andrea studies my face for a minute, then nods. "Hold on... I've got something in my room you can start with."

She jogs back to her room and comes out with a book. "Here. He's become a bit of a hack, and I don't want you running off like a madman with it, but take a read, and if you want... I'll be around to answer questions and talk with you."

I look down at the title. "*Rich Dad, Poor Dad?* Okay...

looks easy enough."

"It is. Not trying to say you're an idiot, Jackson... but you've been fucking off for the four years since high school finished for you. It's a decent refresher. In the meantime though, let's get some breakfast. I thought you were all about protein loading after lifting or whatever it is you call it, and if you don't mind, I'll share an egg or two with you."

I keep the book with me while we eat, then Andrea goes off to class. I've got a while before my afternoon swim, and I was planning on getting out during the evening, so I find a comfortable chair in the downstairs den and start reading. I'm caught up pretty quickly, and I find that I'm in chapter four when Mom comes in, pretty much ignoring me. Not that unexpected, really. "Hey Mom, is Pops around?"

Mom shrugs, not caring, and goes over to the liquor cabinet in the corner and pours herself a straight bourbon. I glance at the clock and shake my head. It's just after eleven. "A little early, even for you, isn't it?"

Mom downs half the bourbon and glares at me. "Considering you caused it, you have no room to say a damn thing," she hisses. "Do you know what the doctors just told me?"

"That you have a surgical addiction?" I shoot back. "That you need a psychiatrist more than you need more collagen in your lips? By the way, you're dribbling."

It's something that's happened to Mom since her most recent round of lip injections. She doesn't seem to be able to close her mouth properly all the time, and is constantly dribbling drinks from the corner of her mouth. Mom wipes away the bourbon with a swipe of her free hand and glares at me some more. "They said they can't do anything else for my waistline. According to them, their ethical guidelines prevent it."

"Maybe they have a point," I say, turning back to my borrowed book. I can feel Mom glaring at me for a little while longer before slamming back the rest of her bourbon and leaving the tumbler on the table. I finish the chapter I'm working on and go looking for Pops. Maybe he's in his office.

Before I get there, though, I hear something crash on the wall. What the hell? I rush down the hall the last little bit and go in, ducking as a paperweight comes flying by my head. "What the fuck?"

"I want her dead!" Pops screams, his face an angry, nearly purplish red. "I want that bitch found and her throat slit!"

I see that Nathan's in the room too, his face grave, but he remains silent. "What's going on? Is this over the photos still?" I ask.

"No, you ignorant, spoiled little shit!" Pops hollers, picking up a tablet and throwing it at me. I'm glad I've got good hands, he just bought this one after breaking the last one with the discussion we had the day after Kat's little limo trick. Even still, I barely manage to catch it, cradling it in my arms while I give the sensors inside a chance to try and figure out which way is up. "That's what I'm talking about!"

The screen stops revolving, and I see that a gossip website is up with a story it lists as *"Breaking News! New Orleans Social Magnate Has String of Mistresses Even While Being Named Family Man of The Year!"*

I read quickly. Most of the affairs are older ones, ones

that I've known about for years, stretching back to my high school days. This time there are pictures though, which I am surprised about. There's Pops in the casino, a couple of girls on his arm... Pops going into a hotel room with what looks like a very young girl, I'd be surprised if she was a month over eighteen at the time... damn. Couldn't have happened to a nicer guy, in my opinion. I'm also glad that Kat seems to have at least somewhat listened to my request, since this leaves the rest of the family totally out of it.

"You knew that accepting the award would bring greater public scrutiny, sir," Nathan says, trying to calm Pops down. "That the press would run with old rumors and play up some photos is expected."

"Bullshit! You know exactly who leaked this, Nathan. If you'd done your fucking job like I ordered you to do, there's no way the press would've gotten hold of those pictures. Hell, I'm friends with the owner of that casino! But now security camera footage of the night they gave me the award is out there. How the fuck does that even happen?"

"Maybe it's someone else," I try to add, knowing it sounds lame as soon as it comes out of my mouth, but I have to try. *Katrina, I hope you know what you've gotten yourself into.* "There have to be a lot of people who might have an ax to grind with you, Pops."

He ignores me, still staring at Nathan. "I don't care what it takes, I want that bitch found. Not next week, not tomorrow, not this evening. I want her found now. I don't give a shit if she's left New Orleans, left the States, or is hiding in the deepest shithole in the darkest back corner of the world. You find her,

Nathan. You find her, and... take Jackson with you. He obviously thinks this is all some sort of fucking joke, so you take him with you. And when you find her, you force her on her knees, and you slit her fucking throat right in front of Jackson here. Show him what a real man does."

A real man? So a real man is a guy who pitches a tantrum and throws things around his office, his potbelly hanging out and his face looking like he's about to have a goddamn coronary? A real man is someone who acts like a preschooler when his shit's exposed? Or is a real man the guy who's cheated on his wife so many times it's fucked with her head to the point she's a fucking basket case, and then when his shit's brought to the light of day, can't even handle it himself, but orders someone else to take care of it for him? All these thoughts flash through my mind, but I keep my mouth shut, even if I can't keep a look of disgust off my face.

Nathan looks disgusted as well, but nods. "I understand, Mr. DeLaCoeur."

"Then both of you get the fuck out. Actually, no, Jackson... you stay here. I want to talk with you."

Nathan gives me a glance, and in his green eyes I see a message. He'll wait for me to finish my conversation with Pops before anything else. I nod just a fraction of an inch, then turn my attention to Pops as Nathan closes the door behind him. "What do you want, Pops?"

He slams his hands down on the desk and screams, his breath stinking and spewing over the space between us. "What the fuck are you doing, disrespecting me like that in front of Nathan? How dare you contradict me in front of the staff!"

Contradict? What the fuck is he talking about? I was trying to deflect him, calm him down. "Pops, that wasn't my..."

"Shut the fuck up!" he yells again, at least taking a seat. "Jackson, it's bad enough that you embarrassed yourself, and yes, embarrassed me. You've been a disappointment your entire life, really. At least Andrea has enough sense to try and make something of herself, even if she does refuse to act like the proper daughter I've tried so hard to get her to be. But you had your uses. It's time to grow the fuck up, and that means seeing that life isn't all parties and limos and threesomes with sluts. Sometimes it means making hard decisions and doing hard things."

"Like ordering your attack dog to do your dirty work for you?" I ask before I even realize what's coming out of my mouth. Pops starts to turn red again, and I decide to just fucking go with it. "You've made your own bed. Now you're upset that someone's calling you on it? What about the rest of the family, Pops? Did you ever think about us in your little tirade?"

He slams his fist on the desk, sending a pen cup flying. He's staring daggers into my face. "I promise you, Jackson, if you ever disrespect me like that again... you'll find that Katrina Grammercy isn't the only person who can have her throat cut in front of someone she knows. Get the fuck out."

I get up, and I make my way out to the hallway. I immediately go looking for Nathan... once again, I have to know.

I find him in the back after twenty minutes of searching, where he's indulging in his other hobby, animals. The plantation still has a stable attached to it, and while it doesn't hold horses any longer, the Great Dane that Nathan keeps there is nearly as big as a pony. "Nathan."

He holds up a hand, and I see in his right hand he's holding a stiff-bristled brush that he's currently using to brush down the dog. "Yes, Maverick, you're a good boy. I know, I promised you a walk this morning, but I've got some business to attend to, so I'm going to have to keep this short. Tonight though, you and I can go for a romp in the back acres all you want. Wouldn't you like that?"

Maverick obviously does, as the giant dog wags his tail briskly. Nathan looks over at me, then back at Maverick. "You think it'd be okay if Jackson comes along?"

Maverick wags again, settling the issue. Nathan reaches over and unsnaps the long lead attached to Maverick's collar, and rubs his head. "Well, come on then. Maybe only a mile or so, then we can head back."

Maverick goes bounding off, acting for all the world like a two-hundred-pound puppy, heading for the door. His dog out of earshot, Nathan speaks to me for the first time. "Your shoes will get muddy. And I'd appreciate it if you'd limit the unpleasant talk around Maverick. He's a big baby, but he's my baby."

I look down and shrug. "I can get others. It's not as important as what you and I need to discuss."

Nathan nods and takes the lead, his long legs eating up the ground. We leave the stables and head north, into the unkempt scrubland that used to be indigo fields two hundred years ago. It's now mostly fields, with a little bit of wild indigo still covering areas of the property, but most of it disappeared after later attempts to turn the fields into tobacco and then cotton before the Civil War broke out. For Maverick, the open spaces are wonderful, even as I feel the first squelch of mud underneath my foot. "So why'd you brush him before this run?"

"We start every day with a brushing, even if it's just a few minutes," Nathan says, and I notice that he's changed into what looks like old combat boots, albeit unlaced. "Like I said, he's my baby, since I've never had children of my own. Lots of nieces and nephews, but none of my own."

"How often do you see them?" I ask, surprised at this insight into Nathan's mind. It's like when we sat down for tea, I'm finding depths to the man that I never knew existed.

"Not often enough," he admits. "Some of it is because I'm pretty busy working for Peter, but also... well, I'm not the sort of uncle that is exactly welcome at the family Thanksgiving table. How do you explain to a five-year-old that the richest member of the family got that way because he's put enough men in the ground to populate a small village?"

"Yet you keep doing it," I say quietly. "I'm not accusing you, just saying."

Nathan nods, his eyes following Maverick as the dog goes sniffing around. "Maverick! Leave that rabbit alone!" he hollers with a laugh, then sobers. "I do. It's all I've ever known, and to try and make myself out to be something more than what I am... I think the ghosts of my past would condemn me even more if I pretended to be something I'm not. But there's a part of me that would like to go back if I could, back to when I was a Green Beret. Yeah, there was a lot of killing then... but we did more than that. I can remember going into what some people call Kurdistan. We were working a black ops mission, this was when Saddam was still in power, just after the Mogadishu op that I told you about. We were supposedly there to reinforce the no-fly zone Clinton insisted on, but really we were there to help the Kurds get on their feet. I spent ninety days in that area, and never fired a shot. But what I did do was help them build three schools, and we dug two wells for villages that were struggling. I'll never forget the look in the eyes of those Kurd children when I pumped the handle, and fresh, clean water flowed out of that pipe. They thought I was Santa Claus and Allah all wrapped up in one that day. I use that image a lot when I meditate, trying to find inner peace."

"And how much meditation will it take for you to find inner peace with what Peter just told you?" I ask. "Hours? Days?"

Nathan stops and turns to face me fully, his scarred eye wide, his right eye arched. "Peter? I think that's the first time I've ever heard you call him anything other than Pops."

"Considering the man just told me that if I ever talk back to him again he'd have my own throat cut, I think that disqualifies him from being referred to by a fatherly name, don't you?" I ask. "But my question stands, Nathan. What are you going to do?"

Nathan turns and watches Maverick bound along. "Did you know the average Great Dane lives only six to ten years? It's why they're also called the Heartbreak Breed, because they're so affectionate, but they die so quickly. But it's also part of the reason I chose Maverick. He's already four, I've had him since he was a puppy. But I know that if I ever piss off Peter DeLaCoeur... there are other men who will do what I will not. Including dropping my corpse into the Gulf. Oh, not that I'd make it easy for them, it'd be a very expensive operation for sure. But I wouldn't want to rob an innocent dog of love and affection, or of too much of his life. You know your... that Peter would have Maverick killed first. It's a poor way to soothe my conscience, but I wouldn't be robbing Maverick of too much of his life if that happens."

"What are you even saying?" I ask, hot. "What type of monster have you become, Nathan?"

Nathan turns back to me, gives me a studied look, and shakes his head. "You miss my point. I can't go after Katrina, not this time. I found her like you asked, and in the course of my investigation, I found out things... well, I found out things that only she should tell you. The only thing I could give you was an address. But I can't go after her for this. I'll delay, and I'll do what I can, but eventually Peter's going to reach out to someone else as well. I can't stop that."

I nod and watch Maverick romp around the fields while we talk. "What am I going to do?" I mutter to myself, the mud squelching as we reach a turn in the little path we're following, and Nathan stops. "What can I do?"

"I don't know if you're asking for my advice or just muttering to yourself, but here it is anyway, Jackson. Stand up. Be a man. I saw how you were last night, coming home from seeing her, and don't try to say that you didn't. But she isn't going to be interested in a playboy. If she's going to be interested at all... it's in the man you could be. You're not dumb, even if you pretend to be for whatever reason. So stand up. It's dangerous, but like you said when you approached me before... it's the right thing to do."

I shove my hands into the pockets of my pants and think. Nathan studies me for a bit, then turns. "Maverick! Let's head back now!"

As the dog goes running by, heading for the stable, Nathan stops next to me. "Don't think too long. I guarantee you, Peter will contact others about this. I've seen him this angry before. You've got a couple of days' head start. At most."

Chapter 11
Kat

CDG- You found me again.

BS- This time it wasn't that hard. You practically were advertising your presence online, if you know where to look.

CDG- I had a reason for that.

BS- I see.

I'm in a chat room, one of my hacker rooms, and I close the main window, dropping into just private chat with Blue Sakura, aka Andrea. I've been looking for her today, hoping she can give me insight into how Peter DeLaCoeur is handling the news that hit the Internet today. Unfortunately, with such stuff, I couldn't get the newspapers to put it out, but in this digital world, it should still carry weight.

BS- What are your reasons?

CDG- I was wondering how Peter took the news.

BS- And how would I know that?

CDG- You know who I am. You don't think I don't know who you are?

There's a silence on the screen for a bit, then Blue Sakura comes back.

BS- Okay, let's lay our cards out. It's been a long time since we used to play in my room.

CDG- Yeah, it was fun. You had a pretty awesome Barbie collection. It seems that we've both changed since we thought that Ryan Reynolds was cute.

BS- What do you mean thought? I still do.

CDG- TMI. So how did Peter react?

BS- Your timing is off today. I haven't been home yet, and I had a nine a.m. class. I haven't heard from anyone at home.

CDG- What's got you out so late? It's nearly seven.

BS- Checking some things. Your reappearance had me chasing some stuff down.

CDG- Anything I'd be interested in?

BS- Perhaps. If I figure it out, I'll drop you a message. Peter certainly doesn't trust me, even less than Jackson. Spoils me rotten, wants me to be his little princess, but he doesn't trust me.

CDG- Speaking of that... I have verification on your history, too. I'm holding it in reserve, it's the sort of bomb that could be spun to hurt Peter badly. But maybe you, too?

BS- We can discuss that later. I need to go for now. Thanks.

CDG- For what?

BS- Discretion.

Blue Sakura logs off, and I sit back, sighing. Discretion isn't my strong suit, and I'm no closer to finding out if I'm closer to my goal than I was when I started looking for Andrea online. I want firsthand verification, I need it. The depression is bad tonight, even though I was able to read all about the social reaction to what I'd dropped on Peter DeLaCoeur's lap. My workout wasn't enough to alleviate it, my endorphins were not enough to push it all back, and for some reason, I can't take my pills. I'm sitting here, staring at them in their plastic bottle, and all I can think about is how I made fun of Jackson for his own self-medication. How can I accuse him of running away from reality when I'm taking my own collection of mind-altering stuff?

Angry, I grab my bottle, get up, and shove it into my dresser, out of sight. I'm going to handle this the old-fashioned way, the same way that the old masters advised. *Purity is something that cannot be attained except by piling effort upon effort.*

Fine. Effort has brought me success. Effort has brought me the ability to bring down Peter DeLaCoeur if I can stay the course. Effort has allowed me to hone myself into the perfect instrument of my vengeance. I can beat this too, dammit.

I go over to my meditation corner, lighting the candle there. It's a new one, a gift from Darcy after her most recent visit, with a fresh ocean scent and supposedly a guaranteed twelve hour burn time. Instead of meditating, however, I stretch out, cradling my head in my arms as I let myself drift, searching for something I can hold onto to pull myself out of the depression.

What comes to mind startles me, and I sit up. Jackson? What the hell? He's a damn playboy, despite whatever he may have said when he visited. Yeah, it was noble, yeah he may have risked the wrath of his father... but he's still wrapped up in being a douchebag.

I lie back down, letting my mind drift again, but it keeps circling back, refusing to let go of Jackson. He can't be all bad, after all. If he wasn't lying about his physique being all natural...

"It's all natural," Jackson teases me, stretching out beside me. "After all, steroids cause shrunken balls. Did they look shrunken to you?" He's got a point. I remember what his cock looked and felt like in the limo, he's certainly not lacking in the size department with either the twig or the berries.

"I guess I owe you some credit for that," I say, reaching out and

touching his arm. He's wearing a white dress shirt and charcoal gray slacks, although since we're lying down he's taken off his shoes. "So why'd you put so much effort into lifting?"

"To escape my sadness," he whispers, reaching out and brushing my cheek. "When you left... you left a hole inside me. That, combined with the rest, I had to pour it out somewhere."

"You... you were on my mind, too," I admit, laying my hand on his side. "I really thought you were special, and that someday you were going to ask me out on a date, not just over to build models or study or play video games."

"I would have," Jackson says, easing closer. We're close, and I can feel the warmth and magnetism of his body so close, my heart beating faster in my chest. I'm not a virgin since I had to practice my seduction and erotic skills on someone, but I've never actually made love before. My heart has never been opened to anyone... but Jackson. And even then, that was a whole different me. "I was going to, and I wanted to kiss you, too. Remember that last time we played in the pool?"

I chuckle, nodding. "You kept staring at my butt. I thought I was getting a wedgie or something."

Jackson shakes his head, his hand stroking down my back to rest on my hip, just on the upper curve of my butt. "Not quite."

I reach my own hand down, fully cupping his ass.

Jackson leans forward, and we kiss, not like in the limo where I was giving him seductive kisses that never touched his lips but real, tender, and heartfelt ones. His lips caress mine, our tongues reaching out, probing each other, as I taste the wonderful, sexy man in front of me.

I moan when his hand comes down and grabs my ass, his strong hand kneading the flesh and muscle. I've always favored my ass over the rest of my body, and Jackson somehow knows, pulling me on top of him and grabbing with both hands as I laugh. "Mmm... you're more aggressive than I thought you'd be after I nearly broke your arm."

"I like to live dangerously," he teases. "Or at least, you inspire me to."

We kiss and grind against each other, Jackson slipping his hands inside the waistband of my pants and grabbing the naked skin underneath. I'm hot, so hot I can't believe it, it's never felt this good before. Even when Carla taught me the Touches, it was never with this feeling inside my chest, never this dam that threatens to explode and consume me with what's held behind it.

I sit up, groaning when my hips straddle Jackson's and I feel his cock pushing up at his pants, my pussy aching for it to fill me. Still, I reach down and begin unbuttoning his shirt, easing the cloth to the side with each button, exposing his perfect chest and stomach. Every muscle is defined, his skin slightly tanned and hairless, not at all like my pale skin that barely sees the light of day most of the time. His nearly white hair and blue eyes gleam in the light of the candle, and as my hand goes over his heart, he lets go of my hips to cover his hand. We don't say anything, just look at each other. There's no need for words, not right now.

I finish unbuttoning his shirt and Jackson sits up, shrugging out of it before wrapping his arms around me in an embrace, the passion creeping out. We're hungry, devouring each other, pushing clumsily at the pants keeping us from what we need. Somehow we roll as we strip, until I'm underneath Jackson, his cock probing at the entrance to my pussy, his eyes sparkling as he looks into my eyes. "How do you feel about me?"

"I loved you then," I tell Jackson, and he pauses, tears in his eyes.

"I love you now," he replies, pushing in. He's perfect, filling me the way that no partner has ever done before. He slides in and out, my body lighting up, his cock giving me sensations I've never felt before. He's just on

the edge of being rough, a little but not too much, driving his cock into me over and over, his mouth kissing me hard, almost bruising. I claw at his back as pleasure explodes over and over in my body, battering at the walls around my heart, electricity tingling along every inch of my skin. Jackson's powerful but tender, rough but gentle, and I'm washed away, giving in to him and submitting to my every desire.

I open up to him, and in that instant, I see it all. I see a future I've never imagined before, of happiness, of growing old next to him, of children running in a park, of snowcapped mountains and high lakes. I see...

It's all washed away as Jackson's cock drives in again and again, pushing me toward the edge. I can feel him trembling, holding back to take care of me, and I kiss him, as tenderly as I can with the way my body is being hammered higher and higher. "Jackson... I'm... I'm..."

I can't say anymore as he pushes me over the edge, and whiteness fills my heart and my mind, driving away the darkness that has been ever present for the past decade. His heart, his love obliterates it, banishing it away, and as my orgasm fills me with light, I feel him shudder and fill me again, his cock exploding deep inside me.

"I'll always love you," Jackson whispers as he gathers me. "There is nothing we should be quite so grateful for as the last line of the poem that goes, 'When your own heart asks.'"

"When you own heart asks..." I repeat, the quote from *Hagakure* echoing in my thoughts as I come back to reality. My body aches, unfulfilled desire aching in my loins and my nipples tight in my sports bra. I sit up, shaking my head again. A fantasy lover, never to be found in the real world. And what's this bullshit about a future? About love? My life is going to be measured in terms of days and hours once I unleash the next broadside against Peter DeLaCoeur.

But I can't deny the depression that was threatening me is pushed back a bit, and I feel a lighter. I'm shaken, though... Jackson? And what about my fantasy... is it true? Did I love him? Do I love him?

I get up off my meditation mat and blow out the candle, heading for my food area. I feel good enough to make some dinner, and then maybe I can get back to work on verifying some of Peter's criminal connections. I'm hacking a casino, the same one that I released the security camera footage from. Unfortunately, their security server is different from their financial server, and the security on it is more closely held.

Still, before I sit down at my computer, I think back to my fantasy. Jackson? Really? But...

A knock comes at my door, and I look up. It's familiar, even if I've heard it only once before.

"Kat! Open up, please! It's me!"

I go over and check my peephole, even though I'm already reaching for the lock. He's outside, and in the dim light of my security light, he looks panicked. "Kat... Katrina! Open up!"

I pull the bolt and open the door, Jackson stepping back enough to let the door open enough for him to get inside. As soon as he's able, he pushes past me and I close the door. "What's this about, Jackson?"

Jackson shifts from side to side, his eyes flicking around the shadowed space of my loft. "Kat, you need to run. Peter's angry, and I don't know if I can keep you safe any longer."

"Talk."

Chapter 12
Jackson

Looking at Katrina in the dim light, the first urge I have is to pull her to me, to hold her and protect her. I resist the urge only by pushing past her and reminding myself of the task at hand. I don't want to be the man whose mind cares about nothing but sex.

"What do you mean, keep me safe?" she asks after her one-word command. She locks the door, and I notice that this time, she didn't have her pistol with her when she answered the door. Why?

"Where's your pistol?" I ask, still looking around. "And is that all you have?"

"It's all I've needed," Kat says in a relaxed voice, going over to her computer desk and taking the pistol out. "I've been doing maintenance on it today."

"Yeah well, I hope it's in perfect condition," I say, wanting to sit down but not knowing where. The loft is nearly black inside, with only the light from Kat's monitor illuminating anything. "Jesus Katrina, can you turn on a light?"

Katrina makes her way past me and hits a switch, illuminating what looks like, of all things, a line of white Christmas lights that stretches around her living area and over her bed. "That's new."

"I used other lights last time. I picked these up because I can run them off a couple of double A batteries if I want," she says, sitting down in her desk chair. "I have enough costs with just keeping my computer going. So what did you mean, Jackson? You didn't show up panicked at my door telling me Peter's going to be coming after me just to see my home lights."

I try to find a place to sit down, finally giving up and pointing to her bed. "May I?"

"Go ahead. But get to talking, Jackson."

I can barely call this a bed, it's so thin and uncomfortable. I think I might be more comfortable sitting on the floor as I adjust myself. "You know, you don't have to bitch at me about it, Kat. I'm serious when I said I'm here for the right reasons. Peter saw your most recent hit on him. Your friends in the online media need to watch themselves also, but Peter knows that he can't hit at them easily or invisibly. He hits you, though... hell, Kat, you don't even exist. Nathan took a week to find you, and he's one of the best in the city at it. And Peter went through the roof at this one. You touched a nerve that he isn't going to let go of."

"I don't want him letting go," Katrina says, her voice intense again. "I want him to latch on so that I can drag him into the light of day with it, then drive a stake through his fucking heart like a vampire."

"Yeah well, I don't want to see you dead because of it!" I yell back, then settle back on the bed. "For fuck's sake, I know you don't care, but I care if you live through this or not."

"And yourself?" Katrina asks, but this time, there's a bit of softness in her voice. "And what's with Peter?"

"He threw a tantrum today... Jesus, how I ever thought that man could have been my father. Throwing things, then he tells Nathan to hunt you down and cut your throat in front of me, because I dared to say that your little act may not have been from you. Then afterward, he tells me that if I ever contradict him in public again, he'll have my throat cut. So I went and talked to Nathan."

"And what did Staff Sergeant Black say about it?" Kat asks, something I didn't know. She notices my surprise, and smirks. "I know all about him, remember? Give me five minutes, and I could have his last commanding officer's home phone number."

I sigh, then half-laugh. She's still a step ahead of me, but I have to get through to her. "He says that he won't come after you. But he also knows that Peter is going to send someone else after you if he doesn't produce results. And he has to look like he's doing something, or else he's going to end up just as dead as Peter wants you to be. There's more than one way to kill someone in New Orleans."

Kat nods, then leans forward, propping her elbows on her knees. "You look more awake than you were before, at least. You understand the stakes of this battle. Either I take him down, or I die. I may die either way."

"I don't want that, Katrina!" I repeat vehemently. "I want you to live!"

"Why? Why give a damn about me?"

Her quiet question, barely above a whisper, cuts me off, and I look at her again. Her hair is totally black in the dim light from the Christmas LEDs, but those eyes of hers... like two tears in the middle of that perfect face. "Because you were one of the only decent things in my childhood, Kat. We met when we were both six, and even then, I knew my mother hated me. She kept telling me how I'd ruined her figure, how it was my fault that Peter was the way he was. I didn't understand it at the time, but I did the math later... Peter was already having an affair with Andrea's mother before I was even born. I didn't understand it at the time, and thought it was all my fault."

"It never was," Kat says, getting off her chair and sitting on the other end of the bed. She crosses her legs, kind of yoga style, or maybe in a meditation pose. "But go on."

"From the beginning, you were my best friend... hell, for a lot of it, my only friend. Andrea didn't even speak English at first when she came to the house, and she and I have never got along all that well, at least until the past few days. We never did really, although I remember that you two sometimes played together. But most of the time you and I played together. I looked forward every day when you would pull up in that Ford Crown Vic that your dad drove, because it meant a whole afternoon or a full day if it was a Saturday where I felt like a normal kid, and not the son of..."

"Of what?" Katrina asks softly.

"Of a human snake," I say after a moment. "Even when I was little, I think I knew about my... about Peter at some level. When everyone else was able to bring their parents to school for those silly days, he was never able to go. Then there were all the other signs... the sports cars, the clothes, the constant pretty girls who kept coming to the house. The son of a bitch didn't even worry about trying to hide his cheating even, although he's gotten worse as Andrea and I have gotten older. And through it all, I was the one blamed by Mom, and more or less ignored by

Peter. To him, I was just an... an accessory, I guess. Something to check off the box, saying he'd done what needed to be done to complete his bucket list on life."

"But with me, you felt different?"

I nod, smiling for the first time in what feels like all day. "Yeah. We clicked from the beginning, Katrina. I mean sure, you and I have our differences. Even back then we had those. But you liked so many of the things I liked, and every time you and I got together... it was magic to me. You know, I'd trade all the groupies, all the cars and the drugs and the parties for another chance to sit down with you and complete that stupid Corvette that I threw out later?"

"So why didn't you try and find me?" Katrina asks, and I can hear the hurt in her voice. "I spent six years in foster care, and a lot of that was hell. Even with Virginia, there was a lot of hell I went through."

"At first, I was just told you were gone," I answer. "Later, when I found out that your parents had been killed, I was told you were sent to live with your grandparents in Vermont. Since I didn't know anything about your grandparents, and I didn't know how much my parents lied to me on a constant basis... I believed it. But without you in my life, without that normalcy... I realize now that I've become too much like my father. I may have all my hair still, and there's a lot less fat around my waist, but in too many other ways, I've walked down his path. Except for one."

"Which is?"

"I don't want you to die, Katrina. You were my friend, and since seeing you..." I stop, unable to finish what I want to say. "I don't want you hurt. You talk about going through a decade of hell, and I don't doubt it. But I've been through my own kind of hell for my entire life, especially when my best friend and the only girl I... liked was taken from me. But if I have to, I'd rather go through that again than have you hurt."

I look down at my shoes, noting that I'm still wearing the same muddy and stained loafers I'd put on this morning, in fact, I'm wearing the same stuff that I wore for my walk with Nathan. It's filthy, and for the first time in years, I don't really care.

Katrina surprises me by reaching out and putting a hand on my arm, and I look up, into her glittering eyes. "I believe you," she says softly. "Jackson... you were the only thing I missed from my old life once I accepted that my parents were dead. But I'm not going to stop, and I'm not going to run. If Peter wants to send his men after me... it's going to cost him a lot to get my head on a stick."

"You sound a lot like Nathan," I mutter, but I can feel her hand through my shirt, and I want her so damn bad. I want to feel her fingers on my skin again, not on my shirt. I want to kiss those lips, to see those tear-colored eyes change to what I know they can be, a clear blue like the Caribbean. I want to hold her and tell her that the pain can go away, for both of us. I want all of that, but I don't move. The hurt and distrust is still too much inside her, I can tell.

"He's misguided, but somewhat honorable still," Katrina says. "You can learn something from him, if you study him closely enough."

"There are other things, other people I'd rather learn from, even if he is interesting," I reply, letting go of my pain some and covering her hand with mine. "Katrina, I want you safe... but if not, I want to be part of your life."

Kat's about to answer, when her computer beeps and she looks over, breaking the tension between us. She pulls her hand free and goes over, pulling up a window. She's quiet for a few minutes as she reads and types, then leans back, her face slack. "Oh my God."

Chapter 13
Kat

I can feel Jackson's eyes burning into me as he tells me that he wants me to be part of his life. I'm lost in those eyes, and the honesty of what he just revealed to me. It's nothing that I didn't already know, I've spent nearly ten years learning everything I could about the way Peter DeLaCoeur and the way he's run his business and family, but to me, it sounded like it was the first time Jackson has ever said it out loud. The way he just opened up, and the weight that drops off his shoulders as he tells me about the pain of growing up in his life... it touches me.

So when his hand covers mine, I feel myself being pulled toward him by his eyes, and I want to lean in toward him. I want to tell him how just hours ago, I was dreaming about him, and about the fact that since he's come back into my life, I feel like there's a chance at a future.

My computer beeps, saving me. I take my hand off Jackson's arm and get off the bed, trying to keep the trembling out of my knees as I cover the short distance. I sit down in my chair gratefully, and see that Andrea has messaged me.

BS- You there?

CDG- I have a visitor. Your brother.

BS- Half-brother. He's making strides, but he's got a way to go before he's my full brother.

CDG- Your choice. What's up?

BS- You know you're not the only one researching Peter's past, right?

CDG- I figured as much. What, did you learn something helpful?

BS- Yes, but it's not something I want to release to the press.

CDG- What?

BS- Can you receive a file?

CDG- Yes. Format?

BS- Encrypted document.

CDG- Send it.

I get a file transfer notice and analyze it quickly. I know Jackson's sitting behind me, but he's being quiet, probably still absorbing everything that we've said to each other over the past few minutes. The file transfers quickly, and I give it another scan before dropping it into a virtual box.

CDG- Encrypt code?

BS- My full name.

CDG- English or Japanese?

BS- English. I'll be in touch after you read it. Goodbye.

Andrea Julia DeLaCoeur... the file unlocks, and a document along with a subfolder pulls up, unzipping and opening for me. I read quickly, and realize what Andrea meant. "Oh my God."

Jackson's next to me in an instant, looking at me closely. "Kat... Katrina? What is it?"

I point, unable to speak. Jackson looks at the window, his lips moving silently as he reads, something he did even as a kid.

Samuel Grammercy, detective lieutenant, New Orleans Police Department. Thirty-eight years old at the time of his death, no suspects ever identified in his death by car bombing.

Michael Ball, forty-eight years old, bartender. Alcohol

server's license states that he works in the Miami area.

The pictures aren't great, all taken from public sources, but there's enough there to verify what Andrea's document tells me.

"They're alive," Jackson says after he finishes clicking through the files. "They... they never were blown up. How?"

"I don't know," I whisper, finally finding my voice. "But Jackson... I remember. I remember the fire, the boom, I remember it all. How is that possible?"

Jackson shakes his head. "I don't know either," he says. "Katrina, can you trust this information? Who sent it to you?"

"Someone I can believe," I reply, not sure why I won't tell Jackson the truth about his half-sister. I just don't think Andrea would want it yet. "But I need to verify this."

Jackson gives me a look. "Katrina, this changes everything. I'm not saying it makes Peter any less of an animal, or any less of a threat to you. But you've spent nearly half your life vowing revenge for something that may never have happened. And if your father's in Miami... you're going to need help."

"Whose?" I ask, shaking my head. "Darcy... but she's got a family now. Virginia's taking care of two new foster kids herself now, she can't help me... I'm alone."

"No you're not," Jackson says, kneeling down next to me and taking my hand. "Kat, you've got me. I already told you that I was going to try and deflect Peter off you... now we've got something else to do."

"You mean it?" I ask, giving his hand a quick squeeze. "It's going to involve money, deception, and lying to Peter.

You'd be signing your own death warrant if he finds out."

Jackson nods, then smirks. "Nathan told me this morning that I need to stand up. Be a man, he said. Maybe this is just my way of doing it."

I nod, then smile. "I like that. Okay, so we work together on this. But I don't have a lot of details. Miami's a big city, and there are a lot of bars there. All I have is a name for him."

"Then we find out together," Jackson says with a smile. "After all, who'd think that Prince Douchebag would actually be trying to do something worthwhile with his time? I mean, besides reading *Rich Dad, Poor Dad*."

"Good book. Myopic, but a decent book," I comment to Jackson's surprise. "You'll find as we spend time together I know more than just martial arts, hacking, and seduction."

"Okay. So where can I start first?" he asks. "This isn't something I have any experience with, so I'm going to be putting myself in your hands."

"First... I need to know more. I need verification, and there's only one person who can do that for me that I know of."

"Who?"

"Nathan Black."

Jackson shakes his head emphatically at first, but then the shakes slow as something dawns on him. "He told me... he told me that he didn't kill your father."

"Not that he didn't set the car bomb. So find out what happened. Meanwhile, I'm going to go to some of my other sources, help narrow down the Miami end of things."

Jackson thinks for a moment, and I understand. He suspects how dangerous Nathan Black is, but I know exactly how dangerous he is. On the other hand, Jackson knows more about Nathan's state of mind than I do right now, which is why I'm asking him to talk to Nathan directly. It's still dangerous, however.

Finally, he hums, then grins. "Deal. How do you want me to pass along what I know? I mean, coming here all the time is great for me, but puts you in more danger, right?"

I nod, then hold out my hand. "Phone."

He takes out his phone, and I quickly go to his address book. "Here, under Grace Miseria. It's another one of my aliases. Jackson... not too many people have this number. I normally give out one of my rotating SIMs."

He nods, and looks at the number for a moment, then puts his phone back in his pocket. "I understand. Let me talk to Nathan, and I'll be in touch as soon as I have something."

Jackson walks to the door and unlocks it. In a moment of deja vu, I'm up, running to the door before he leaves, this time though catching him before he gets the door all the way open. "Jackson... wait."

"What is it?" he asks, turning back to me, his face still full of concern. We were yelling at each other at the beginning, and now I want to kiss him. Weird.

"Just... I wanted to say that I'm sorry. I'm sorry about getting your junk in the papers."

Jackson smiles and shakes his head. "Thank you for the apology, but I'm not angry about it anymore."

"Why?"

"Because it brought you back into my life. I think that's more than worth the price of a few pictures. Goodnight, Kat."

"Not Kat. Not for you, at least," I reply, taking his hand and give it a squeeze. "I was thinking, after you used it a few times... I kinda like hearing you call me Katrina again."

"I like that, too. Goodnight, Katrina."

Jackson leaves, and I watch him for a moment before closing and locking my door. My computer beeps again, and I see that it's Andrea.

BS- You okay?

CDG- Yeah. Took me a minute to read it over, and then to discuss what to do next with Jackson.

BS- He knows?

CDG- He knows the info. Not who sent it. That's up to you.

BS- Thank you. Maybe in time, but I've my own plans. Not sure if he's to be included.

CDG- I understand. Do me two favors?

BS- I can try.

CDG- He's going to talk to Nathan about the bomb. Keep an eye on him.

BS- If I can. And two?

CDG- Rich Dad, Poor Dad? Really?

BS- LOL. I just gave him that to give him some easy fluff to see if he was serious. It seems like he's been snapped back to reality.

CDG- It does, doesn't it?

BS- You sure you're okay with this?

CDG- I'll try and be. Hey, I just thought of something. If there's an emergency... call me on Viber. 864-885-9073. I check it often. Goodnight.

BS- Goodnight. And thank you.

Chapter 14
Jackson

I'm unsure of how to approach Nathan as I get back home. The sun went down hours ago, and Peter is probably gone. Growing up, he almost never spent evenings at home, usually going to see "friends," as he would put it. So there's a chance that Nathan might be with him if he's actually conducting business.

On the other hand, if Peter's out with any of his current mistresses, he'd leave Nathan behind. Now that I've admitted to myself and to Katrina that he's a philandering, lying son of a bitch, I'm able to recall little details about the way he does things, things that I'd overlooked or never really cared to think about before. Like dyeing his hair, or the fact that he changes secretaries on a roughly yearly basis. Or the fact that when he's going out to fuck around, he leaves Nathan behind.

I'm encouraged when I see that Peter's Porsche is gone. That thing only has two seats, and unless Nathan's riding shotgun, he'll be home. Of course, Peter never lets anyone else drive that German showpiece. I park my Audi and go inside. And here I thought my car was pretentious...

The first person I find is Andrea, sitting in the dining room with her textbooks in front of her. She's stripped out of her power suit and looks more like the twenty-year-old that she is. Shows me how fifteen hours can change someone, I guess. "Hey, Andrea."

"Whatcha want, Jack?" Andrea asks, grumpy. Studying must be going bad for her. She's always been moody, but normally she's never outwardly hostile to me unless I'm being a jerk to her. "Don't tell me you finished *Rich Dad*."

"No, I got to chapter four before everything sort of kicked off this morning. Since then, I've been... well, busy. How was your day?"

"Sucked. Got my midterms back." Oh yeah, she said something a while back about preparing for her summer midterms.

"Andrea, you go three semesters a year, you've been doing that since junior high school. Don't you think, well, maybe you can let go of a test or two? Nobody can throw perfect games each time out. I've had bad lift days, shit like that. Besides, what'd you score?" It is one of the things that I've never grasped about Andrea until meeting Katrina again. Her drive is superhuman, and she's getting her MBA at twenty because of it. Still, it can't be healthy, having graduated high school at sixteen, getting her bachelor's at nineteen and now being more than halfway through her MBA. I've never worried about it before, mainly because I've been too much of a self-absorbed manchild to give a damn. Well, that's going to change. "Come on, Andrea. What'd you score?"

"Only 83 and 87," she grumps, slamming her book closed. "Happy now?"

"Whoa, whoa, Andrea. I wasn't trying to piss you off," I hurriedly apologize. I want to snap at her in return, but something, maybe something that rubbed off from Katrina's talk with me, holds me back. "Okay, so you didn't get As in them.

And I know, the shitstorm I've raised this past week and a half or so hasn't helped much."

Andrea takes a deep breath, then nods. "Thank you, *oniichan*. Sorry, too. Margaret was bitchy when Peter left tonight. We had an argument, which is why I'm out here instead of in my room. She's insisted that she hold court over the entire family wing of the house, and threw me out. It was either study here or in the kitchen, and the kitchen's too hot."

I smile and pat her shoulder. "I understand, thanks for the heads-up. I'm sorry you had to deal with that." She looks started at first, then nods gratefully. Mom's always treated her like shit, but I've never really bothered to empathize before, I guess because I was always too wrapped up in my own bullshit. That's going to change. "Quick favor. Have you seen Nathan?"

Andrea nods. "After Peter left and Margaret's blow-up, I heard him say something about getting a workout in. You'll probably find him out there, or maybe in his workshop."

"Thanks. And I owe you a hot chocolate later or something, something to help you stay awake while you study."

"Sounds good. And Jackson..."

"Yeah, Andrea?" I ask, already heading out the door. I pause, and look back.

She looks like she's going to say something, then shakes her head. "Just... when you get back, if you'd like to talk about what you read, I'll make some time."

"Thanks. We'll see."

I leave the dining room and run up to my room, changing clothes quickly. I didn't get a second workout in today yet, and I could use a sweat myself. It only takes me three minutes, and I jog outside. I can hear Mom drunkenly singing to herself in her room, so slurred I can't even make it out, but it sounds like blues. I leave the drunken singing and the main house behind, heading out to the gym. Andrea's right, I find Nathan inside, stripped down to just some compression shorts and pounding on a heavy bag. He puts a lot of thirty-year-old athletes to shame. He's still pretty ripped, and I can only hope to be in that kind of shape at his age.

A timer goes off, and Nathan stops, stepping away and seeing me for the first time. "How goes your warnings?" he asks, surprised when I don't answer. "What?"

"Did you?" I ask, surprised at how calm I say it, despite my anger. "Did you set the bomb?"

The timer goes off, and Nathan turns back to the bag. His first punch is a jab, but still, the hundred and fifty-pound bag jumps like it's just been shot, only to be followed up almost immediately by a thunderous right hand that shakes the beam the bag is attached to. The foot-thick wooden beam groans and I see dust shake down around him as Nathan continues with his assault on the bag, driving fists, elbows, knees and his bare feet into the leather sides. When the timer goes off again, he looks surprised that I'm still standing there watching him.

"I'm going to repeat myself, Nathan. Did you set the bomb that blew up the Grammercys' car? No matter how much you want to try and scare the shit outta me by beating up the bag, I'm going to get an answer."

"You sure about that?" Nathan asks. The timer goes off again, but he ignores it, still looking at me. "You think you can beat an answer out of me?"

"I'll do what I have to, succeed or not. I thought you were a better man than that. Why'd you lie, Nathan, when I asked you about the bomb before?"

"I didn't lie," Nathan says, stripping off his gloves. "What I said was that I didn't kill Katrina's parents."

"Considering her father's alive and running a bar in Miami, no shit. Now, are you going to tell me what really happened?"

Nathan goes over to the locker that contains the boxing equipment and pulls out one set of sparring gloves. "Let's see if you really are ready for the answer. You survive two rounds, and I'll tell you a bedtime story."

"What are the rules?" I ask, catching the gloves as he tosses them to me.

"Boxing. I don't want to actually hurt you, Jackson. But you'll have to earn the truth if you want it. Coming in here and demanding things from me doesn't show me that you're ready for the truth. So I will test your resolve."

We walk over to the matted area, which is about the closest thing we have to a ring without throwing down outside on the grass. Nathan sets the timer, then pulls his gloves on. "On the bell."

"No mouthpieces?" I ask. Nathan shrugs, and I get his point. I don't even have one here in the gym, and it doesn't matter anyway. If something gets knocked out, I'll go to the dentist.

The electronic bell goes off, and I come out. I've got size on him, at least twenty pounds, and I'm an inch taller, but I'm taking nothing for granted. He might not want to hurt me, he might be tired and sweaty, but he's not an idiot. In fact, he's perhaps the deadliest man I know.

I lose track of what's happening after his first combination comes whipping toward my head. All I know is that he's a whirlwind, fists coming through every gap in whatever defense I set up. I keep my hands high, protecting my head, hoping that all the crunches and other stomach training I do can keep me from getting put down with a liver shot.

Nathan does notice, and I'm eating punch after punch to my stomach and sides, and I run, dancing and shucking and jiving as best I can. I had decent moves in my last fight, easily avoiding the guy I fought then, some football player from Tulane who thought he was a little tougher than he actually was.

But Nathan's no college football player with more balls than brains. He's trained, he's a professional, and as the bell beeps to signal the end of the first round, I'm already staggering as I head back to the corner.

"You can't take an ass whipping like that again," Nathan says, barely breathing hard while I kneel in my corner. "Give up."

"Not until you tell me what you did to the Grammercys." I get to my feet, my stomach on fire and my legs shaking. "Come on, I won't just be a punching bag this round."

Nathan's eyes gleam with something that I think is either respect or perhaps pity, or maybe he just thinks I'm out of my fucking gourd. The bell rings and I step out, flicking a jab. It's not much, but I hope it's enough to keep him from just steamrolling me again.

No such luck. In a sweet little move, he switches his

stance, his right hand becoming his lead and catching me over my punch, his fist crashing into my jaw. I feel something work loose, and the coppery tang of blood fills my mouth. I stagger back, trying to duck away, covering up. The world is spinning, and suddenly I hit the mat, knocked down.

"One... two... stay the fuck down... four..." Nathan says, and I at least take a little comfort in the fact that he's breathing heavier than he was before. It'd be so easy, giving up. But Katrina would never give up. She's willing to die for her vengeance...

I don't know how I get to my feet, but suddenly I'm up with my fists out, and for some crazy fucking reason, I'm waving Nathan over. "Come on! Is that it, old man?"

Nathan shakes his head and steps forward again, this time back in his typical left-handed stance. His left jab catches me between the eyes, and I eat it, ducking into the punch and throwing everything I have into a right cross that catches him in the side, just under his armpit and causing him to grunt.

He steps back and shakes out his arm. Nodding in respect, he unleashes hell, and I'm forced to just defend again before another sledgehammer explodes in my stomach, and I'm down on one knee.

"Stay the fuck down!" Nathan gasps, stepping back. I hold my stomach and look up at the clock, seeing there's still thirty seconds left. I can survive thirty seconds, hell he's gasping for breath as much as I am.

I get up, my left hand holding my ribs, and wave him in. "I got a lot more."

Nathan spits to the side and steps forward again,

throwing what he probably thinks is a mercy shot, a looping overhand that if it lands is going to put me into dreamland for quite a while. I weave, coming under the punch and unleashing everything I've got left into a left hook. As weak as I feel right now, it catches Nathan with probably all the force of a sick grasshopper, but still it catches him, and I feel a sense of accomplishment as the bell rings.

He steps back, and wipes a bit of blood from his nose, while I work my jaw and spit, bright red splattering on the mats, but at least no teeth come out. "I did it."

"You did," Nathan says, stripping off his glove. He sticks his hand out, and I reciprocate, shaking hands with the man. "I didn't think you had it in you to get up from that second one."

"Bullshit, you didn't think I'd get up from the first one," I reply, rubbing my jaw. "Think we can get something to ice this thing? I'm not sure I won't lose a tooth still."

"Yeah. Let's sit outside, and I'll get you an ice pack."

We go out by the pool, Nathan going inside and coming back out a minute later with a bag of frozen peas and a couple of bottles of mineral water. I notice that Andrea's still at the dining room table, watching us as Nathan hands me the peas and sits down. He cracks one of the mineral waters and passes it over. "Sorry, no ice packs, but the peas work just fine, too."

"Thanks. How's the nose?"

"Not bad, didn't break anything. You got my respect for that one," Nathan says, cracking the other mineral water and taking a drink. "Now... I owe you a story."

I nod, and swirl some water around in my mouth, washing out what's left of the blood before spitting it onto the lawn. "What makes the grass grow green?" I joke, and Nathan chuckles as I finish the line, ingrained for him but just a movie quote for me. "Blood, blood, blood."

Nathan takes another drink of his water then leans back. "Samuel Grammercy isn't the saint that his daughter thinks he is. Then again, considering the man left his own daughter behind in this city's foster care system, I guess you already figured that out. But Samuel wasn't even the good cop that the papers made him out to be."

"What was he?" I ask. "Nathan, I never really got to know the man. And I missed the timeline on his death, which is something I still regret since I missed Katrina going into the system, too."

"That was Peter's plan," Nathan says quietly. "The truth is, Samuel worked for Peter, or perhaps it'd be better to say worked for Peter's friends. You see, while Samuel got plenty of busts, the vast majority of them fell into two categories. Either he was busting the guys who were enemies of his employers, or he was doing an end around."

"What's an end around?" I ask. Nathan smirks and gives me a look. "Seriously. I've been deluded for years, so don't just assume I know fucking everything."

"Okay. An end around is when Samuel would arrest or bust someone, but then before the case went to trial, something would get screwed up, charges were never pressed, whatever. The key part of an end around though happens in the evidence room. Say that a week ago, the cops made a bust for ten guns. Then Samuel pulls the end around, and in checking in evidence from his bust, things get mixed up, and when the charges are dropped, the evidence is returned to the suspects, but the first case shows only five guns on their bust now. Guess where those other five guns went? Right into Samuel's friends' evidence."

"And this was profitable?" I ask, surprised. "Seems like a lot for five guns."

"Oh, Samuel pulled end arounds for more than just five guns," Nathan said. "He was damn near an expert in doing that sort of evidence tag switch on stolen property, too. Computers, art, currency, anything except drugs. It wasn't that Samuel had a problem with drugs, it's just that NOPD policy is to destroy drugs regardless of whether charges stick or are dropped. He had a whole other funnel system in place for that one."

"What happened?" I ask.

"He got greedy and lazy. One night, the evidence clerk was some Dudley Do-Right who saw the Detective Lieutenant doing the switcheroo. He went to Internal Affairs, who started to gather evidence on Grammercy. Peter's connections in the NOPD heard about it, but at the time the ADA in town was just as righteous as you could get. Also, this was just a few months after Hurricane Katrina, so the feds were still in town in force. Samuel felt the jaws closing in on him, so he came to Peter for help."

"A faked death."

Nathan nods. "We set it up nearly perfectly. The horse show was one of the first big events at the Fair Grounds after the hurricane, and Samuel got his wife to leave her phone behind to give them a reason to send their daughter back and out of the way. Theresa, Katrina's mother, was opposed to it, but Samuel browbeat her into going along with it. Katrina was the perfect witness to leave behind. Young, innocent, and traumatized enough that she didn't notice some of the details. I'd pulled similar jobs faking deaths in the Green Berets, so I was the one tasked with setting it up. I was actually there, although in disguise so Katrina didn't recognize me. After they sent her back, Samuel and Theresa jumped over a concrete wall that was there into a dump truck that was parked below, landing in a giant pile of kitty litter. When Katrina picked up her mother's phone, I hit the switch, blasting the car all to hell. She, of course, didn't see that there was nobody inside, although later two bodies were planted in the wreckage. That was actually done by the first firefighters to respond, a crew that also covers up arsons in that area for Peter and his friends."

"So what happened to Samuel and Theresa? And how the fuck could they just leave their daughter like that?"

Nathan shakes his head. "That I don't know. I spent weeks unable to sleep after I had to hold that little girl, sobbing in my lap before the cops arrived. She was so distraught she never realized, even though she'd seen me... what, by then it had to be hundreds of times. I took her home more than once, you know."

"Why was that?"

Nathan sips at his water again, and sighs. "Peter isn't the only DeLaCoeur who has had a few affairs. Not that I blame Maggie, with the way Peter's treated her over the years. But some of those play dates or business meetings... well, Samuel was doing more than having drinks with Margaret. I doubt she knows about the faked deaths. Peter probably wouldn't have filled her in, since it would hurt her more to think Samuel died back then."

"What do you know about them now?" I ask, sipping my water. Nathan's showing at least a little bit of guilt, and as long as I have that, I'm going to drive with it, trying to use it to the best of my advantage. My jaw aches, but the peas help some. I'm more numbed by the idea of what Samuel did to his daughter, though. "Where's he live?"

Nathan shakes his head. "After the bomb, I only saw Samuel Grammercy one more time. Peter had gotten him some top-flight fake IDs, good enough to pass anything short of the FBI, and I delivered it to him at the airport. He and Theresa were booked on a flight, but I never troubled myself to find out where. Safer and less guilty to not know."

"Miami," I inform him, sitting back on the lounge chair. "That's a hell of a burden to carry for the past ten years, Nathan. I have a feeling it's not your lightest, either."

"I've seen some things," Nathan agrees. "Your point is?"

"You said it yourself. Maybe it's time to start balancing your ledger. I know that you can't stop Peter from sending other men against Katrina. But that doesn't mean you can't help us, too."

"Us?"

I shrug. "Regardless of if she's doing it for the right reasons or not, her cause is noble. I told her I'd help her, too. I'm asking you... whose side of this are you on?"

"Seems like an easy choice," Nathan says after sitting still for a few minutes, watching the moon reflected in the black mirror of the pool. "On one hand, there's Peter, who's made me a rich man, a lot richer than I'd have been if I'd stayed in the

Army, or if I'd gotten a job with a more legitimate employer as a real security officer. He's connected, and one of the most dangerous men along the Gulf Coast. On the other hand, I have a crazy twenty-two-year-old girl, with barely a dime to her name most likely, and my employer's son, who until just about an hour ago, I thought was more or less a spoiled little bitch."

"Bitch, huh? I would have thought I at least rated being called a spoiled little prick, but all right," I joke, not as offended by his words as I would have been even a week or so ago. Now, it means nothing to me. I have something more important than my ego to worry about. "It does seem like an easy choice."

Nathan nods. "It does. So... how best can I help you guys?"

"Let me find out what Katrina wants to do, and I'll be in touch with you. Until then, I'd say just keep trying to distract Peter from finding her."

"I can do that. Now, if you don't mind, I need some meditation and a little shut-eye. Goodnight, Jackson."

"Goodnight. Oh, and Nathan?"

"Yes?"

"Would you mind if I joined you for tea tomorrow? I'd like to talk more about... things."

Nathan nods and gives me half a smile. "I'd say that would be possible. But first, make sure you do your reading for your sister. I'd hate to disappoint her."

"How'd you know about that?"

Nathan laughs. "I'm the head of security for this house. It's my job to know as much as possible. Goodnight, Jackson."

Chapter 15
Kat

I've never been to Darcy's house since she and Jeff got married. It isn't that she never wanted me over. In fact, she's invited me multiple times. No, the reason that I've never been to this neat little two-bedroom house in the Leonidas neighborhood is that I didn't want to put Jeff in a bind. He's her husband, but also a good cop. Not that any cop can be totally clean in a town like this, and Jeff's helped out Darcy more than once, but I've never wanted to push it this far before.

So it's with no surprise that Bo, the three-year-old brown and white pit bull Darcy got as, for some reason, a baby shower gift from one of her friends, is wary of me as I stand outside the fence, waiting for Darcy to let me in.

"Hey little mama, you lookin' good enough to eat with a biscuit," a young guy, maybe my age or maybe a little younger, says as he goes by before stopping to see if maybe he has a chance.

"Not interested," I say. "I have a man," I add, before letting him respond.

I'm surprised when he actually moves on, and Bo the pit bull watches the guy for a moment before turning his attention back to me. I think about the lie I just said, chuckling a little to myself. Maybe I do, or I will.

Darcy comes out just after the guy moves on, calling to Bo. "Bo... get your butt up here on the porch," she hollers, still smiling as she walks down the short concrete walk. Bo immediately turns and runs up, wagging his tail and grinning at his mistress, begging for affection. "Okay, okay, you big puppy, you protected the house. Now, I'm going to let my friend in, and you are going to behave. This is my friend Kat that I told you about, okay?"

Bo wags his tail again like he understands and runs off to the back of the house, while Darcy watches him go. "He looks like a hundred and ten-pounds of badass, but he ain't nothing but a baby," she tells me as she opens the gate. "You scratch him behind his left ear and he'll love you for life."

"Hint noted," I say, giving her a hug once I'm inside the gate. "Thanks for letting me come by."

"I knew it would happen someday. Just wish you hadn't called when I have laundry in the living room," Darcy half-jokes as we go inside. I see the basket, but it's mostly folded, except for some toddler's clothes. Henry is napping in a partially reclined chair, his chubby cheeks puffing out with every little exhalation.

"He's even cuter than the pictures," I whisper softly, kneeling in front. He's a beautiful little boy, Darce."

"Yeah, but hell in my workshop," she says with a little smile. "That boy has an unbelievable knack for being able to crack the connections on video cards that I just got lined up."

I chuckle and sit down in front of the laundry basket, taking out a tiny t-shirt and starting to fold it. "Then I guess I should be glad you haven't brought him by. He'd have a field day with my setup."

Darcy laughs and nods. "So what's up?"

I start folding another shirt, but the emotions are too much, and I keep fumbling it, turning the tiny little Elmo shirt into a ball. Finally, I give up and toss the shirt back into the basket, and bury my head in my hands. The tears are hot, bitter, and I don't even realize they're flowing until I can't see anymore, and I feel Darcy put her hands on my shoulders, pulling me into a hug. Her casual accent is gone, and she's back to being her normal Darcy, calm and supportive. "Shh, Baby Girl, shh... you just let yourself cry. I'm right here."

It's been years since I last wept, so long I can't even remember it. I know it was after Virginia took me in, but that's about it. I didn't even know I could cry still, but sitting there, Darcy holding me close like I was her own child, I cry, all the pain and anger of the past twelve hours flowing out into her tank top. I don't know how long I cry, but when it's gone, I feel hollowed out, cauterized. "Thanks."

Darcy nods and hands me a hand towel from the basket. "Here, wipe yourself down. I'd get you a tissue, but I know you hate those things. Ain't got a handkerchief around, though."

"This is fine," I say, wiping my eyes. "I hope Henry won't mind me borrowing it."

"Oh, that one's Jeff's," Darcy says with a little chuckle. "But no, he won't mind. Now, what's going on?"

"My parents... they may be alive," I say, looking up into Darcy's big brown eyes. "At least... my father might be."

Darcy blinks, absorbing the information. "He faked his death?"

I nod. "That's what it seems like. I got a message from a source last night, and Jackson says he confirmed it with Nathan

Black. The bomb that went off, it was a ruse. They... they abandoned me."

The words start fresh tears, more sad than angry and bitter, and I'm crying for the six years of foster care, of the decade of pitiless training, of obsession that I'm still not free of. I wipe at my eyes again, not letting myself lose control. Darcy hums, then gives me an intense look. "So you want my help?"

I nod and fold the hand towel in half to get rid of the snottiness. "Yeah. According to the source, he's living in Miami under the name Michael Ball. Now, I remember you mentioning you've got some connections in Miami. Familywise, even."

"I do, a few cousins, an ex-boyfriend, too," Darcy agrees. "You want me to use my resources?"

"Would you? I mean, I'll work my end, but you've got feet on the ground already in Miami."

"Sure. For you, I'd go to Miami myself and track your daddy down. Can I ask you a question, though?"

"Shoot," I say, reaching into the laundry basket and taking out the Elmo shirt I screwed up before. The words about my parents out, I find that I'm able to actually fold the shirt halfway decently.

"If this is true... what's that do to your plans?" Darcy asks. "You've been gunnin' for blood for a decade, but is it still worth blood?"

I think about it, then shake my head. "I don't know anymore. I know Peter needs to go down still. The entire DeLaCoeur network needs to be dismantled. But..."

"But you've got complications now," Darcy says simply, nodding. "You're thinking about what this means to Jackson, to

Andrea. And I'm going to be blunt, you're thinking more than just about what you did to Jackson."

"I… I don't know," I reply honestly. "It's like you said, complicated. He's an ally, that's for certain. Considering he went toe to toe with Nathan last night in boxing, he deserves at least that much."

Darcy hums knowingly, and I give her a look. "What?"

"Nothin'. Just glad to see that you're maybe considering that there's more to life than death and revenge. Listen, if you've got a few hours, I can get to work on reaching out to my contacts now. We might have something for you by the time Jeff gets home, he's working a double today."

"Ouch, double shifts? What's up?"

Darcy shakes her head. "Contract talks are coming up, and a lot of guys are calling out sick because they think the new contracts are going to take away their built-up sick days. Jeff isn't mad though, the day shift's doing community outreach at one of the elementary schools, then just catching up on paperwork. His sergeant's looking out for him."

"When is Jeff going to go for sergeant?" I ask. He's a year younger than Darcy at thirty-one, and has been on the NOPD for eight years now, so I'm curious. "And yeah, I can hang out a little bit."

"Good. And Jeff thinks that maybe a sergeant slot's going to open up pretty soon. He's already a training officer, he thinks he can maybe make a shift sergeant slot as soon as the new fiscal year comes up. A couple of guys are slated to retire, and he's one of the top training corporals. If not, he'll look for an Academy slot, see if he can maybe get a daytime only shift job for a year or two."

"That'd be nice. With Henry going to preschool soon and all. You sure you don't need more help with him?"

Darcy shakes her head and chuckles. "You know how it is, Kat. I make more than enough with my work that I can afford to spend time with Henry. Besides, I do too much and it starts to look strange to the IRS. Don't need them sniffing my backtrail."

"You're legit now," I remark, putting the last of the clothes in the basket. "You really think they'd chase down BlakDhal1A?"

"I think after I cracked a couple of government d-bases three years ago that I haven't told you about totally, they'd chase me for quite a while," Darcy says. "Come on, let's get these put away, and I'll start making phone calls."

* * *

Darcy's still working her connections when Jeff comes in, his blue on blue uniform causing me to sit upright before I realize who it is. "Hi."

"Hi," he says, obviously confused. "Uh, you are?"

I get up off the couch, where I've been reading some Clifford the Big Red Dog to Henry, who's more interested in chewing on the foot of his teddy bear than my reading.

"Sorry, I'm Katrina Grammercy. I'm a friend of Darcy's. Nice to meet you." I offer my hand, which Jeff shakes with a smile.

"It's been too long since I heard your name for the first time. Nice to finally meet *the* Baby Girl."

I roll my eyes as Jeff laughs. "Is she going to call me that for the rest of my life?"

"Shit!" we hear from the back of the house, and we both look. Darcy comes out, her brown eyes slightly red with frustration and embarrassment. "Sorry. Sorry Henry, Mommy's just upset."

Henry mumbles something, turning over. He gets off the couch and comes over to Jeff, his arms out for a hug. Jeff sweeps his son up and into his arms, covering his little face and tummy with kisses. "Daddy silly!"

"You make Daddy silly," Jeff says, giving his son another hug. "Now, hang out for a second with Kat and let me get this uniform off. You don't need to be messin' with anything Daddy's got on."

I notice that Jeff's not carrying, and he meets my eyes. "Since Henry was born, I leave it in my cruiser," he explains. "The take-home policy on the cruiser is a bit expensive, but the neighbors like it, and it's safer for Henry. I can leave both my Smith and my shotgun in the trunk there."

"Nothing for home defense?" I ask, and Jeff shakes his head. "Wow... gutsy."

"Not all of us are willing to keep a Glock 18 in our living room," Jeff replies, telling me he knows more about my operations than he might otherwise have. "Don't sweat it, I understand. Just... be careful with that thing, okay?"

"I am," I answer, taking Henry from him and holding the squirming little boy, who promptly grabs a handful of my hair and yanks. "Ouch, glad I don't wear earrings either."

"So what's the cursing about?" I ask, carefully pulling my hair free from Henry's grip as Darcy comes in. He's got strong little hands, and even my two inches of hair stings as he yanks. "You need to get him into arm wrestling ASAP."

"Don't encourage him," Darcy says with a chuckle. "But I'm having problems with my contacts. Seems it's been too long since I checked in with them down there, some have moved out, some have dropped out of the game, some are just... not available. And my ex-boyfriend's getting married. Feel bad for whoever that poor girl is."

"So nothing?" I ask, and Darcy quickly shakes her head. "Well, what then?"

"Something, but it's going to be slow. I don't think you've got the leeway to sit around waiting," Darcy says, "not with what Peter's surely getting ready to send after you."

I nod, then shrug, helpless. "Can't do much else. If I have to, I'll go running, take down Peter, then worry about my parents later."

"Or you could ask for help from someone else," Jeff says, coming out of the master bedroom. "Darcy, I've never helped you before like this, but you've never asked for it."

"Wanted to keep you out of trouble," Darcy replies. "Plausible deniability and all that stuff."

Jeff comes over and wraps his arms around Darcy's waist from behind, chuckling. "I lost all sense of plausible deniability when I married you, Darce. Besides, this doesn't sound all that risky. What're you looking for?"

"My parents," I say, and Jeff gives me a questioning look. "Yeah, I thought so too until yesterday. Seems they ghosted on us, and they're in Miami. Darcy's been trying to use her contacts to help me find them."

"Well, I've got some contacts, too," Jeff says, going over to the counter and opening his cell phone. "Ones who can legally do what you guys are trying to do."

Jeff taps at his phone, going over to the couch and sitting down. Darcy and I exchange looks, and she shrugs. She doesn't know what he's doing either. Jeff ignores us for a moment and talks to someone on the other end of the line.

Darcy snaps her fingers in recognition and leans over, whispering. "Gabriel Hawkins, he's an Academy friend of Jeff's, and he's one of the sysadmins for the NOPD's connection with the national crime database."

I nod and sit down on the carpet while Jeff talks. "Okay, yeah, I'll owe you some barbecue, that's all good. Thanks, man. Sure... name..."

"Michael Ball."

"Michael Ball, not sure on the spelling of Michael. Age? Between forty-five and fifty claimed."

"Jeff knows a lot," I comment, looking at Darcy who nods.

"He's been interested in the case ever since he learned of our friendship. He knows more about the case than most."

"Just a second, Gabe," Jeff says, then covers his phone. "Any more information?"

"White male, five-foot-eight, brown/brown, and... he might be a bartender," I say, recalling everything from memory.

Jeff gives me a thumbs up and uncovers his phone, repeating what I told him. "Yeah, that's what I was thinking, cross-referencing the name with the ABC list of bartender licenses. The ID's false, but probably good enough to get by the

ABC. Yeah, you can do that? Cool. No, I'll wait."

Jeff sets his phone down and gives me a smile. "He's running the search now."

We wait for a few moments, and Jeff's phone makes some noise, and Jeff picks it up. "Yeah, I'm here, Gabe. Really? Three hits in the Dade and Broward counties? Yeah, send me their info, I'll pass it along. Honest man, I'm not making a dime off this, this is a favor to a friend. Thanks, Gabe, I owe you."

Jeff hangs up, then waits a minute until his phone buzzes. "Here you go," he says, reading the message. "Three matching that description in the area. Two of them are listed as married. How do you want it?"

"I'll write it down myself. You don't need any more of an electronic trail on this than you've already got. Jeff, you're sticking your neck out on this one."

He nods, and passes his phone over to me. Darcy brings me a piece of paper and a pen, and I start copying the three addresses down. "Any phone numbers?"

"He could get them, but I figure you've got those skills. As to your comment, well, I've broken the rules before with Darcy, just not like this. It's about justice, and sometimes the law and justice don't always see eye to eye," Jeff says, sitting back. "Now, I've got one more question for you."

"Sure, what's that?" I ask, tucking the folded paper in my pocket and handing the phone back to Jeff.

"You staying for dinner or not? No offense, but you're skinny as a rail, and I'm pretty sure that we can scrape up something that'll put a little meat on your bones."

I laugh and sit back, nodding. "Fine. But you know that

saying, whether it's true or not. We can never be too rich or too thin."

Jeff rolls his eyes and looks over at his wife. "I see why you like her."

Darcy, who's playing with Henry, hums her assent and smiles. "She's got skills, too. You should be careful, hun. You push her too far, you may end up using your sick time actually being sick, as in recovering from a broken arm."

I give Jeff a wink, and the cop in him blanches slightly. "Don't worry, I haven't had to break an arm in months."

"Uh... so what do you like on your pizza?"

Henry, hearing the word pizza, looks over, cheering. "Yay! Pizza!"

I look over at Henry, who's got two little fists jammed into the air, a giant smile on his face. "I think whatever he wants works for me."

Chapter 16
Jackson

"So... three names?"

I'm in extreme pain, something I didn't think could happen with working out anymore. But this is the good sort of pain, the pain of hard work.

I'm trying to balance on just my hands, my legs resting on Katrina's shoulders while she stands and I do incline pushups. The burning is mostly in my stomach area, which has to hold everything in a totally straight line from my ankles to my shoulders, or else. I found out the hard way what 'or else' was a while back when Katrina kicked me in the stomach. Thankfully she didn't kick me too hard, since it was just meant as a warning when I let my back sag.

"Twenty. And yeah, three names," she says, keeping a silent count as I start my next descent. Each pushup is timed, three seconds down, hold for two, then an explosive push up. And apparently, this is just the warmup. "Jeez Jackson, I thought you'd have gotten more functional muscle with all that mass you're carrying."

"Didn't... think... I was deficient," I grunt as I hold my down position, my forehead a fraction of an inch off the floor. I push, exhaling and grunting. "Did fine before."

"All right, twenty-one's enough, relax and shake out. I'll use my chair for mine."

Katrina squats down so that I can pull my legs off her

shoulders, and goes over to the chair she's talking about. She kicks her legs up and does the same thing I just finished, the only difference being the height of her legs. Most women I know can't even do twenty regular pushups. Katrina, in one of the sexiest displays of feminine fitness I've ever seen, cranks out the twenty timed and elevated pushups like they're nothing. When she brings her legs down, she looks up and sees that I'm staring. "What?"

"Uh... nothing," I say, taking a swig of water. Still, she blushes a little, and I feel heat rise in my own cheeks. In the days since joining forces, we've grown closer again, and I'm realizing that my feelings for her are more than just friendly. The problem is, we're not twelve anymore, and I have a lot more on my mind than building model cars. I shake my head and sip my water again. "What's next?"

"Jackson..."

"Don't even start," I say, cutting her off. "We're doing this together. If for no other reason that I want to make sure you've got someone watching your back."

She gives me a look, and I shake my head and stick out my hand. "I told you, Katrina. We're partners on this. After what he did to you, after what he's done to so many others, Peter needs his comeuppance."

Katrina thinks, then nods. "And what is that comeuppance, Jackson? You know if I take him down, that means jail time for him."

"Fine," I say, and she arches an eyebrow. "What?"

"What I have evidence on... it means freezing his assets too if he gets arrested. Jackson, you've made tremendous strides, but are you ready to give up the money, too?"

Katrina, in her normal way, has pierced right to the heart of what's been troubling me. When I think about it, of course, I don't want the dirty blood money. Thinking about what it's come from, and what it's done to other people, especially what it's done to Katrina, makes my blood boil.

But at night, when I've been lying on Egyptian cotton sheets that cost a few thousand dollars, and a mattress that cost several thousand more, or when I woke up this morning and put on an outfit that probably cost more than what Katrina makes in an average month... I can't help but admit that I *like* living the good life. I like driving a one-year-old Audi, and eating the best food I can. I like having the bling, and the comfort of knowing that even with a psycho asshole for a father, I can still have money.

So yeah, I'm torn. But still, looking at Katrina, I know what to say. "We'll take him down, Katrina. We can discuss the details later. First, let's use those finances to get to Miami and take care of finding your parents first."

I can see she's not happy, but she nods in acceptance, like she expected this from me. It hurts, but I can't lie to her. Too many people have lied to her already, and I won't be a part of that.

"Okay," she says after a moment. "Well let's finish up, and we can discuss travel plans."

* * *

Back home, I find Nathan in his workshop, where he gives me a knowing smile as I make my way inside and take a seat. "How go the new workouts?"

"Painfully," I groan. "Tell me you did rougher stuff in the Green Berets."

"Doubtful," Nathan replies, going over to his tea collection. "Remember, we weren't as motivated. Dedication and fanaticism are just a hair's breadth apart sometimes. Here, this should help. It's a blend that has plenty of antioxidants and a good shot of caffeine. And it tastes pretty damn good, too."

He mixes the tea and brings me a steaming mug, which I sip. It's got a fruity tang to it, and I hum in appreciation. "Good shit."

"Thanks. Technically, it's not actually tea at all, but an herbal blend. I like it enough to keep it with my others, though. So what did you want to see me for?"

"I need some misdirection," I say, setting the tea aside. "For a trip."

"Oh really? And where would this trip be?" Nathan's unscarred eye twinkles in good humor as he asks me, then grows serious. "I'm asking because I need to know how much of a distraction I need to provide."

"Multiple days, maybe four or even a week. We think we've found Sam Grammercy."

Nathan thinks, then nods. "The only way I'll be able to pull that off convincingly is if I know where you're going, Jackson. I don't need exact details, but something more than just that you're taking off for four or five days."

I sigh, thinking. Would Katrina trust Nathan? Do I? Finally, I take the plunge. He's already risked his life just delaying and lying to Peter for this long, and if it helps Katrina, then so be it. "South Florida. We're thinking Miami, maybe."

Nathan nods again and sips at his tea. "One more thing. For the past few days now, you keep using the pronoun 'we'. I want to caution you, Jackson. Your emotions are becoming cloudy in this."

"This is an emotional situation, Nathan. You have to admit that."

"I do," Nathan says, then sighs. "You know, I never have told anyone in this family exactly why I left the military. Or at least, the real reason."

"I figured you'd just had enough of the military life, or maybe the long hours for terrible pay," I reply, listening carefully. If Nathan really is telling me something that nobody else knows, he trusts me as well. "You went to work for Peter for long hours but better pay."

Nathan smiles slightly at my joke, but shakes his head. "The pay wasn't the issue. I was only twenty-nine when I got out, and I had plenty of money. Special Forces pays decently well, even for a Staff Sergeant. I had hazard pay, special operations pay, deployment pay... I was making pretty good money for my lifestyle. No, it wasn't the money, or disillusionment with the system. I told you about my mission with the Kurds, but I didn't tell you all of it. Her name... her name was Aisha. She was a native girl, although I guess you can't call a twenty-four-year-old widow a girl. Before we met, she had a husband and a little girl, I never found out their names... they were killed by the Iraqi forces. Aisha dedicated herself to trying to kill as many of Saddam's men as she could. So of course, when my team was sent into Kurdistan to help them, she and I were paired off. She was officially our translator, a rare position for a woman in a country that is, at least culturally, very conservative."

"You two... hooked up?" I ask, drawn in. The idea of Nathan Black ever being in love is just insane, though, and I have a problem even using the word.

Nathan though nods. "We fell in love. Or at least, that's what we told each other. My team leader, Lieutenant Edwards, didn't care as long as Aisha was effective. I was always professional regardless of our sleeping arrangements. For three months, she and I were together... until the Republican Guard came around."

"You guys didn't take them on, did you?" I ask, shocked. "That'd be suicide. I mean, they were Iraqis, so not on your level, but they had to have had a serious numbers advantage."

"It was. Six Green Berets and one Kurd translator against a battalion of the Republican Guard, all rolling in BMPs? No, we weren't that stupid. When Lieutenant Edwards ordered us to fall back and disappear into the desert for a while, move out of the area, we all understood. I thought Aisha understood too, as she helped us pack our trucks and get ready to pull out as soon as darkness fell. I thought she was with the LT in his truck, like normal... until the first rest stop and he got out of his truck and came back, asking for her help. She'd told LT that she was riding in my truck."

"Where'd she go?"

Nathan swallows another mouthful of tea and sighs. "We found out four days later when we could circle back and the Republican Guard was gone. She'd hit them, and hurt them pretty badly. Sniper attacks at first, and she ambushed a patrol sent out to try and stop her. She'd taken a couple of frag grenades with her, made them pay. In the end... well, the villagers we talked to never knew for sure, but they think she took out five or six before they got her. The Iraqis were... not kind to her body."

I look down at my tea, and take a deep breath, setting my tea aside. I don't want it anymore. "Why are you telling me this, Nathan?"

"After that, I just didn't have the heart to serve any longer. My contract with the military was up soon afterward, and I just couldn't do it anymore. You see, Aisha had a cause, one she was willing to die for, Jackson. Katrina does, too. Just... be careful. That's all."

* * *

Nathan's words are still on my mind the next morning when Peter finds me in the dining room. "Well?"

"Well, what?" I ask, sipping my protein shake. I skipped my morning workout in our gym, my body is too damn sore, and I can barely lift my arms past my shoulders. It's got me in a bad mood, especially since I slept like hell last night.

"Have you and Nathan found the bitch?" Peter asks, rubbing at his bleary eyes. I wonder if he's started his drugs and drinking early, or if he's just still coming down from his fucking around last night. "It's been nearly a week."

"New Orleans is a big city, and it takes time," I answer, drinking some more of my shake. I've already had my morning oatmeal to go with it, but I need the extra protein if I'm going to recover at all. "Besides, she isn't in town."

"Well, where the fuck is she?" Peter yells, slamming his

hands on the table. "Or have you and Nathan been spending all that time together just sipping tea and sucking each other's dicks?"

I'm on my feet, pissed off. Seriously, this is just too much. "Shut the fuck up, Peter. If you'd calm down and stop acting like King of the Big Easy, I'd be able to answer your question."

I find that I'm pissed, but it's a *cool* pissed, if I can explain it. It's like I'm supposed to be pissed, and even though I'm pissed, I'm still under control. My body is exactly where it's supposed to be, standing up, my shoulders squared, showing him I'm not intimidated by his bullshit. My voice is loud, but not shrill, and I feel like I'm the one in control of the conversation.

Peter senses it too, and he wavers. "Fine," he says after a minute. "So where is she?"

"We've got a lead in Savannah," I say, pulling a city out of my head. Peter doesn't have any connections in the Savannah area that I know of, and it's far enough away that I can disappear for a few days and he's not going to suspect anything. "Nathan and I were confirming our information, and we were going to take off soon as we could."

"Well, what the hell are you waiting for?" Peter asks. "Keep me posted. I want updates as you get more info."

He leaves, and I chug the rest of my shake, rushing off to find Nathan before Peter can trip me up. Thankfully, Nathan's out walking his dog, and I find them in the stable again. "Road trip time."

"Oh?" Nathan asks. "And where are we going?"

"You're going to Savannah," I tell him, reaching down

and petting Maverick behind the ears. The huge dog woofs softly and pants, happy for the attention. "You think you can be okay by yourself for a few days, Mav?"

Maverick woofs again, but Nathan shakes his head. "If you're heading to Miami, I'm taking Maverick with me to Savannah. I'll take my Tahoe."

I remember Nathan's Tahoe, an older SUV that is certainly big enough for the giant dog to stretch out in if he puts the back seat down. "Fine by me. I need you to just check in with me from time to time, in case I do need backup. Think we can do that?"

Nathan nods. "I'll go tell Peter, like I just got the information confirmed. I assume you're telling me this because he approached you?"

"He did."

"That's fine. When do you want to head off?"

"Let me check with her, and we can get going this afternoon. I was thinking you drive, we'll fly."

"Deal. Well, let me take my dog for a walk, and we'll get ready."

Chapter 17
Kat

"You don't have a problem with flying?" Jackson asks quietly as we wait in line for the TSA check. "I mean, you said you don't even have a library card."

"I don't," I whisper back. "But Kit Misery does."

I'd prepared for this contingency, and actually have a few false IDs set up, although I doubt any of them are as elaborate as what 'Michael Ball' has. The TSA tends to be overworked and understaffed, and as long as one of my IDs doesn't get flagged for a terrorist watch list, I'll get passed through. I don't have the time to go into it with Jackson here, but he nods and we get through. Ironically, Jackson is the one tagged by the gate agent for an additional pat-down, and he flushes a bit red when the bored, obviously rushed agent cups his balls perhaps a bit differently than the book says.

"How'd you like the grope show?" I chuckle as he grabs his bag and we head down the hallway. "Looked like fun."

"Yeah... not something I'd like to do again," Jackson grumbles, until he sees me chuckling. "What?"

"Even if I were the one doing the groping?" I tease, and Jackson is surprised. "Come on Jackson, we need to keep up the appearance of a young couple going on vacation, if anyone wonders. A little... banter isn't out of place. We show up at the hotel looking like two strangers sharing a room, and we're going to create more questions."

Jackson blinks, then nods in understanding. "You're right, of course. But do I have to call you Kit the whole time?"

I shake my head. "Nope, the hotel reservation is totally different, and it's one of those places that doesn't ask too many questions."

Jackson stops and pulls me to the side. "Katrina, are you sure you want to go slumming the whole time? I mean, no offense, but wouldn't it be nice to treat yourself to at least a night or two in a decent place? Hell, even a Marriott?"

I smile and pat his cheek, he looks so cute. "It's the way I operate, Jackson. Now, maybe it doesn't look nice, but the way I live provides me something your lifestyle doesn't."

"What's that?"

"Freedom," I tell him, reaching down and taking his hand. "Besides, if there's time, maybe we can do some nice things. They just have to be untraceable and paid for in cash. You put anything on your credit card, and Peter's going to wonder just what the hell you're doing in Miami."

Jackson thinks about it quietly as we walk, hand in hand. Sure, it's part of our deception, but to be honest, it feels nice, and when he gives my hand a squeeze, I squeeze back, taking a look over at him. He's smiling, and I can't help but smile back. "What?"

"I understand what you're saying. By the way, you look dynamite today, even if it is the first time in weeks that I haven't seen your belly button."

I look down at my t-shirt and jeans, chuckling. "They're too damn tight. Only reason I have these is because I can wear them without having to put on a belt. I hate going through metal detectors."

"You could have worn those martial arts pants you've got."

I shake my head and laugh. "I look strange enough as it is. I wear those, and I'd for sure get attention from the authorities."

The flight to Miami is pleasant, and I notice that Jackson pulls out a book a few minutes into the flight. Andrea was true to her word. *Rich Dad* has been replaced with *Think and Grow Rich*. "How's it coming along?"

"I think I'm getting it," Jackson says. "I mean, reading the other book, I was a bit off because he's always focusing on the real estate aspect. But this guy, he's different. He's talking about the market, and using your own ideas to build your business. It makes a lot more sense to me. Maybe because I'm just not into real estate."

"And what ideas do you have?"

Jackson shakes his head, unsure. "Not ready to really think about that yet. I mean, I've spent four years since high school being a party boy. I've gotta figure myself out before I start throwing around money in investments. Still, if you had to push me on the subject, I'd say... well, the one thing I know is training, unless you're talking partying and maybe a little bit about cars. And fashion, how to dress for success. Maybe I could be a style consultant or something," he says and frowns.

"Those are good starts," I advise him, leaning in and giving him a nudge.

"Gee, thanks," Jackson says, still giving me a little smile. We alternate between reading and chatting during the two-hour flight, landing without a problem at the airport and heading toward the car rental counters. Thankfully for me, Darcy was willing to put one of her credit cards on the reservation to secure our car, and Jackson peels off the cash for it out of his pocket.

We drive to the hotel, which isn't as bad as Jackson feared it would be. Sure, it's not going to show up in the Yelp or Zagat's guide to Miami, but the room is clean, and the bed is a king. Jackson stops when we put our bags down, looking at the bed. "Uh... Katrina?"

"Yeah?"

"There's only one bed," he says, pointing. "Only one bed," he repeats.

I laugh and sit down, sinking into the pillow top mattress. Ooh, nice. I don't think I've ever had a bed this nice before, in fact. "It's okay, Jackson. Remember, we're here supposedly as a couple. Now, it'd be strange for a couple to get a room with two beds, don't you think?"

"But... okay. You're right," Jackson says, taking his shoulder bag and putting it against the wall. It's weird with him acting this way, and I wonder if it's just for show. "I guess I can sleep on the floor or something, it'll be okay."

I laugh and push back on the bed, stretching out. This feels heavenly, and Jackson's being so cute I can't help but laugh more. I'm almost positive he's trying to bait me into saying he can sleep in the bed with me, and if he is, I'm falling for it. "You will do no such thing. This bed is big enough for both of us."

"So I'm not going to wake up with a broken arm?"

"If I had problems with you and my personal space, I wouldn't have held your hand in the airport," I remind him, "nor would I have let you into my loft for our workout the other day. I'm just saying, Jackson... it's okay. You packed your PJs, I assume?"

Jackson nods. "Good, and I can wear my pants and a t-shirt myself," I reply, grinning. "Now, are you going to join me on this thing, or do I get to roll around by myself for a while?"

Jackson chuckles and stretches out on the bed next to me, lying on his side to give me some space. Still, it's nice, and I turn over, looking at him. He's close, but there's still maybe a foot or two of space between us, and he's giving me this strange little smile. "What?"

"You look different, lying there like that," Jackson says quietly, that strange little smile still on his lips. "It's nice. You don't look so... pissed off or intense. And I can't recall a time that you've been smiling so much in this way."

"What way?" I ask, and Jackson chuckles.

"Like you're actually having fun, and not laughing sarcastically or ironically. You look like you're actually having fun, and enjoying what you're doing innocently."

Jackson reaches out, then stops, his hand frozen halfway in between us, then starts to pull back before I reach out and take his hand. "It's good to spend time with a friend again," I tell him, squeezing. "Really."

"Well, then maybe I can convince you to have dinner with me at a decent restaurant before we start work tomorrow?" Jackson asks. "We can even do a workout here in the room beforehand if you want to make sure the calories are consumed wisely. Just no pushups, I can't handle any pushups."

"Today's a leg day anyway," I tease him, then nod.

"Okay. But we can skip the workout. I think we've earned a three or four-day vacation. Instead, maybe we could do some sightseeing or something? I don't think I've ever done that before."

"Sure," Jackson says, giving my hand another squeeze. "Where do you want to go?"

"Uh... well, I've always wanted to try hanging out in the trendy places, with the beautiful people," I tell him. "To be honest, it was a little cool being Kitty in that dress the first night. I felt... pretty."

I wouldn't admit it to myself then, but I did enjoy that part of dressing up. Sure, I was trying to be a seductive vixen, but I did enjoy being pretty. At the time I was too angry and driven to let myself feel it, but afterward, I had to admit that I enjoyed that part of the whole operation. I expect Jackson to look upset or maybe angry, but instead, his smile spreads and his eyes are deep blue with meaning. "You don't know just how pretty you are, Katrina. But yeah, I think we can do that. How about we get changed, dress up a little, and head over to Ocean Drive. If anything, there's probably some shops that we can stop by, they'll have stuff that will look amazing on you."

The idea of shopping for a reason other than pure functionality is strange and leaves butterflies in my stomach, and I nod. "Can I just wear my normal gear until we find a shop?"

Jackson chuckles and nods. "Only if I get to wear what I want."

I nod and we get off the bed. I go over to my bag and look inside, taking out my second best pair of pants besides the jeans I wore for the flight, a baggy set of denim blue cargo pants and a skin-hugging white cotton crop top. I look at the top, then at my t-shirt, and decide to go with the crop top. Miami's a place where people can show a little skin, right?

I take my clothes inside the bathroom to change, while Jackson stays in the room to do his thing. "So how long did Darcy say it was going to take to verify the addresses?" Jackson asks as I take off my jeans.

I glance toward the door and notice with a start that it's not totally closed. I'm sure I closed it before, but maybe the latch is broken or something, and in the little gap in between, I can look out into the room. I don't mean to be a voyeur, but seeing Jackson stripping down to just the boxer briefs he's wearing sends a warm tremble through my belly. He's muscular, which I knew, but I didn't realize just how muscular until just now. Now I can see every ripple of muscle, even down to his lower back and along his spine. Yeah, I may have joked with him a little the other day about being nonfunctional, but looking at him now, I can think of plenty of functions that Jackson's body is more than capable of doing well. I clear my suddenly dry throat and cough once. "Sorry, what was that?"

"I asked how long you think it'll take your friend to verify the addresses?"

The mention of our purpose for being in Miami clears my head, and I pull on my normal pants, cinching the belt that's already in the belt loops. "Maybe another day. I'll be honest, if she doesn't get back to us by tomorrow, I want to check out a couple of the addresses ourselves. It's more dangerous, but at least it's foolproof."

"You sure about that?" Jackson asks. I pull my sports bra

on, then the light top that I'm wearing on top that'll protect my arms. I'm pretty pasty white. I haven't been spending a lot of time in the sun. "I mean, if they went the whole mile, they could've gotten plastic surgery. They might look completely different. I know Mom looks a lot different than she did from even ten years ago."

"I doubt either of them have gone off the deep end like Margaret has," I reply, to which Jackson laughs. I know he doesn't have a lot of affection for Margaret, who's treated him nearly as badly as Peter has. Imagine treating your own son like he's the reason your husband cheated on you? Despicable. "Besides, I'd know."

I go out into the main room, stopping when Jackson turns around. He's pulled on some aqua blue shorts with a white linen belt, and a tropical printed shirt that makes him look like a native. He hasn't buttoned it yet, and I can see the ridges of his chest and stomach muscles through the gap. He looks down. "Sorry, you're a little fast."

"Not a problem," I say, going to my bag and reaching in for the sunscreen I made sure to purchase. SPF fifty or bust. "Besides, I'm showing off my belly, why not show off yours, too?"

Jackson shrugs, letting his shirt stay open. "Okay. What's that?"

"Sunscreen. That is, unless you want me to look like a mint candy tomorrow, all red and white stripes. Think you can help me with my lower back?" Jackson comes over and holds out his hands, and I squirt a glob of the lotion into his palm. I turn around and pull my top up a little, making sure he covers it all. "I can get the rest, if you need."

"Okay, this might be a little cold," Jackson says, and then his hands touch me. I can't help it, it feels so good to have him touch me, and I shiver slightly. His touch is gentle, rubbing my skin lightly, and I bite my lip to keep myself from gasping when his fingertips brush lower, just into the edge of my belt, on top of my hips. I hear Jackson's breath catch, then his hands come around, rubbing my sides before pulling back with reluctance. "I... I think I got it all."

I turn around, seeing the same look in Jackson's eyes that I'm feeling inside me, and it's with a slightly shaky hand that I take the lotion back from him. "Thanks."

I do the rest of my lotion myself and pull out my sunglasses and hat, fully suited up for the Miami sun. "You going to do any sunscreen?"

"I did some while you were changing. Just SPF ten, I've got some tan already. You know, all those hours being a douchebag by the pool with nothing to do but read."

I chuckle and put my glasses on, casting the room in silvery darkness. "I won't take back what I said, you were a douchebag, but I think my opinion of you has changed a lot in the past few days."

We leave the hotel, driving down to Miami Beach and going to Ocean Drive. I've seen the place before of course. Any computer geek who hasn't played *GTA: Vice City* at least once is no geek to me, and the game was modeled after the real Miami. But still, seeing all the art deco buildings and the shops is really cool, and after we find a place to park, we go for a stroll, just walking. It's fun, and when Jackson takes my hand, I just go with it, relaxing and enjoying myself. "Hey, do you have a camera?"

"I've got my phone," Jackson replies, pulling it out. "Sixteen megapixels and enough memory to put a two-hour high-def video on it."

"What do you need with a two-hour high-def video?"

"You don't really want to know that," Jackson says with a playful tone, and I realize exactly what sort of video he's talking about. "I guess what I'm saying is... yeah, I've got a camera."

"Well, can we get some pics together then?" I ask, letting his little faux pas drop. Hey, he's trying. "Like, maybe a selfie or something? I bet my friend Darcy would love it."

Jackson brightens a ton and fiddles with his phone, then nods. "Sure. Where?"

We pose in front of one of the shops, and in a spur of the moment I put my arms around his neck and hug him while we wait for the camera to count down. He turns, and we're forehead to forehead when the timer goes off, and as the image comes up, I love it. We're smiling at each other, and I'm looking into Jackson's blue eyes while he looks into mine. "That... is a great shot," Jackson says. "I'm posting this one on my Instagram for sure."

."Very funny," I counter, popping him lightly in the shoulder. "Don't make me hurt you in South Beach."

Jackson rubs his arm and laughs, and we keep walking. Jackson stops in front of a boutique, and I look in the window, surprised. I see what he's looking at, and shake my head. "No way, Jackson. No way in hell."

"Why not?" he asks, pointing out one of the skirts in the window. "That would look amazing on you. And it goes with your top."

I shake my head but give in, letting Jackson drag me inside. The clerk looks bored, but when Jackson explains what he wants me to try on, the woman perks up. "Oh, that would be perfect on you!" she exclaims, her unnaturally red dyed hair bouncing. "You've got the midsection that this sort of skirt was designed for. It's meant to hug the hips and flare out from just below, so you get to show off your, ahem, assets while still having that breezy, flowy feeling."

"Will they go with these?" I ask, looking down at my shoes, my black minimalist Nikes that I wear a lot for working out, or when I'm not expecting to need boots. The clerk hums, then shakes her head. "Well then, we might have a problem."

"No we don't," Jackson interjects, holding up a pair of sandals. "You're a size nine?"

"Yeah... how'd you know?"

"Lucky guess. And these are exactly a nine. Come on, my treat, Katrina."

I roll my eyes and take the skirt and the sandals into the changing room, trying them on. The way the cotton hugs my hips is sexy, and again, without even knowing it maybe, Jackson's made me feel pretty. I make a mistake putting the sandals on, forgetting to take off my socks until the little thong that goes between my toes gets stopped, and I adjust myself quickly, thankful that the sandals have a little bit of elastic that goes around my ankles to keep them from flapping around. I step out, and Jackson's expression is worth any sort of discomfort over being in such strange clothing. "Well?"

"We're getting it and the sandals," Jackson says

immediately, going over to the register. "In fact, she's wearing it out. Can you bag up the other stuff?"

I'm blushing and trying to back into the changing room again, and Jackson rushes over, taking my hand. "Come on Katrina, please?" he asks quietly, the clerk giving us space. "I'm serious, you look amazing in it, and it'd go so well with dinner. You said you wanted to look pretty. Well, right now you're the prettiest woman I've ever seen in my life."

I nod, and our lips move closer, and I don't know who's closing the distance but I want it. He's so close, inches away, now just an inch...

My phone rings, and I step back, shaking my head. "Sorry, I... sorry."

"No, it's okay," Jackson says, letting go of my hand. "Listen, I'll go take care of this with the clerk. Just bring your stuff up from the changing room and we can get some dinner."

I see that the call's from Darcy, and the reality of why I'm in Miami comes back to me, and I answer the phone. "Yeah, Darcy?"

"I just got a call from my cousin. They got out to all three places, they had the pics you gave me of your parents. They got a visual on your mother. They're living at the second address you gave me, down in Coral Gables I'm told."

"Thanks, Darcy. We'll go check it out."

Darcy hums, then replies. "You sure you don't want any backup on this? I mean, I know Jackson's trying to be a good guy, but this could be... difficult."

"No, I'm sure. Let me talk with Jackson, and I'll get back to you."

"All right. You take care, you hear? Bye."

Darcy hangs up and I put my phone back in my pants pocket, tempted to duck into the changing room and put on my pants again. In the end, I remember another line from *Hagakure*. *Matters of great concern are to be treated lightly. Matters of small concern should be treated seriously.*

I fold up my pants carefully and carry them along with my shoes out to the front, where Jackson's face is haunted when he sees me. "Good news?"

I nod, and Jackson sighs. I reach out and tap him on the shoulder. "We'll talk about it over dinner. Tonight, though... we're going to have a nice dinner together, and we can worry about Darcy's phone call tomorrow."

We go on our way, and as we walk out of the store, he takes my hand again. "Are you sure?"

"It's all right. I don't want to rush in all emotional, and this will give me a chance to calm down and enjoy time with you. So, where are we going for dinner, anyway?"

"Figured Cuban food tonight. This area's famous for their Cuban places, and there's a spot that I went to last time I really liked. Don't worry, it's been years since I've been to Miami, so I doubt anyone will recognize me. Especially since my cock isn't hanging out."

His joke breaks the tension, and we laugh, heading back to the car to drop off my stuff before enjoying the rest of the night. "Okay, let's enjoy the night."

Chapter 18
Jackson

Despite Katrina's kind offer to share the bed with me, I sleep like shit. It's not that the bed is too soft, or too hard, or anything like that. The room's nice enough, and the air conditioner works fine.

The problem is Katrina. I wake up three times in the night, each time in a cold sweat worried that something is wrong with her, looking around. I lie back, trying my best to relax and not wake her, but I can't help it, and I toss and turn for a while before dropping off into a light, disturbed sleep again.

My mind keeps whirling with images from last night, of her smile as she and I walked along Ocean Drive, or the way she enjoyed the Cuban food we had together, and especially how beautiful she was in her new skirt. Finally, at five in the morning, I give up and turn over, peeking over the blanket we've rolled up and placed between us, watching Katrina in the early morning sunlight. She really does have the face of an angel, and in sleep the constant tension she carries almost all the time is gone, making her look softer, more vulnerable, and achingly beautiful.

I think back to that moment, right before the call from her friend Darcy, when we were so close. Was I making the move to kiss her, or was she? I know I wanted to, and at that moment I'd have been willing to risk a shattered nose or a broken arm to kiss her.

As the morning light brightens our hotel room slowly, I

calm myself by studying Katrina's face. Okay, fine, I'll admit it to myself. I have feelings for her. In fact, they're more than just feelings. And as much as my cock stirs at the thought of her touching me the way she did in the limo, I want to hold her and protect her. Even though I know that if the zombie apocalypse ever does break out, she's probably the one who'd end up protecting me. I want to give her the happiness that's been denied her life for so long, and I want to see her smile more like she did before she got that phone call.

Katrina stirs, a little smile coming to her features, and she opens her eyes, seeing me looking at her. "Good morning."

"Good morning," I answer. "Did you sleep well?"

"Better than you did," she replies, reaching over and taking my hand. "You tossed and turned a lot."

"Sorry," I apologize, thrilled by the touch of her hand in mine. "Did I disturb you?"

She shakes her head and gives me a soft smile that sends warmth flooding my chest. I'd kill for this woman at this very moment if she asks me. "No, I was okay. Actually, I've slept a lot worse than tonight. My first few weeks in the loft, I had a hell of a problem with rats and mice."

"Oh? The place looked spotless every time I've been there."

Katrina nods and her smile becomes a little more predatory. "You'd be surprised what you can do when you sleep light and you have a decent pellet gun by your side. That was before I got my Glock."

I chuckle and shake my head. "So what's the plan?"

"Breakfast, then we head down to Coral Gables," she

says. "It's going to be a long day. I'd prefer to not just kick in someone's front door without some sort of verification."

Our first stop is, in fact, a Burger King, where we get breakfast sandwiches and talk. "So my plan was to use the Metro today," Katrina says as we munch. Burger King does at least have decent tater tots, although I think the sandwich itself sucks. "I mapped out the address the other day, there's a station just a few blocks away. I think it'll make our work a lot easier and less conspicuous."

"If you think so," I say, sipping at my drink. "What about sun and heat?"

"We'll stop at a 7-11 or something like that, and stay mobile," Katrina replies easily. "Also, I was thinking, on the way is a shopping mall. They've got to have a sporting goods store, so we'll stop and get a pair of binoculars or a spotting scope or something. Something small, so we can still look inconspicuous."

"You seem to know a lot about doing surveillance on places," I note, and Katrina grins. "Wait, don't tell me... you did ninja training, too?"

She laughs and shakes her head. "No, but I did intern with a private investigator for a summer. I didn't do a lot, mostly made sure he stayed awake during night stakeouts, oh and one time I acted as a plant for him as he was working a divorce case. Seems the husband supposedly had a taste for teen girls."

"Did he?"

"Maybe, but never for me. That was where I met the girl who taught me the Touches, and you know how useful those are."

I shiver at the memory, and she gives me a little smile. "Yeah, they're pretty effective."

"I think it's the person giving them as much as the technique themselves," I say, and then grin. "Sorry... I guess that's a little too personal."

"No, I appreciate it. In fact, I appreciate everything you've done the past few weeks," Katrina says quietly. "Maybe Darcy was right."

"About what?"

She shakes her head, and finishes her juice. "Later. Come on, let's grab some drinks, make sure we're protected. You've got your sunblock?"

We take the Metro to the mall, where we get a pair of palm-sized binoculars and get back on the Metro, going two stops past The U and getting off. It's not far, less than a mile, and to be honest, it's not a great neighborhood. "I wonder why a man who stole so much from the city lives in such a fucking bad neighborhood," I ponder as we leave. "Seriously, you'd think he'd have kept enough to live a bit better than this."

"That's probably why," Katrina says, pointing out two coeds who go walking by in short shorts and bikini tops. "Let's face it, if he had an affair with your mom, he's probably not above cheating on my mother with other people, too. And this is... a neighborhood with a lot of scenery."

"I've seen better," I reply, giving Katrina a meaningful look. "Besides, you could probably kick both of their asses, and their boyfriends', too."

"Well, yeah, like... duh," Katrina replies with a fake bimbo accent that has me in stitches. "Point taken, compliment accepted, and thank you. But we're being pros right now, okay?"

"Okay," I agree, following her. Katrina's dressed in her work clothes too, the same pants she wore yesterday along with her long sleeve crop top, baseball hat and sunglasses, although the light training shoes have been replaced with lightweight mid top boots. She's ready to kick some ass if need be, and I wonder if somewhere in those baggy pants is her Glock. I mean, we flew, but still, who knows what tricks she's learned.

We get to the apartment complex, the Palm Garden Apartments, which is a five-story stucco building with what looks like maybe some sort of green area and a pool in the middle. "Well?"

"According to the address, the apartment's most likely on the third floor," Katrina says, taking out our new binoculars and giving the building a quick scan. "Let's walk around, see if we can spot anything."

We can't get to one side since there's another apartment in the way, but we do find a way to circle around, and I see a problem. While the building has only one main entrance/exit, a security gate that connects to the parking lot and the walkway to the sidewalk, the apartments wrap all the way around. "There's no way to watch all four sides at once."

"Then we focus on the entrance-exit," Katrina says. She looks around, and points. "There, that looks decent enough."

The 'decent enough' spot Katrina points out is a little bookstore with a coffee bar in front, sort of a Barnes and Noble clone, and we settle in. I'm glad for the shade and air conditioning, and the shop owner seems happy enough when I go over and slip her fifty bucks, as well as ordering some tea and scones. I'm not really hungry, but we are using the shop's seats, after all, and I don't plan on buying any books.

We keep watch together for about an hour before Katrina taps my arm. "Hey, instead of both of us, let's take thirty-minute shifts."

"I'm not confident enough to identify your parents if they walk by, especially your mom," I admit sheepishly. I don't like admitting I'm not Superman. "I mean, I'll help when I can, but I might be calling for your help."

Katrina considers it, then grabs the binoculars. "Wait... there he is!"

I look across the street and see a man, roughly fifty or so with a rather large, angry pink bald patch on his head, just about Katrina's height, with a bit of a potbelly and a slouch coming down the street, wearing jeans and what looks like a bowling league shirt heading toward the security gate. "You sure?"

"He's got the same birthmark on the left side of his neck that my Dad had. He's gained weight, gone to seed a lot, but it's him."

"Great, so how do we get in?" I ask, stopping when the shop owner brings us more tea and scones. I guess she thought that my fifty was asking for repeat service, not that I mind too much. "I doubt he'll just answer if we buzz that we're UPS or something."

"Actually, that's pretty close to what I was thinking," Katrina says, sipping her tea. "What do you think?"

I take a sip of my tea and grimace. "I think I've picked up Nathan's tea snobbery. This stuff is terrible."

Katrina chuckles and downs her tea quickly. "Come on,

we can take the scone with us in your backpack."

We cross the street, and Katrina studies the security gate. "Hey, we won't have to do anything. It's not buzzered or anything," she says, and I see she's right. There's a simple latch, but that's it. I guess it's not the sort of apartment to have all that much security. "Cheaper place than I thought. Come on."

We go inside, stopping at the mailboxes, where we see that apartment 302 is listed as 'Ball'.

"You ready?" I ask Katrina, who looks suddenly nervous. "What is it?"

"I... I don't know," she says, looking over at the stairs. "I mean, it's been ten years. And while I know there's a lot of things to not be happy about... it's my parents, Jackson. What if, what if there's a reason they did what they did? What if I can't do it? What if..."

I pull Katrina close and hug her tightly, cutting off her self-doubt. "You'll do the right thing. I know this much about you, Katrina. Live in the moment, and don't let your self-doubt stop you."

She stiffens for a moment, then hugs me back. It feels amazing, and it feels even better when she sets her head on my chest. "This is why I'm glad you're here, Jackson. Thank you."

"It's no problem," I reply, my nose filling with the scent of her hair and stirring emotions deep inside me. "I'll be right by your side the whole time."

Katrina squeezes me tightly and lets go, stepping back. "Okay. Then let's go see what's going on with my parents."

Chapter 19
Kat

My feet tingle as Jackson and I take the stairs up to the third floor of the apartment complex, and twice I stop, Jackson waiting patiently for me to find the guts to continue. I didn't think it would be this hard.

Never in my entire decade since seeing them supposedly blown up have I felt as much fear as I feel right now. I've spent nearly ten years training, focused with burning intensity on one goal, and until Jackson came back into my life, I thought that focus, that intensity, would never waver. Now I'm seeing that my blind devotion has left me weak, at least in some areas, and I'm glad that Jackson is here with me.

We reach the third floor and we walk to our left, following the unit numbers as they drop from 310 toward 302. We get to the door, and Jackson takes my hand again. "Remember... live in the moment, focus on the goal. All that stuff you've been reading and training for, it applies here, too. Okay, Kat?"

At my assumed name, Jackson's words jolt me into place, and I nod, determined. I turn back to the door and knock three times, pleased that I don't sound weak at all. I'm ready to take this on, and as I hear footsteps approach the door, I'm strong, ready, and actually a little bit pissed off. These people left me behind.

The door opens, and I see, for the first time in ten years,

my mother. She may be nearly forty-five now, and the years have added some stoop to her shoulders and some gray to her hair, the exact color as mine, but it's Theresa Grammercy. "Hello?"

"Mom... it's me," I say, probably the stupidest reply in the history of the world, but I haven't exactly had a chance to practice this before, you know?

"Theresa Grammercy?" Jackson interjects, and Mom's eyes flitter to him, and before she can even start to protest, I see the truth. She knows who we are. "My name is Jackson DeLaCoeur."

Mom's eyes come back to me, and there's guilt there, at least a little bit, but she doesn't move. "You shouldn't be here."

"And you shouldn't have left me in New Orleans to live in foster care for six years," I shoot back, keeping my voice low. "Now do you let me in, or do I have Jackson call the cops now? I know for sure that Michael and Theresa Ball are not legal identities."

Jackson plays along, taking out his phone, even though there's no way in hell I'd call the cops. That would bring attention to me, and I don't have a legal identity right now.

Mom doesn't know that though, and backs up, letting us in. "The Lord teaches us to submit to the will of those in authority above us," she mutters, and I see just how sad Mom looks. She'd always been pretty conservative, foregoing makeup most of the time, but she looks positively mousy now, her hair grown out, but hanging in two thick and limp braids that stretch halfway down her back. She's in a dress that I think might have started its life as a very ugly couch. Pale blue and pink rose patterns dominate the shapeless bag of a dress, and she's wearing house slippers. "You're breaking the Lord's will."

"And I'm pretty sure if I dig in the Bible long enough, I'll find something that says that faking your own death and abandoning your daughter is also against the Lord's will, too," Jackson replies, thankfully. Listening to her speak, I'm too angry and sad at the same time to form words. I want to scream and cry, but I'm paralyzed, not saying much at all. "Where's Samuel?"

"He don't live by that name no more," Theresa says, but points anyway. "His name's Michael now. Like the archangel."

"Theresa?" a harsh voice booms from the living room. "What the fuck are you babbling in there? We got visitors?"

The way Theresa flinches motivates me to speak, and I step forward, going toward the living room of the apartment. "Yeah, some ghosts from the past," I say, walking into the living room. Samuel is sitting in a cheap recliner, his eyes going wide as I walk in. "Hello... Daddy."

"Katrina..." Samuel whispers, then plasters a big, fake smile on his face. "Oh honey, it's so good to see you!"

Theresa and Jackson are right behind me, and I restrain myself carefully as Samuel gets to his feet and holds his arms out, coming over to give me a hug. I hold my hand up, and he stops a few feet away, realization dawning on his face that I'm not here for a happy family reunion. "I guess I should have expected that," he says, dropping his hands and sighing. "Well, will you have a seat at least? We've got a lot to talk about."

I look at Jackson, who arranges his body in the short connecting hallway, blocking most of it with his bulk while Theresa sits down in a wooden rocking chair, her hands folded in her lap and her legs jammed together. Her head is hanging slightly, but whether it's in shame or if she's praying, I can't tell. Jackson gives me a nod, and I grab an ottoman from the couch area and squat down on it. I don't want to be backed up against anything. "All right... talk. Start with why the fuck you faked your deaths and left me in New Orleans to go through six years of hell in foster care."

"You will not use foul language in this house, young lady," Theresa interjects, a hint of hysteria in her voice. "The Lord despises a foul mouth."

"And a liar?" I ask. "Besides, after what I've been through, if there is a God up there, I owe him an ass kicking."

"Katrina, your mother has... she's become very involved in the church," Samuel says, trying to explain. "We've been through a lot of stress the past ten years, honey. Theresa has found that it comforts her. After the mob came after me, I knew I couldn't stay in New Orleans, and the only way to do it was to leave you behind. I thought that they'd ignore you if they thought I was dead."

"Oh, bullshit. You left me behind. Why?" I look at Theresa, ignoring Samuel for a while. "Huh, Mom? Him, I can understand, what with what I've learned... but you? Why did you go along with it?"

"*Wives, submit to your husbands as you do to the Lord,*" Theresa shoots back. "My husband's will as head of this household is the final say. He said that this was the plan, and I obeyed him."

"The very next paragraph though says that husbands should love their wives as Christ loved the church, and that they should ensure that their wives are pure and blameless, to love them as their own bodies. I don't think faking your death and abandoning your daughter follows that particular teaching," Jackson says quietly. When I look at him in surprise, he shrugs. "I've been to my fair share of church in my time, too."

"Regardless, you're still lying to me," I add, looking back at Samuel. "Why?"

"You need to go, Katrina. It's not safe," Theresa says, her control wavering. "You can't be here. You need to go."

"I'm not going anywhere. Not until I have answers," I say, my own calm evaporating. "For Christ's sake, you two left me! Why?"

Theresa starts crying, sobs shaking her shoulders, but I feel no guilt, no pity for her as she trembles and shakes. She's muttering to herself, and as I catch words of it, she's praying or quoting the Bible or something like that, which just infuriates me more. I jump to my feet, having had enough. "Shut up!"

"That's enough!" Samuel half-screams, getting to his feet as Theresa sobs harder. "We did it to protect you, Katrina! The mob was after me, and I couldn't think of any other way to protect myself and my family!"

Protect his family. His words are yelled with such vehemence, with so much passion that for a moment, I want to believe him. But then I remember what Jackson told me Nathan Black said, and what I went through going through foster care. Virginia may have trained me, but it was tough love from the beginning, and there was nobody there to protect me for the six years I lived under her roof. The pain of the past ten years protects me from being swayed by his lies, and I square up, looking at Samuel, who I realize I am now actually taller than in my boots.

"You lie, Samuel. You were a corrupt cop, and if you were running from the mob, why'd you go to Peter DeLaCoeur for help? Why'd you get Nathan Black to rig the whole thing? Peter's as much in the mob as anyone else."

Samuel stops, then starts to go red, his anger at being called a liar turning him the color of old brick. "Fine. If that's the way you want it, you miserable little whelp, then I guess I'm going to have to throw your ungrateful ass out of my house."

Jackson goes to move, but I hold up my hand. No, this is my battle. I tilt my chin, cracking my neck, and nod. "Then come on. Maybe while I'm kicking your ass you can finally tell me the truth."

Chapter 20
Jackson

I'm tempted to move from my position on the wall, but Katrina's gesture stops me, and I remember how well she can handle herself. I settle back, waiting. Actually, I do have to admit, part of me is looking forward to this. It could be better than a Bruce Lee movie.

"So why'd you do it, Sam?" Katrina asks as Samuel raises his hands and tries to come after her. Katrina moves with a ballet dancer's grace, avoiding his grab and spinning out of the way, pushing him on the back as she does, causing him to stumble a bit. "Was it that the FBI was going to come after you? Internal Affairs?"

"I was a good cop!" Samuel yells, turning and coming after Katrina again. She's backing up, light on her feet even in her boots, and I can see she's toying with him. It's hot actually, watching her move. She's graceful, not like a dancer or a stripper, intentionally working her body to tease, but instead she's graceful in an unconscious way, like she's focused on something greater and her grace is just a means to an end.

"You were a dirty cop," Katrina replies, ducking as Samuel grabs a little knickknack off the top of the television and throws it at her. Katrina moves so quickly that it almost looks like the porcelain projectile passes right through her, exploding on the wall behind her. "You were a dirty cop who worked for Peter more than you worked for the people of New Orleans."

"You don't know a damn thing about what I did!" Samuel screams, trying to grab Katrina again, who blocks his hands, slapping them away before shoving him in the chest. Samuel stumbles back, and gets ready to charge Katrina, who I can see is obviously ready for him. Before he can, though, Theresa is up and out of her chair, trying to get in between her daughter and her husband.

"Michael, no! Stop!" she yells hysterically, grabbing his arm and yanking. Samuel's not in good shape, hell, I'm worried the man's going to have a heart attack if this goes on much longer, but Theresa's scrawny. Maybe Katrina doesn't understand, but I do. She might get some of her height from her father, and I can see a little bit of his face in hers, but the hair, the slender frame... that's all from Theresa Grammercy, and that body's been worn down by a decade of guilt, so what was once thin has become bony and weak.

Theresa tugs, but Samuel barely moves at all, except for turning and pushing his wife, sending her sprawling. "Shut up, bitch. You're half the fucking reason I left anyway, you and that constant harping on me, threatening to go to Peter and tell him about me and Margaret. If you were a good wife, I wouldn't have had that problem!"

Samuel turns to kick Theresa, and I start to move, but before I can even take a step, Katrina's right there, spinning him around and sweeping his legs out from underneath him. "Don't touch her!" she screams, stomping down on Samuel's left ankle. I don't hear anything break, but that doesn't mean it doesn't probably hurt like hell. "You have no right!"

Unfortunately for Katrina, while she's an expert in the

martial arts, she probably hasn't watched as many cop shows as I have, and she forgets one of the main cop rules in a domestic disturbance, which is never ignore anyone. Her own mother, who should have been grateful for her daughter's assistance, instead throws a shoe at her. It catches Katrina in the chest and surprises her just enough that Samuel is able to grab her ankle, sending her tumbling to the floor next to him with one hard yank. Theresa's still trying to get involved, but I grab her, dragging her away toward the bedroom.

"Sit down!" I say, shoving her into the bedroom and closing the door. It's not great, but it's better than nothing, and before she can push the door open, I grab a bookcase and jam it under the handle. It's not much, but it'll give me a minute.

I run back to the living room, and watch as Katrina flips Samuel over neatly, landing on top of her father, anger and rage etched on her face. "You son of a bitch! You fucking bastard! You left me, you cheated on your wife, and you try to pretend that you're the victim! I hate you!"

Katrina starts pounding him in the face, vicious elbows and forearm blasts that batter away at his arms. He's beyond trying to defend himself, he's out of shape and exhausted already, but Katrina isn't letting up. Samuel's just got his arms up over his head to try and absorb the punishment, but I can tell from looking at Katrina's face, she isn't letting up.

His arms slip, and one of Katrina's elbows slices through, shattering Samuel's cheekbone, and his head drops back, stunned. His arms fall to the side, and she grabs him by the throat, a look of murder on her face. "Katrina! Katrina, stop!"

"No way, Jackson," she hisses, her eyes locked on

Samuel's face. Her fingers start to tighten, and he hacks, trying to grab at her wrist, but her grip is too strong. "He's got to pay."

"By turning you into a murderer like him?" I ask, coming next to her. I can't grab her, she's so high-strung right now that I'd probably just make her angrier, but I lay a hand on her right arm, just above her elbow. "Katrina, do you want to become as bad as he is? To become like him?"

"He took ten years of my life away," Katrina hisses, twisting Samuel's hand with her left when he finally gets a grip on her wrist. I hear something snap like dry twigs, and Samuel's gasps and coughs weaken as he gives a pained whine. "I think I deserve that much, with interest."

"Then do it the right way," I whisper, closing my hand on her arm. Her arm is thin, wiry with muscle, and I can close my fingers all the way around it, but I don't tug. I have to try, to let her do the right thing. "Let him go, Katrina. Do it the right way."

Katrina's face is still etched in fury and anger, but her fingers relax, and Samuel coughs, a little bit of blood dotting his lips as he does. He starts to raise his head and Katrina throws a palm strike, catching him between the eyes and bouncing his head off the floor, knocking him out. "Fine."

Katrina gets up, her knees shaky as she looks down on her father's laid out frame, and I hold her carefully, supporting her as she starts to walk away. The door to the bedroom finally gets opened and Theresa comes out, running to her husband and looking back at us in an expression that's so pathetic and miserable I actually feel slightly sorry for her. "How can you do this to your own father?"

"My father died ten years ago... along with my mother," Katrina whispers. "I swear to you, though, you two will pay for what you did. If I were you... I'd start running before he even wakes up."

"Come on, Katrina," I say softly, holding her arms. "We don't need to be here any longer."

We leave, and I have to half-carry her to the stairs, where she starts to recover, brushing my hands off. We run down the stairwell and out the gate, not stopping until we're around the corner. Slowing, we begin walking, Katrina looking straight ahead. "You okay?"

"No." Her voice is steel-hard, her eyes emotionless. I look down, and see that her hands are balled up, her forearms still tense and corded with effort at restraining herself.

Okay, fine. I understand that, and that's what I'm here for right now, helping her when she's not totally in her right mind. "Let's get back to the hotel, figure out what to do next."

"The Metro station's just up the street."

We walk in silence for a little bit, and I feel more confident as we put some distance between us and the apartment that we're not going to have Miami-Dade cops come rolling up to arrest us. Part of me is turned on, Katrina was so sexy and beautiful as she unleashed only the smallest bit of retribution on her father. However, it was scary too, watching her so close to going over the edge.

"Jackson," Katrina says as we reach the station, and I still can see in her eyes a lot of steely hardness, but also a hint of my Katrina coming back.

"Yeah, Katrina?" I ask, taking out my wallet to pay the

ticket machine.

"Back there, talking to me. You were right."

I put the money in the machine and look at Katrina, who's still got her hands balled up. "I swear to you that you will get them. And Peter."

Katrina nods once. "Let's get back to the hotel."

Chapter 21
Kat

I hold it together pretty well on the ride back to the hotel, although I need Jackson to open all the doors for me. I can't get my hands to unclench, and I know I'm still stalking as we walk up the stairs to the second floor to our room. It's only once we're inside that I start to tremble, and I look around, looking for something I can vent my rage and fury on.

Jackson notices, and grabs one of the cushions from the room's chair, holding it against his body like a shield. "Go ahead, let it out."

My first punch isn't enough to satisfy me, so I punch again, and again, and again. I'm losing count, my hands barely cushioned by the foam Jackson's holding as my hits thud against his body. I know he's taking some of the blows, but he nods, encouraging me as the tears start to flow.

"The motherfucker!" I yell in between punches. "How could they just lie to me like that? How could they look me in the eye and lie?"

"I don't know, Katrina," Jackson says, wincing again as I punch him directly in the chest through the cushion. "I'm sorry."

"No, they're the ones who are going to be sorry!" I yell back, punching again. Jackson takes a step back, and I follow, raining punches into the cushion. "I'm going to see them both in jail for this! I'm going to destroy them! I'm going to... argh!"

The dam finally breaks inside me, and the tears start.

Jackson puts his hands on my shoulders, but it only makes me cry harder. "It's okay, Katrina," Jackson tries to reassure me, but the tears won't stop. I sit back, sobbing at all the pain and loss, but Jackson slides down next to me, wrapping his arms around me and holding me closely. "It's okay, Katrina."

I clutch at him, crying for untold minutes until I'm able to pull myself together again. "Why, Jackson? Why'd they do it?"

"It doesn't matter, Katrina," Jackson says softly, his strong arms holding me safe and secure. "It doesn't matter. What matters is that you're who you are, and that's pretty damn amazing."

I sniff and feel fresh tears as I think of the lies. "Then why don't they love me?"

"I don't know, and it doesn't matter," Jackson says again. His fingers come to my chin, and he turns my face to look into his eyes. He's close again, and this time, there's no denying what we want and need.

Our lips touch, hesitant at first, but it feels so right, and it becomes stronger. My hand comes up to his neck and we grow deeper, our tongues coming out to caress each other. I'm lost, and I've never felt this before, never felt this level of trust and desire inside my body.

We part, and Jackson looks guilty. "Katrina, I shouldn't be taking advantage of you."

I chuckle and shake my head. "I... liked it. It's a great first real kiss."

"What?" Jackson says, surprised. He shifts back, and I feel heat on my neck and face. "What do you mean, real kiss?"

"I mean... I'd never had a *real* kiss before," I answer,

getting to my knees in front of him. "I've had one purpose in my life, and everything I've done was to help achieve that goal."

"You mean you've never... well, you know, had sex?" Jackson asks, and I blush, but laugh at the same time.

"I'm not a virgin, Jackson. But it never had meaning. There was no emotion."

I lean in, putting my hands on his shoulders and kiss him again, our lips melting around each other. "Can I tell you a secret, Jackson?"

He nods, and I smile. "You were the first boy I was ever interested in. Actually, I guess you're the only boy I've ever been interested in."

Jackson smiles and pulls me closer. We raise up, our bodies pressing closer, and I feel a tingle in my body as my breasts press against his chest, my nipples tingling at the pressure. His fingers trace around my ear, and I shiver with desire.

"Katrina," he says softly, like I used to dream a lover would when I allowed myself such dreams. "So beautiful, so strong. Amazing."

I bite my lip. "Jackson... it's always been you. You make me feel pretty... you make me feel like..."

"Like what?" he asks when I don't answer. He smiles, and kisses my cheek, trailing his lips toward my ear as I tremble in want. "It's okay. Tell me."

"You make me feel like... like there's a chance for a future," I whisper as his lips find the curve of my jaw and kiss, nibbling on the skin and finding the lobe of my ear, where his tongue traces the sensitive curve. I feel every caress of his tongue on my skin, and I'm hot, more aroused than I've ever been. "Oh God..."

Jackson smiles as he sits back, getting to his feet and helping me up. "Come on, Katrina. Let me show you what a future can really be."

I reach up, taking his hand, and he pulls me up, confident but gentle at the same time. Standing, he pulls me into an embrace, kissing me with that same confidence, with more passion than before, turning me slowly so that I'm backed against the bed, and I tumble down, laughing as my legs fly up and I literally *floomph* onto the bedspread.

Jackson chuckles and kneels down, taking my right boot in his hand and untying it slowly, his hand cupping my calf as he eases it off my foot. My breath catches as he pulls my sock off, and with careful, almost meticulous attention, he kisses my toe before setting it down, his fingers still lingering on my calf. "I wanted to touch these since that first visit to your place," he says as he unties my other boot, pulling it off before cupping both calves and massaging them with his fingers. "You have no idea how sexy you really are."

Jackson kisses my knees through my pants as I scoot back, and he joins me on the bed, lying on top of me as we kiss. I'm running my hands through his hair, moaning softly as he finds the pulse of my neck and licks, tasting my skin. Oh, it feels so good...

I feel his hand come up to cup my breast, and suddenly I'm filled with fear, my desire wilting inside me. No, this is too fast, this is going to complicate my mission...

"Wait... wait, Jackson, please, get off," I beg, pushing him away. "Wait... it's too fast, too fast."

Jackson rolls, giving me space, getting off the bed and stepping back. "What's wrong?"

"Too... too fast," I gasp, my heart racing in my chest. I'm not able to make any other words, I'm so confused. My body's tingling, and I want him so badly, but I'm afraid, my body and my heart and my head warring with each other. "Jackson... I can't. Not yet."

He looks like he wants to protest, and my body wants him to. My body wants him to disregard my words and shove me back into the mattress and get back on top of me. But my heart is afraid. I've never let anyone in this close before, and my head is against it, knowing that if I do, my mission becomes that much harder.

He must see the confusion in my eyes, because he nods. "When you're ready."

Chapter 22
Jackson

It's not the ocean, but the lake is beautiful, and according to the guy I asked at the supermarket where I bought the supplies, there's no problems with snakes or alligators. The blanket we snatched from our hotel room, and Katrina carries it folded over her arm as we walk toward the shore, holding hands. "A picnic, huh?"

I shrug. "I know that I come off as a rich boy," I say, thinking about the skirt that Katrina's put on again. She looks so fucking sexy in it. "I know that I like to make it rain sometimes, but I can enjoy the simpler things in life too, you know."

"I know," Katrina replies, giving me a meaningful look. "Jackson, my opinion of you has changed from a few weeks ago. Yeah, I know you still enjoy the money, but this... this is very nice, too. Come on, let's enjoy."

Katrina spreads out the blanket while I arrange my backpack, which we filled with items grabbed from the supermarket's deli: fried chicken, potato salad, and sweet tea, with a tub of banana pudding for dessert. A certifiable Southern feast. "You're really willing to risk that stuff calling itself tea after what happened earlier with the stuff at the cafe?"

"As long as I keep telling myself it's not tea, I can live with it," I say. "Besides, it's better for us than Coke, and you said you don't drink alcohol, right?"

"No, I never drink it by choice," Katrina says, curling her

legs underneath her. "I know, it's weird."

I sit down and open the container of chicken. "Actually, if it doesn't cause you pain, I'd like to hear more. You've told me some, but you're still a mystery."

Katrina thinks, then nods. "Okay. Well, you kind of got the basics. After the bomb, I was pretty screwed up, and bounced to two foster homes before landing with Virginia. She's had her own issues, and while she never told me all the details, let's just say she had her own vendetta that she dealt with. But through her, I learned to channel my anger and frustration, to focus on what was necessary. But it also blinded me to some things as well."

"It's fine," I dismiss, handing her a paper plate with food on it. "Go on."

"Well, the first thing she taught me was mental focus. I was taught to use my anger to burn away everything that wasn't focused on my goal. I was taught a meditation, one that, thinking about it now, does give me some regrets."

"How's it go?" I ask, and Katrina shakes her head, embarrassed. "It's okay. I won't be upset, no matter what it is."

Katrina looks at me, her light blue eyes questioning, and reaches a decision. "Okay. Here's how it goes.

There is no peace. Peace is a lie.

Freedom is a lie.

Happiness, love, and the future...
are lies.

The rage is the truth. Rage gives

me power.

Anger gives my power focus.

I have my target.

Rage... Power... Anger... Focus.

DeLaCoeurs... Vengeance is mine.

Pretty morbid stuff, isn't it?"

I swallow, hearing the icy rage in her voice as she repeated the mantra, and nod. "Yeah, but I understand now. After today... I understand more."

"Well, from there I learned to let go of a lot of concerns about legality. I learned to evaluate things more on what's moral rather than what's strictly legal. I learned about computers as you know, and more martial arts, and the Touches... well, those you know about." Katrina looks shy, and I love it. "I guess nothing all that useful."

"Oh, I think one of those is useful," I say, grinning, but I realize it's probably not the best time. "No, but seriously, I had a silly image last night, during one of the times that I woke up, before the dream got disturbing."

"Oh? What was it?" Katrina asks, and I wave her off. "Come on, it can't be that silly."

"Well, I had a dream that you and I opened a gym together," I tell her, sipping at the tea. It's horrible, but not as bad as the stuff this morning, maybe because it's still pretty much ice cold and a lot of the sweetness is numbed. "You taught women how to kick ass like you do, and I taught people how to get ripped. Oh, and you taught me some of your tricks."

"You seem to have a pretty natural skill, I don't think you need the Touches," Katrina jokes.

"Doesn't mean I wouldn't mind feeling them again," I say, grinning.

* * *

I'm lying in bed after reading for the past hour and trying to get my mind on anything other than today's events. Going to Katrina's parents' apartment, the beat down, and running away are part of it, but instead, my mind wants to go back to the feeling of her in my arms, the way she felt when we kissed, and the desire that flowed through me the rest of the day.

I look over at Katrina, who's sleeping, her lips slightly parted, so soft and kissable...

"Shit," I mutter, lying back on my side of the bed. I can't get up and go to the bathroom to beat off, that's fucking shameful. I haven't had to beat off to alleviate blue balls since... well, ever. At least I'm not standing at attention right this second, although my cock is awake and telling me all sorts of things it would like to do right now.

I close my eyes, hoping that maybe I can get some sleep, and maybe I do drift off, because the next thing I'm aware of is a light Touch on my forearm, sending warm sparks through me, and I hum slightly. "Mmm..."

"Shh," Katrina whispers in my ear, her hand touching another area, and even though I'm in a fantasy, I know I'm also awake. My eyes open, and I see that Katrina's turned on the little lamp next to her side of the bed, and she's taken off all of her clothes. I blink, making sure I'm not imagining things.

"Katrina?"

"Tonight... I want there to be a future tonight," she whispers, her voice choked with feeling, and I notice she's pulled the bedspread down, removing the barrier between us. "Tonight... show me what it can be."

She touches me again, and I'm fully awake, fully aware of what's happening, but still clear-headed, my desire for her completely natural, not manufactured by what she's doing. She leans down, her body sliding over mine, and looks into my eyes. "Katrina..."

"Be my first, Jackson," she pleads, her eyes filled with emotion. "Be my first real lover."

I nod, and she lowers her lips the last few inches, and we kiss. What I don't tell her, what I want to tell her, is that I've never had a real lover either, not the way she's talking about anyway. And in that kiss, she's my first as well.

Chapter 23
Kat

When we get back to the hotel after our dinner, I'm torn more than ever. The dinner, the kiss, all of it, I'm feeling different than I have in my entire life. Even telling Jackson earlier that with him, I feel like there's a chance at a future, it's not enough.

The reality is that when I'm with Jackson, not only do I feel like I have a future, but I feel regret. I feel regret about the past ten years, and the senseless bullshit that drove me to what I've become. I want those ten years back, those years that I should have spent doing normal girl things, like having my first kiss with Jackson like I'd wanted when I was twelve.

We get ready for bed casually, like there's no tension between us, but I can feel it in the air. It's in the way he lies in bed trying to read, but spending ten minutes on a single page before turning to the next, and in the way he keeps glancing over at me every time I move. When I switch off the light, I close my eyes to meditate, hoping that maybe by focusing and pretending to go to sleep I can relieve some of this tension. Jackson closes his book and sets it aside after a few minutes, and I can hear him turn over onto his side too, but after a few minutes, he mutters to himself.

"Shit," he lightly curses, then shifts again. His breathing evens out though, and I think he's drifted off into a light doze, and I open my eyes, turning on my side to look at him. I can't see much, so I turn on the lamp next to my side of the bed, and watch him in the soft light, amazed at how handsome he is. Even in sleep though he's tense, and his lips are constantly moving. It takes me a while, but I realize he's saying my name, although in desire or fright I'm not sure.

I make my decision, knowing that regardless if it's right or wrong, it's necessary. Carefully I get up, and take the rolled-up blanket from between us, then I strip down, taking off everything I'm wearing before stretching out on the bed again. I see his forearm, and I Touch him lightly, his tension easing before he hums, the desire growing inside him. "Mmm..."

After he wakes, I look into his eyes, and ask him the most important request I've ever asked anyone in my life. "Be my first, Jackson. Be my first real lover."

He nods, and I lower my lips to his, the two of us kissing again. He's gentle, and I feel my heart warm as he strokes my back, slowly waking to the desire inside us. Suddenly, Jackson's hands are surer, more powerful and demanding as he realizes what I want. I giggle as he rolls us to the side, and suddenly I'm underneath him, his eyes sparkling with humor as he looks down on me. "Now this is not what I ever expected."

I chuckle and nod. "Neither did I. You're still wearing your clothes." I'm thrilled as Jackson pulls his t-shirt off, then pushes his boxers down. His cock is already growing, nearly fully hard, and I feel a wetness start to form inside me. I'm ready, anticipating what's going to happen, and I smile, my heart warming. Jackson sees my smile and stops, just watching me.

"Every smile you give, you look more and more beautiful," he tells me before we kiss again. His skin is warm, amazing to feel pressed against me, my body thrilling at the sensation of our bodies touching. I wrap my legs around his waist, moaning as Jackson starts kissing his way along my throat, finding my ear again and nibbling. "Mmm, you like that."

"Oh yes..." I groan as he traces my earlobe again. Feeling naughty, I plant my left foot and roll us again, giving me full access to his body, gasping when I feel his cock bump against the entrance to my pussy. "Jackson..."

"Condom?" he asks, letting me go. "I... I think I have one."

I look down at him and shake my head. Tonight is about the future, and in my mind, my future with him does not include condoms. Besides, with every training partner I ever had, we used condoms. I want my first lover to be different. "No," I reply, pulling him up as I scoot back. I adjust my legs and sit in his lap, straddling his waist, his cock sandwiched between us. He scoots us back until his back is resting against the headboard of the bed, and I stroke his hair, emotion choking me. "I just want you to know... I... I... "

"I know," he says, and we kiss, harder and more passionately than ever. Jackson wraps his arms around me, his hands supporting me as we stay like this, devouring each other. Planting my knees, I reach down, grasping his steely cock and groaning in need. I lift up and position him at my entrance, coating him with my natural juices before lowering down slowly, shivering as he stretches me open. I look down and see him looking me in the eyes, his own heart visible as I sink deeper, my body and soul filled as we come together.

Settling in, I feel my clit grind against the base of

Jackson's cock, and I tighten around him, smiling as his fingers pull at my back in response. Leaning me back, he kisses down my throat to my breasts, sucking on my nipples in turn and nipping at the skin. I feel so many sparks shooting through my body that I have no idea where they're coming from.

His raw desire and passion combined with his natural skill sets my body on the trembling edge of ecstasy. His lips are electric, his tongue teasing my breasts until I'm lost, delirious and clawing at his hair, wanting to both pull him in tighter and push him back so that I can kiss him again.

Finally, Jackson releases my left nipple and I jam his head back, bouncing it off the headboard and crushing his mouth with a kiss while I lift my hips, sliding up before riding his thick, perfect cock down again, my clit dragging against him the whole time, a match igniting the fire inside me. I ride him, my hips moving on their own, up and down, back and forth, squeezing him with every movement.

I'm dripping in sweat, my body already driven past any feeling it's ever had before, and Jackson's still there, holding and supporting me. His mouth finds my neck again and I'm caught, trapped between the feeling of his lips on my throat and his cock inside me, riding back and forth. "Jackson... oh, Jackson.... give me more."

We slide down the bed, until he's on his back and I'm riding him, our fingers entwining as he supports me. He's looking up into my eyes, and I lean down until our noses touch, stopping my hips. "Take me, Jackson. Please."

Without letting go of my hands, he wraps me up, pinning my arms behind my back as he rolls us again, putting me on my back, my legs spread and open to him. He's slipped out from the roll, but in a single long thrust, he splits me open again, both of us gasping at the feeling. Letting my hands go, Jackson pushes my ankles up toward my head, and I grab behind my knees, holding on as he starts pounding me with his thick cock, his powerful hips shaking my body with every thrust. I egg him on, "Come on, that's not all you've got," I say, even though I'm already hissing in pain and pleasure with every slap of his hips against mine.

Jackson's groans and gasps are in perfect unison with mine as he speeds up, driving into me harder and harder as my words give him even more encouragement. My hands clutch at his back, my nails scratching and clawing at his skin as Jackson fills me perfectly again, my body never feeling this way before, never feeling this good. I'm caught on the edge of coming, and Jackson knows it.

I'm reduced to grunts, unable to speak but still capable of feeling, begging for the last bit to push me over into paradise. I feel him swell bigger within me, and with a final shuddering groan he comes, his cock filling me and sending me crashing into climax, my body electric white with sensation. It's never been this good, this meaningful before, and as I cry out, I want to form the words that I've never said before to any man, not in the past ten years, but to Jackson I want to say them. I want to tell him how I feel, but before I can, darkness overwhelms me, and I'm driven into unconsciousness and sleep.

* * *

At first, I'm confused waking up. I've never felt this before, claustrophobic and comforted at the same time. There's a warm weight pressed against my back and a strong restraint around my waist. At first, I want to struggle, but then Jackson hums, and I realize what it is, and comfort takes over. I snuggle into him, relaxing in the few minutes we have before the needs of the day takes over.

"Good morning," Jackson whispers in my ear. He kisses my neck, and a little thrill runs down my spine. "How'd you sleep?"

"Better than I have in my entire life," I answer honestly, taking his hand off my stomach and kissing it. "Last night... was amazing." I turn around to look him in the eyes. Even sleep-tousled and with a little bit of sleep crust around his left eye, he's handsome and wonderful and sexy as hell. "You opened up new frontiers to me last night."

"Then let's explore them today," he invites me, his hand going down to cup my hip.

"You trying to wear me out?" I laugh, purring when he cups my ass. His hands feel so good, but I want to draw it out, make it last. "Come on, we've got time. Go get a shower while I make a few phone calls, and we'll plan out the rest of the day."

Jackson shakes his head. "Only after a good morning kiss. Then I'll go. If not, I'm dragging you to the shower where I'm going to seduce you, and then I'm going to do it again on the bed afterward before you can make your phone call."

I chuckle and kiss him, loving this side of him. It's something I've had so little time for. It feels nice. "There. Now go, and if my phone call goes quickly enough, maybe I'll join you for the last part of the shower."

Jackson grins and gets up, giving me quite a show of his

naked butt as he walks into the bathroom, and I roll off the bed, finding my phone. I know who I want to contact, and I need Jackson out of the room to do so. I wait until I hear the shower start, and through the crack in the door I see him get in and start washing. Opening my apps, I see that Andrea has tried to contact me via Viber, and I return her call. She's online, and maybe she's got a smartphone like me, so I don't have to wait.

"Hello?"

"It's good to hear your voice again, Andrea."

"It's been too long, Katrina. How is Savannah?"

"Actually, we're in Miami. That's what I wanted to call you about. I found my parents. They're alive."

"Whoa. I suspected something with the way Nathan and Jackson bounced so quickly, but that's one I didn't think of."

"Yeah well, Peter helped my parents fake their deaths. Nathan's already told Jackson about it, and it's a stake in Peter's heart if I can prove it. Andrea, I'm going to need your help."

"What can I do?"

"I've never been able to crack Peter's home computer, or wherever he keeps whatever electronic files he's got. If I can get something to tie him to my parents' faked deaths, and to the dirty dealings my... that Sam Grammercy was doing, I can bring him down quickly."

"What's the rush? I mean, besides your life being in danger."

"I'm ready to move on from all of this. But I have to complete it first. I've put too much into this to just give it up. Andrea... can you help me?"

"Damn right. Let me get to work."

"Thanks. I'll have another friend working it too, so if you

run into someone online called BlakDhal1A, chill. That's my girl."

"All right, I'll be in touch. For now, though, I've got class in ten. Enjoy Miami."

Andrea hangs up, and I set my phone back in my bag. I hear the shower turn off and Jackson get out. "Any longer and I'd turn into a prune," he calls. "But if you want, you can help me dry off."

"Hmm, maybe I can," I tease, going into the bathroom where he's dripping, gloriously naked, his cock hanging long and thick between his legs, and twitching as he sees me. "What, did you think I'd get dressed?"

"I wasn't sure, but I'm glad you didn't," he replies, kissing me when I come close enough. "I thought you wanted to take your time?"

"I do. This is just a little foreplay," I say. He's already rock hard and ready to go at it, but we've got things to do. "Come on. Let's get dressed, go get some breakfast, and then we'll have all day to have fun before we head back to New Orleans and put this whole damn thing behind us."

I leave the bathroom, Jackson lagging behind as he wipes down, and I get dressed quickly. I'm hungry, and after having sex, I'm looking forward to a big breakfast before coming back for more.

"Actually, I was thinking about that in the shower," Jackson says nervously. "Uhm, is there a way that maybe we can get your vengeance without Peter going to jail?"

I've got my pants on, and my sports bra is half on, but I pause, shocked at what I just heard. I finish pulling my bra on and reach for a t-shirt, since it's closest. "You must be joking, Jackson. What do you want me to do, kill him?"

Jackson blanches, and shakes his head. "No, no. What I mean is... what about just the two of us running away? We live well, and safe from his influence. Isn't that a better revenge than destroying him and hurting others?"

"Others?" I ask, sensing where this is going. "You mean hurting your ability to drop five hundred bucks on a skirt and sandals for me, don't you? Didn't think I noticed the price tag?"

Jackson blushes, but shakes his head. "No... not just that, Katrina. I mean, there's my mother, and as bad as she was to me, she can't survive on her own. And Andrea, she's still in school, and then there's the other people who may..."

"Stop it, Jackson. Just... cut the bullshit," I snap, pulling my t-shirt on. I sit down and pull my socks on, looking for my boots. "Jesus, I had hoped we were past this point. It's not about the fucking money! Life isn't about that!"

"It isn't about blood and revenge either!" Jackson yells back, still naked. "You told me to be better than him, well, you need to be, too! Stop worrying about your goddamn vengeance and live your life! Let it go, let us be able to let it go!"

"I can't!" I yell back, furious. "I'm not looking for his death anymore, but that asshole stole ten years of my life! I can't get that back, and I'm not the only one. Maybe he didn't kill my parents, but he's killed how many more? How much of that money you're so worried about is blood money? And don't try to fucking lie, telling me it's not the money you're worried about!"

"So what are you going to do? Blow the whole damn thing up? Burn the house to the ground? Because if you send him to jail, you might as well! You know the feds and who the fuck else is going to civil sue the shit outta the estate. What then? Living broke?"

"I've done it," I reply coldly, standing up. I go to grab my bag, and see the skirt sitting on top. I yank it out, and rip it in half, tossing the pieces onto the carpet. "It isn't as bad as you think. Might just make you stronger, Jackson."

Before he can answer, I grab my backpack and leave, pissed and trying not to cry. I'd suspected, I'd feared since yesterday, but hearing his words, I know that I can't trust Jackson to not interfere in the rest of the plan. He cares for me, I know that. But right now... he's not ready.

* * *

"This seat taken?"

For the first time in my life, I'm well on my way to being drunk. After storming out of the hotel, I grabbed a taxi, going toward the beach, not with any purpose but to get some distance and to calm down. Distance and perspective are important for any warrior in a fight, after all, and I hoped that watching the waves on the sand would help me find some temporary peace and clarity.

The problem is, I can't calm down. I used the prepaid card I have with me to take out a couple hundred dollars, most of what's left on that card, and crash at a fleabag hotel, putting myself through a workout that leaves my body dripping in sweat, but my mind no more settled.

Jackson's tried to call me half a dozen times, and texted me more. He's apologetic, but I can read between the lines, he still wants to protect the fucking money. Finally, about two hours ago, I gave up and shut off my phone. Instead, I headed here, one of the first bars that I saw, and walked inside. Fuck it, it works for everyone else, why not me, too?

I'm about four drinks in when I hear the voice, and I turn my head, three-quarters drunk, seeing two people standing there. I have no idea who they are, but don't really care. "Go 'way. Not good conversation."

"I can see that, Katrina," the one person, a woman I notice, says gently. At the mention of my name my head whips back, and I reel to my feet.

"Who the fuck're you?" I ask.

"It's me," the woman says, stepping closer into the light. "It's Andrea."

I squint, and I realize that it is Andrea. The straight black hair, the almond-shaped eyes, but the same dark blue as Jackson's... "Well hey! It is you! How'd the hell you get here? Who's yur big friend?"

I blink, but in the dim light of the bar, I can't make out his face. "Who are you?"

"A man who owes you a lot more than I can ever repay," he says. "Come, let's talk. Away from the alcohol."

"My tab though..." I protest, and the bartender, who's been watching with a leery eye, waves me off. "What?"

"We're pay as you go," he reminds me. "We're square."

Andrea reaches into her pocket and pulls out another bill and puts it on the bar. "Just in case, and for taking care of her," she says. Coming closer, she takes my arm and puts it around her shoulder. "Come on, Kat. How much did you drink, anyway?"

"I dunno... less than a bottle," I say, swaying along with

Andrea's help out onto the streets. It's later than I thought it'd be, the moon is nearly fully overhead. "Hey... what time is it?"

"A little before eleven thirty," Andrea says. The sidewalk is mostly empty, but this is the beach area of Miami, and I guess along A1A, the traffic and pedestrians don't go to bed until much later. "Sorry it took us so long to get here."

"How did you get here?" I ask, the clear air helping me at least not slur my words. The man stays behind me and Andrea, and I sense that he's giving us security. I wonder who he is.

"Well, after you called me, Jackson called Nathan here after you two argued, Nathan gave me a call. I figured it was enough of an emergency, I booked a flight and boogied while Nathan hauled ass in his Tahoe."

"Nathan?" I ask, turning around. I recognize him now, Nathan Black. The bastard who helped my parents fake their death. My hand flashes out, catching Nathan in the face with a slap, but he takes it without even reacting. "I should try and castrate you."

"You should... but there's a line on people who want my balls, Miss Grammercy," he says softly, calm. His eyes are a strangely disconcerting green, giving him almost a reptilian look in the streetlights. "Besides, Andrea and I are here to help you. After that... you and I can settle accounts between us."

"Fine," I say, turning back around and almost falling. "Where are we going?"

"To where I'm staying," Andrea says. "I don't know where you're at, Jackson didn't tell Nathan."

"How'd you find me?"

"The Viber account. I called the number, did a GPS ping

off the towers. It got us here, and we've spent the past three hours checking around."

I nod. It's a good trick, and one that I should have thought of.

"Now, let's just get you out of here, and you get to meet Maverick."

"Who?"

"My dog," Nathan says with a touch of affection. "I'm glad we were able to find a place that's pet-friendly."

"A dog, a half-Japanese business student, a former Green Beret... I pick such interesting people to hang out with," I mutter, relaxing as Andrea helps me over to a taxi. I let it all go as the taxi pulls away, Nathan crunching in up front with the driver while Andrea comforts me. I know I cry, although Andrea doesn't ask me why, and Nathan stays quiet the whole ride. We end up out by the airport again, although on the other side than where Jackson and I were staying. Driving past a bunch of houses, I'm confused. "Where're we going?"

"AirBnB," Andrea explains as we pull up to a house. "Easy, casual, and more anonymous."

"Good idea. Shoulda thought of that myself," I mutter, clarity starting to come back. I feel like an ass for losing control so much, and inside me, I can hear some of my instructors telling me off for putting myself in so much danger. I'm lucky that Andrea and Nathan wanted to help, and not put a bullet in my head. "I'm hungry."

"There's food inside, and I'll brew you some tea," Nathan says. "If you need to rest, we can. Then we'll talk."

"I don't need rest," I reply as Andrea helps me inside.

We're greeted by what has to be the biggest damn dog I've ever seen, who's bouncing and wagging his tail excitedly, barking loudly when Nathan comes in behind us, closing the door. The barks drive icy daggers into my ears, and I groan. "That's not a dog, that's a fucking horse. Oh, my head."

"Maverick!" Nathan says quietly, snapping his fingers. The dog quiets immediately, and when Nathan points, he retreats, laying down in what I guess is the living room of the house. "Sorry, he's energetic after being in the Tahoe all day."

Andrea leads me into the kitchen, where she has me sit down and comes back with some cereal in a bowl. "It's not much, but it's all we've got right this second. Didn't do any shopping, we were kinda busy looking for you."

"Thanks," I mumble, picking up the dry little rings and munching on them. It's not a lot, but it'll help. "I can't believe I went and got drunk."

"Emotions do that to us," Nathan says quietly, no condescension in his voice, which surprises me. He goes to the stove and starts a pot of water, and leaves the room, coming back with a metal canister. "Thankfully, I keep my travel stash with me, and it's strong and black."

"No coffee?"

Andrea chuckles and snatches a piece of cereal from my bowl. "Despite the long New Orleans tradition of some of the finest French Roast in the entire United States, Nathan here is a total heathen who only drinks tea now. I think it was all those years of bad Army coffee that got to him."

"A Japanese girl calling someone a heathen for drinking only tea," I remark, shaking my head slowly. "Maybe I drank more than I thought."

"Hardly, I just like giving Nathan a hard time," Andrea says. We're quiet, and Nathan finishes his tea brewing, bringing big mugs for all of us. "Thanks, Nathan."

He takes a seat at the table and sips, sighing contentedly. "That's as much for me as you guys. You might want to let yours cool some though, Katrina."

I nod my thanks and keep munching on the cereal until the bowl is empty. Andrea gets up and grabs the box, bringing it over, and I see that it's probably been left behind by the last renters since it's mostly empty already. "Fine dining."

"The finest," Andrea agrees quietly. "I don't want to pry... but do you want to tell us about it?"

"Tell me what you've found first," I order, pouring another bowl of cereal and emptying the box. "And we might need a food run."

"There's a twenty-four-hour place down the street, I saw it driving from the airport," Nathan says. "I can go later. As for what you're asking, I believe you're talking about the files on Peter's personal computer you asked Andrea about?"

I give Andrea a raised eyebrow, and she shrugs. "Nathan and I talked after meeting up at the airport and while we've been looking for you. We laid it all out between us, making sure we're working toward the same goal. We want Peter to pay as much as you do."

I look sideways at Nathan, who nods. "I know. Like I said, we'll discuss it later."

"Fine. And, what have you found?"

Andrea shakes her head. "Peter kept nothing. I've had his

password for a while, and copied a lot of his server a while back for... personal reasons. But he kept nothing about the bomb that was used for your parents."

"However, I did keep information," Nathan says before I can get upset. He takes a memory card from his pocket and sets it on the table. "I've kept it and a few other e-mails as insurance against Peter going too crazy on me. I don't know what you've got, but this could easily put him behind bars for a long, long time."

I take the chip, and look at it. "You know that if you give this to me, you're putting yourself in my hands?"

"I should have done that as soon as I found your loft address," Nathan says quietly. "I should have done it again after Jackson came to me and asked me not to turn you into Peter, and then again when he asked for my allegiance in covering this trip. So don't worry about that part."

I nod, then take out my phone, putting the chip inside. I copy the files, and then upload them to my cloud server, making sure there are copies in multiple locations. Darcy knows about the cloud. She can get the files if something happens to me. "Okay. So what now?"

"Now we take him down," Andrea says with intensity. "The only issues are timeline and method. What about Jackson?"

"He's... not on board," I say softly, trying not to let my mood falter. I'm in work mode, and I can't be worried about Jackson right this moment. "He... he's still got some things to let go of."

Nathan nods in understanding, then sips his tea. "Then I have an idea... one that protects him, protects you, and brings the authorities in relatively quickly."

"I'm listening."

Chapter 24
Jackson

I'm frantic with not knowing what to do. I've tried calling Katrina for the past two days, and I'm paralyzed with worry.

At first, when Katrina walked out, I thought she was just pissed off. I mean, I've pissed off women before, but I figured she'd come back after cooling off. It wasn't until after I got dressed that I realized her bag was gone too, and by then, it was too late. I searched the area around the hotel, but she wasn't there.

I tried text messages, calls, everything as I took the rental car around the hotel's neighborhood, hoping that maybe she stayed close. Two hours of driving later, and I tried other places as well. But nothing, which shouldn't really surprise me. Miami's a big city, and I'm looking for one woman.

Nathan calls me back, and I'm glad for his help. He came down from Savannah as soon as he could, arriving just after midnight that day, meeting me for breakfast the next morning. He searched in his Tahoe all day yesterday, and now I'm desperate.

"Nathan... what have I done?" I ask as he mechanically shovels hash browns into his mouth. We're at a diner, and I realize with a start that I haven't eaten since lunch yesterday, and I call the waitress over for a pancake breakfast. Fuck the carbs, I need food. "What have I done?"

"Sounds like you pissed her off," Nathan says quietly,

sipping his orange juice. "She may have ghosted on you."

"No, I can't accept that. Not after... well, after what happened between us," I say. He doesn't need to know all of that. "I have to find her."

"Maybe she went back to New Orleans," Nathan offers. "I mean, she could have jumped on a flight back home just as easily as hanging out here."

I shake my head, sighing in frustration. "No way, Nathan. I don't know how I can say that, just... it's a feeling. She's here in Miami, I know it. After the incident with her father, there's just no way she'd just leave town without at least something pulling her back. Being pissed at me isn't enough."

The waitress brings me my short stack, and I cover the whole thing in syrup. The first bite is sweet, but bitter, because I should be having this meal with Katrina and not Nathan. Nathan watches me for a minute, then speaks again. "Jackson... are you letting your emotions get the better of you?"

I half-slam my fork down and look him in the eyes. "You're goddamned right my emotions are involved in this, but fuck you if you think that it's a bad thing. My entire life, I've kept my emotions, my real emotions, behind a wall. Now that I've let someone past them, no way am I giving up on that person."

Nathan takes another bite of hash browns and sets his own fork down. "Okay. I ask because I need to know how far you're going to take this. We stay here in Miami much longer, and your father is going to start asking what the hell's taking us so long."

"Let him ask," I grumble, taking another bite of pancake. "I don't care if I blow him totally out of the water on this. For fuck's sake, don't you see how wrong I was?"

"Not really. You haven't said much other than that you two had an argument, and that we're supposed to look for her. Hell, I don't even know much about what happened here in the city. Just obviously you found Samuel Grammercy."

"Michael Ball now," I correct him, then shake my head. "I guess it doesn't matter what the argument was about. What matters is what I've learned over the past two days."

"And what's that?" Nathan asks curiously. "That you want to run away with her, make lots of little DeLaCoeur babies, and soak up some sun rays in a tropical paradise?"

I have to chuckle at his light jab, and shake my head. "No, although the tropical paradise part sounds pretty good. But I do know one thing... there are things more important than money."

Nathan nods in acceptance, and we finish our breakfasts. "Okay, so what's the plan for today?"

"I'm going to go back down toward the University area," I tell him, thinking quickly. "It's where her parents are living, and maybe she's going to try and do something. What about you?"

"I'm going to dig down in the industrial areas, maybe in some of the computer shops," Nathan says. "If she is staying in Miami, she's more likely to go to the cultures and areas she's familiar with. That's the poor, the techies, and the industrial areas. So I'll start canvassing there. Do you know if she speaks Spanish? It might make certain areas more penetrable."

I shake my head. "Honestly Nathan, I have no idea. Do you speak Spanish?"

The former Green Beret gives me a smirk and nods. "*Si.*

He estudiado durante diez años, y puedo hablar en niveles cercanos a nativos."

"I have no damn clue what you just said, but I'll take you at your word. All right, stay in touch."

Nathan nods while I wipe my lips with my napkin and stand up. "If I find her?"

"Stay close, get in contact with me," I tell him. "She doesn't trust you, I think. Also... I need to apologize to her, and tell her some very important things."

"I understand. See you later."

I leave the diner and get in my rental, driving down to the University of Miami. I drive as slow as I can over the neighborhood, even going through the U itself. A couple of girls give me looks, but I'm not looking for ass, I'm looking for Katrina. Finally, I pull over into a diagonal parking space, and I walk around campus a little, seeing if maybe I can spot her. Lots of girls, none of them look at all like Katrina, and I sit down, frustrated. I stare at my hands, wishing I could take back what I said, what a dumbass I was being.

"Hey man, you look like you need a friend to talk to," someone says, and I look up, seeing what could only be the typical college campus bum. Slightly soiled shirt flaps untucked over his old jeans, and he's wearing Birkenstocks for fuck's sake. I take it back, he's not a bum, he's a Social Justice Warrior, probably. "Wanna talk?"

"No... well, okay," I reply, and the dude takes a seat on the grass. "Just... it's about a girl."

"What about her?" the SJW asks, relaxing back onto his hands. "Like, did she cuck you or something?"

"What? Cuck? Hell no," I say, startled into laughing. "I just fucked up, that's all."

"How so?" the guy asks, and I shrug.

"We... we're trying to get something done, something really important to her and really to me too, but I chickened out. You see, if she does what she wants, then there's a good chance I'm out a ton of money. It's not good money, it's dirty as hell actually, but still... I've been living the good life for a long time, and I panicked. I tried to talk her into a safer path. She walked out on me, and since then, I've been trying to find her."

"If you do, what will you tell her?" the SJW asks. I'm reminded of my conversation with Nathan this morning, and I chuckle.

"I'll tell her the truth. That she's more important to me than any money, that I woke up the past two days miserable because she's not there, and that if it means following her to hell, I'd rather do that than have all the money in the world."

The guy nods, then leans forward. "My advice is to tell her all of that, as soon as you can. That, and probably beg forgiveness for being an idiot."

I laugh once, harshly, and look at the guy. "I thought guys like you were supposed to be all about being nonjudgmental."

The guy laughs and gets to his feet. "If I was who I look like, maybe. I'm just a psychology doctoral student doing a study. Thanks. And don't worry, this isn't going in any paper. Good luck, man."

The guy leaves, and I get up, determined to find Katrina even if I have to tear Miami apart. I head back to my car to start my search again when I feel my phone vibrate and my ringer go off. I look, and it's Nathan. "Yeah, you found her?"

"Yeah, she's by the Miami Dade North Campus, close to Opa Locka," Nathan says. "I'm uploading you a GPS location of where I am now."

My phone buzzes and a map pulls up. I didn't even know the thing did that. I look, and realize I can get there in about twenty minutes. "Okay, I see it. I'm at the U, I'll jump on 95 up to there. Keep her in sight, Nathan."

"Will do," Nathan says. "She's been talking to some people, but I'm out of her direct sight. Don't worry Jackson, I know what I'm doing."

"No doubt. I'll be there ASAP." I start my engine and rush to the interstate, jumping on and driving north as quickly as I can. The traffic isn't bad, it's midday and the rush hour isn't for quite a while, so I make good time, getting off at Opa Locka in only fifteen minutes. I find Nathan's signal, and see his Tahoe parked in the parking lot of a flight school and what the sign says is a pilot supply store.

"Nathan," I say when he rolls the window down. "Where is she?"

"Parking lot over there," Nathan says, pointing across the street. I look, and see nothing. When I turn to look at him, he smirks. "Seriously. She went inside the tan building over there just five minutes ago. I think it's a small airline, maybe a puddle jumper type place."

"What for?" I ask, and Nathan shrugs.

"Most likely she's close to being tapped out financially, and those sorts of guys can sometimes work deals."

The door to the building opens, and I see Katrina step out, her backpack over her shoulder. She's changed shirts, wearing something almost normal, but there's no mistaking that angel's face or the short hair. "There. Come on Nathan, I can't let her go."

Nathan nods and I get into his Tahoe, seeing Maverick in the back taking a nap. "Rough day for him?"

"He'll get a walk later," Nathan says nonchalantly, starting the engine. "You ready to do some groveling?"

"Damn right," I say with a laugh, feeling lighter than ever. I'm eager to talk to her, to tell her it doesn't matter about the money, that I need her in my life.

We're just about to cross the street when my phone buzzes again, and I pull it out, wondering who's texting me now. My heart jumps into my throat when I see that the text is from Peter.

Never, ever lie to me again. You're next.

"What the fuck?" I ask, but before I can show the text to Nathan, a red sports sedan pulls into the parking lot, the side windows rolling down. "No... NO!"

The shooter fires four times, the shots loud in the muggy Miami air, one of them catching Katrina in the forehead, where a giant fountain of blood goes flying. She crumples to the ground, and I'm trying to jerk the handle on my door, but Nathan's already slammed his foot to the gas, throwing me into my seat. "What are you doing? She's hurt!"

"She's dead!" Nathan yells, following the red sports car. "But we can get this bastard!"

His words sink in, and I look out the front window,

nodding. "Get him."

Nathan's Tahoe is big, and he's kept it in good shape, but the sports sedan is thousands of pounds lighter, lower to the ground, and more agile as it weaves through the traffic in front of us. We chase for over a mile, and in the distance, I can hear police sirens approaching. The car whips around a corner, and Nathan tries to follow, but his Tahoe is too big, and we spin out, nearly tipping over.

"No... no, NO!" Nathan yells, getting out of the driver's side and reaching to his hip, but his gun isn't there, and he realizes it. I'm out too, but the red car is gone, out of sight turning another corner, and I sink to my knees, going into shock. Nathan comes up and grabs me, dragging me to my feet. "Come on, Jackson. There's nothing we can do here. Let's go."

"Go?" I ask, stupefied. "Go where?"

"Out of here for one," he says, pulling me toward the Tahoe where Maverick is up and barking loudly. "You can't get whoever did this if the cops find us. Let's go."

Chapter 25
Jackson

It takes Nathan eighteen hours to get us back to New Orleans, mainly because we couldn't just get on the road and go. First, he drove me quickly back to the hotel, where I spent ten minutes grabbing my shit before we peeled out. In the panhandle, at around one in the morning, he pulled into a rest stop to crash for a few hours, power-napping.

I'd like to say I was helpful during the drive, or at least coherent. Instead, I was sitting in a state of shock, sleeping some of the time, staring blankly out the window the rest. I ate when Nathan passed me a cheeseburger, and I drank from a straw, but that was it.

About an hour outside New Orleans, Nathan pulls into another rest stop, and shuts off the engine. "Jackson, we need to talk."

"About what?" I ask listlessly. I just saw the woman that I wanted to make a future with catch a bullet to the brain, and now you want to talk? What the fuck is your problem?

"About what we're going to do when we get back to New Orleans. I was thinking... I'd like to drop you off at Katrina's place for a few days. I know it's going to have painful memories, but you don't need to be at the plantation right now."

"Why not?" I ask, turning my dead eyes to Nathan. "I just need five minutes. Go in, you lend me your 1911, and I put five rounds in Peter. Last one in the brain, just like he had the shooter do to Katrina. Balances out."

Nathan shakes his head slowly and clears his throat. "Do that, and you'll be dead before you even reach the front door. You know I'm not the only person working security at the house, and I am sure that he's got someone else watching his back now at all times."

"Who gives a fuck?" I protest, anger at least somewhat burning the lethargy of the past hours away. "She got her fucking brains blown out, Nathan. He deserves to die simply because of that."

"Is that what she'd want you to do?" Nathan asks quietly. "She was willing to die, I know that. But did she want you to die, too? Or did she do everything she could to make sure that you stayed safe and protected as well? I know what I saw, even if it was from a distance."

I think about it and shake my head. "It doesn't matter. She deserves justice."

"That may be, but I'm going to say something else, and you may not like it, but I'm doing this because I've come to respect you, Jackson," Nathan says quietly. "Katrina trained for what, nearly a decade, and she was still caught dead by Peter's men and money? You're pissed off and untrained. You need time to let this soak in, and to plan what to do next."

I think about it, and nod. "Fine. Take me to the loft. But keep me up to date with what's happening at the house. If things calm down, or if I think I can tolerate it, I'll come back for a bit."

Nathan nods, and gets back on the interstate. "I'll pitch Peter a bullshit story, although I guess not completely. You're angry, upset, and are taking some time off to live on your own. He'll probably be happy, and it'll give you space as well."

We get to the loft, and Nathan leads me upstairs, carrying my backpack for me. He has to jimmy the lock, but it doesn't take him long. He looks around, nodding in appreciation. "Not a lot, but I've lived in worse. You gonna be okay?"

"I'll live," I reply, going over to Katrina's bed and lying down. "Maybe later...maybe I'll give you a call."

"I'll be in touch. And don't worry about the landlord, I'm sure we can work something out with him, too," Nathan tells me. He leaves, shutting the door behind him. I can smell her on the pillow underneath my head, and as I fall asleep again, I cling to her essence, treasuring it.

* * *

"Jackson..."

I sit up, hearing her voice, surprised. "Katrina?"

She comes in from out of the darkness, a little smile on her face and wearing her skirt, but without her sandals, her bare feet whispering on the wood flooring of the loft. "Yes, it's me. How'd you sleep?"

"I had the most horrible dream," I say, getting off the bed and moving over to hug her. "You wouldn't believe how terrible it was."

"Well, that doesn't matter now. So are you ready?"

"Ready for what?" I ask, confused. Katrina laughs softly and ruffles my hair, smiling.

"For our big day tomorrow, silly," she says, holding up her finger with the glittering diamond ring on it. "You know, we're getting married?"

I feel a stupid grin break out on my face, and I shake my head. "I must have slept harder than I thought. Or maybe I'm still sleeping."

Katrina laughs and kisses me, her lips so soft and perfect. "Don't worry, I'll always be with you."

I step back, and look into Katrina's eyes. "I love you, Katrina. From the time I was twelve, you've been the one. I want..."

A knock at the door interrupts me, and Katrina steps back, fading into the darkness of the loft. I want to follow her, but for some reason, my feet won't move. Just before the shadows swallow her, she raises her hand, palm up to me. "I'll always be with you..."

"Katrina, don't go!"

"Don't go!" I yell, sitting up, sweat pouring off my body. I'm alone, but the knocking continues, and I realize someone's trying to get me to open the door. "Go away!"

"*Oniichan*, it's me," I hear, and I get off the bed, going over and opening the door. Andrea is there, and I notice that it's raining, hard. "Can I come in?"

"Of course," I tell her, sort of ushering her inside. She's dripping wet, and I wonder where her umbrella is. Then I realize knowing Andrea, who tends to be her own woman no matter what, she probably rode over here on the Honda scooter she bought a year ago. I glance outside, and my suspicions are confirmed, the distinctive funky tubular frame and dual headlights making it stand out in the downpour. "Why'd you bring the scooter?"

"It didn't start raining until I was halfway here," Andrea explains, twisting out her long hair over the sink in the kitchen area. "When Nathan told me where you were, I didn't take the time to read the weather report."

"Why'd he tell you where I am?" I ask, instantly suspicious.

Andrea sighs and gives me a look before finishing

twisting out her hair and then whipping it back. "I'm dripping wet, soaked to the skin, and to be honest, cold as hell since I had a whipping case of wind chill from riding over here as fast as I could. You mind if I at least dry off a little bit and maybe get something to prevent hypothermia before you start the interrogation?"

That's my Andrea, sweet and supporting one minute, sarcastic and bitchy the next. I nod and look around, realizing that I have no idea where Katrina even kept her towels. I go over to the cheap dresser and open the top drawer, trying not to cry again as I see the single sports bra inside, and a pair of red panties that I for some reason know were from the night we got together in the limo. There's nothing else, she packed and took it all with her in that backpack. I close the drawer quickly and pull open the next one, and can't take anymore. Inside is the pair of black drawstring martial arts pants that she wore when she was relaxing or working out, and I walk away, leaving the drawer open.

The lights deeper in the loft aren't on, but I can see the post in the middle that Katrina had wrapped in padding and tires, and I punch, letting my rage and sadness out. It's not enough, and I punch again, the pain of my knuckle smashing against the unforgiving tire rubber helping a little. Another punch, and another punch, each blow letting me vent my emotions. I feel something split on my hand, and it helps more, so I punch harder and harder. I'm gasping, crying, sobbing maybe, but I keep hitting the tires until I can't anymore, and then I punch a few more times before I drop to my knees. The lights overhead turn on, I guess Andrea's found a light switch somewhere, and I see that the tires in front of me are glistening, dark with my blood, and I drop my head, puking at the horror of the image in my mind of Katrina's head exploding as the last bullet blew out the back of her skull.

Andrea comes over, kneeling next to me, and rests a tiny hand on my back. "It's okay, Jackson. I'm here for you, too."

"Why?" I sob, my stomach turning again before I retch. There's nothing inside anymore, just hot, burning stomach juices that barely splatter out. "Why, Andrea?"

"Because Peter DeLaCoeur is a snake who deserves to spend the rest of his life in jail," Andrea says softly, but with steely intensity. "That's why she died, and why I'm here."

I sit back, and look at my half-sister, who's spent most of her life in a sort of uneasy rivalry with me, but in this instant, there's no taunting, there's not even the sort of dismissive mentor look she had when lending me books on business. Instead I see a supportive, caring person, and in her blue eyes, I see something that I've missed and overlooked for too long. Peter and Margaret might be my parents, but they're sure as hell not my family. Andrea is. "What can we do?"

Andrea stands up and offers her hand. She takes my hand, and there's a deceptive strength in that grip and steel in her eyes as she helps me to my feet. "The first thing we do is get you cleaned and bandaged up. You busted the hell out of your hands, and we need to bandage them. Then... then we'll discuss what I've been doing for the past six years."

* * *

"What do you know of my childhood, Jackson?"

I've taken off my shirt, washing it out in the sink before

hanging it from the end of Katrina's bed frame, while Andrea's changed as well, pulling on one of the t-shirts that Katrina kept in her dresser. Despite Katrina being slender and liking shorter shirts, she was still a lot taller than Andrea, and the shirt hangs past her waist, looking almost oversized on my half-sister. I'm sitting on the bed, my hands stinging from the disinfectant and half dozen bandages that we borrowed from downstairs. Andrea is in one of the chairs, the blanket from the bed wrapped around her shoulders to let her stay warm.

"You came to us when you were still really young. I can't remember exactly when, but I was young myself, I couldn't have been more than three or four."

Andrea nods. "I was brought here from Osaka when I was eighteen months old. The Japanese government was pissed, but since I was brought over on an American passport by agents of my biological father, there was little they could do. I'm an American citizen after all, with a birth certificate from the State of Louisiana even. But that's beside the point. What do you remember about my mother?"

I shake my head. I was so little. "Nothing. I mean, I know some rumors, but I personally remember almost nothing. I know she had an affair with Peter, obviously, but other than rumors, I can't say."

Andrea nods. "I remember almost nothing, too. My grandmother got to send me a few packages when I was smaller, and before my grandparents died, I got a few things. In my room at the house, I have a picture of my mother, back in '94 before she had me, maybe before she met Peter, I'm not sure. She's wearing her student chef's whites, and posing in front of Emeril

Legasse's restaurant. In the photo she's throwing up a peace sign of course, since that's something Japanese people often do when they get their pictures taken. She looked so excited and happy, and it was from wanting to read the letters from my grandmother about my mother that led to my own studies of Japanese. But what really drove me was trying to figure out who she was, and why she died."

"What happened?" I asked. "I mean, I heard she committed suicide."

"That's what the official story is, and after the arguments that she had with my grandmother and grandfather, it's a pretty reasonable story," Andrea says painfully. "My grandmother wrote about her eternal shame and regret that she and my mother argued about her affair with Peter the night before she died, and that she said that I shamed the family. Then there was the note that they found in my mother's dress, tucked into the belt, where she said that she could no longer live with the same."

"You said official story. There's something more?" I ask, and Andrea nods. "Tell me, please."

"Peter was involved. I mean, besides the fact that I was kidnapped out of Japan and brought here, he was involved. I've never been able to prove that he had a direct hand in my mother's suicide beyond a phone call where he basically told her that she was outta luck, but I have my suspicions. What I do know is that my mother's death wasn't a suicide."

"How?" I ask, and realize I may sound like I'm doubting her. "I mean, how'd it happen?"

"Security camera footage showed two men visiting the apartment building where my mother and I lived. It took me a very long time and a lot of connections to obtain it. Later, both men were busted by the cops on an unrelated charge, but what was interesting was that the handwriting of one of the men perfectly matched the handwriting used in my mother's suicide note. Even the grammar and word choice was the same. My mother spoke and wrote in the Kanto-style dialect of Japanese, and from some of her earlier school writings that my grandmother sent me, she had pretty, almost dainty writing. The note was written in a heavy, sloppy hand, and was written in Kansai-ben, the Osaka style of Japanese. The differences are small to foreigners, like using *ore* instead of *watakushi* to refer to herself, but I really applied myself with my language studies... there's no way that Aiko Mori wrote that note."

I gawk, and Andrea nods. "Yeah. So you see why I've got a sword to grind against Peter DeLaCoeur as well. For the past six years, I've been pretty much doing the same thing Katrina was, gathering information. I was just looking to finish my MBA before taking him down. When I heard about what you were up to, I approached Nathan when he came back by himself today. He told me where to find you."

I should be pissed that she's kept this secret from me for so long, but I'm not. Instead, another question comes to mind. "So why have you called me *oniichan* for most of my life, if you hate the family so much?" The Japanese term for older brother is probably only one of maybe five Japanese words I know. However, I know I'm the only person Andrea uses familial Japanese terms with. Peter hates it when she speaks Japanese since he doesn't understand it and never bothered to learn any, and Andrea would never call Margaret her mother in any language.

Andrea gets up off the chair and comes over, sitting next to me on the bed. She puts an arm around my shoulder and gives me a squeeze. "Oh Jackson, I've never hated you. You've pissed me off plenty of times and disappointed me, sure. Mainly it hurt that you spent so much of your life living in denial of who we are and what sort of family we lived in. But I have never hated you. You're my big brother, and I love you. Right now you need my help, and I'm going to be here for you."

I hug Andrea back, fresh tears coming to my eyes, and soon I'm crying again. I wish the little waif in my arms was about six or eight inches taller, that the long black hair was short and brown, and that Andrea was Katrina. Still, it helps, and Andrea holds me back, letting me vent. When it's over, she kisses my forehead, and gives me a smile. "Better?"

I nod, and wipe at my nose. "Yeah. I think I need to invest in some tissues though. I don't see any. I don't think Katrina ever cried."

"I bet she did," Andrea counters. "I've done plenty of crying myself. Now, you know why I'm here. I've got some computer skills too, and with your permission, I want to combine what I've gathered with what Katrina's got. Together, I'm certain there's enough dirt there to put Sam Grammercy and Peter DeLaCoeur away for the rest of their lives. There has to be."

"Let's do it," I say, anger filling my voice. "I don't care about the money anymore. Those bastards took Katrina from me, they need to rot."

"And our money?" Andrea asks.

I shrug. "Doesn't fucking matter anymore. Maybe I'll take what I can before the cops move in, I'm sure I can do some wire transfers or get cash advances on my credit cards that he's paying for, but I honestly don't give a fuck. I'll walk out tomorrow with five bucks in my pocket if I have to."

"Well, we can do more than that," Andrea says with a chuckle as she gets off the bed and goes over to Katrina's computer. She sits down and takes a look, and I can tell, she's impressed. "Whoa... this thing is fucking... I think we could rename this thing Skynet."

"Can you access it?" I ask, and Andrea nods. "Really?"

"I know more than just business. This might take a little while though, unless you know the system, too."

I shake my head, chagrined. "I saw her use it, but she didn't tell me much."

Andrea flips a switch, and the computer hums to life, a glow forming from the flat panel display. "Well then, this might take a little while to get into. Do you have any money on you?"

I pat my hip pocket, and pull out my wallet. I honestly wasn't even sure it was there until I take it out. Opening it up, I see a few bills. "Maybe fifty bucks, why?"

"Because I skipped lunch to argue with Nathan and find this place, and I'm hungry. I saw a minimart on the corner if you turn left when you hit Market Street. Think you'd be willing to make a grub run while I get cozy with the HAL-9000 here?"

"Skynet, HAL-9000... you're a geek, Andrea."

She turns and gives me a smile, and I realize something. I love her, too. "Thanks, *oniichan*. Take a hat or something, I can hear the rain still."

* * *

It actually takes Andrea three weeks to crack the system, during which I can do little more than sit around, read the business books that she brings me, and fuck around on my own laptop. Nathan gives me a call once in a while, but my cover story of just being pissed at Peter is holding pat, and Peter hasn't invested too much effort in finding me yet.

I also start exercising again, copying the movements that Katrina and I went through, and trying some more that I make up from the stuff laying around the loft. I find that the pain of the exercise eases the pain in my heart, and that in doing so, I find myself closer to Katrina. I can understand more about what she put herself through for so many years, and I can begin to understand what drove her to become the woman she was. It's both sad and beautiful, and as I drop the sandbag that I've had over my shoulders, not all the water dripping down my face is sweat.

"You keep pushing yourself like that, you're going to end up with rhabdo," Andrea says from over by the computer, where she's been working for four hours. "I'd prefer to not have to drag you to the hospital on the back of my scooter."

"You brought my car today," I reply, dropping down into a burpee and kicking out before pulling back in and jumping, touching the beam that's over my head. I'd found the two rope handles that Katrina had tied around the beam yesterday for pullups, and realized there were so many little things I still wanted to find. "Besides, rhabdo mostly hits untrained individuals."

"And athletes who refuse to accept that their bodies may

not be as strong as their minds," Andrea notes, turning back to the computer and typing away. "I'm just saying, don't kill yourself over there."

I ignore her and finish my set, stopping when the world swims in front of my eyes and I'm fighting for my balance. Enough, it's enough for now... maybe I can do more later. "How's the process going?"

"I've nearly... got it!" she says, sticking her hands in the air.

I stagger over, sitting on the bed while Andrea clicks away madly with the mouse, typing occasionally. "You're not going to believe all that she's got here. Holy shit, I thought I had information."

"What do you mean?" I ask, staring at the blanket while the world still swims. I lie back, and the spinning slows enough that I can focus on what Andrea's saying.

"I mean, I have gigs of data, lots of documents, and I thought I had a lot. But Katrina... it's going to take me a while, but this thing... she's got just one file folder named 'PDLC' here that has over a terabyte of data. That's like twenty full-length Blu-Ray movies of information."

"What's it all say?" I ask, covering my eyes. It helps some more, and I think that maybe in a minute or two I might even be able to sit up. "I think I might puke."

"That happens," Andrea says dismissively. "As for the info... I haven't had time to go through this all yet. Like I said, if this was a movie, it'd run for about forty hours, just this one folder. I don't even know what the hell else is still on here. I need time."

"Take all the time you need," I reply, sitting up slowly. "Is the computer locked?"

Andrea taps, and shakes her head. "It can be. What do you want the password to be?"

I think for a minute, and know there's only one answer that fits. "Make it... Hagakure. It was her favorite book."

Andrea types, then nods. "Done. First letter capitalized. *Oniichan,* I know that this is important to you, and it is to me too, but I've got some other work I need to get done. Can I leave this in your hands, to start going through the data?"

"Sure, I'll stick to the PDLC files only though."

"Good. By the way, when I come back tomorrow, I'll bring another book for you to read. It's a good one on business evaluation."

I give Andrea a confused look. "Why?"

Andrea grows serious as she gets up and grabs her backpack. "Jackson, we're going to take down Peter. But the best way you can honor Katrina... is to be everything she saw inside you, the same potential I see. I won't let you waste it."

* * *

I barely sleep that night, absorbed by the data that I read. Andrea was right, Katrina's pure amount of gathered information is staggering. I start with the documents, mostly a lot of PDFs, but also text files, copied e-mails, and all sorts of other data. The names I see attached to each are disgusting, and I realize finally just how far deep down the rabbit hole I've been living.

He may not have been responsible for Katrina's father, but Peter's had at least a dozen other men killed. Some of them had families, and some of them were for simply business reasons. Some of them, perhaps the most disgusting ones, were ones he had killed merely because they pissed him off.

After my eyes go bleary from reading text, I switch to some of the audio and video files. I listen to intercepted conversations as Peter tells people what to do to maintain their criminal empires. Most of them sound like Katrina was using some sort of microphone or listening device to get them, and I wonder just how many years she crept around, gathering her data before she was sure she was ready to strike.

Finally, just before dawn, I drop off into a light doze, waking up when I hear someone knocking on the door again. I sit up, realizing I've spent the whole night in front of Katrina's computer, and check the time, seeing that it's nearly eight in the morning. I've only been asleep for about four hours.

"Yeah?" I ask at the door, opening the peephole. I see a black woman outside, tall and statuesque, with intense eyes and a solemn cast to her face. She's pretty, but she wears the same gravity on her face that I've come to recognize on my own face in the mirror. "Who are you?"

"A friend of Katrina's," she says. "My name is Darcy."

I remember the name, and unlock the door. "What are you doing here?"

Darcy steps inside and lets me close the door behind her. "I should ask you the same thing, but I know the answer. Peter's sources may have kept it minimized in the news, but I know what happened. Of course officially, it was just a random shooting without even a body, the bastards. And I know you've had some help, there's no way you got into Katrina's computer without it. It's a pleasure to finally meet you face to face, Jackson."

"Katrina mentioned you, the pleasure is mine," I reply automatically, remembering a little bit of my manners. "How'd you know I was here?"

Before Darcy can answer another knock at the door comes, and I hear Andrea outside. "It's me. I've got breakfast."

I open the door, and Andrea looks startled when she comes in. "Who's your visitor?"

Before I can say anything, Darcy introduces herself. "Darcy Weaver... also known as BlakDhal1A."

Andrea looks surprised, but I'm even more surprised when she offers her hand to shake, since she rarely does that. "Andrea DeLaCoeur... Blue Sakura."

I hold my hands up, confused. "Okay, I'm now officially lost. What the hell's going on, and Darcy, why are you here?"

Darcy points to Katrina's computer. "I helped her build that thing, and I taught Katrina a lot about how to become a world-class hacker. And I had a tag on it that let me know if the computer was accessed. It was a request from Katrina, since she knew what might happen to her. She told me if she disappeared, I was supposed to come here and unleash everything, including what's in her cloud."

"She's got a cloud, too?" Andrea asks, and Darcy nods. "Just how big?"

"Only the juiciest stuff. And her gate controls."

"Her what?"

Darcy smiles. "She had media contacts, network connections, the whole works. The gate controls are that and more. Basically, if we use them, we can shotgun everything we need to take down your father, along with Samuel Grammercy, and a lot of other very bad operators in this town."

Andrea looks at me, and I realize they're leaving the decision in my hands. But it's not really a decision at all.

"Give me twenty-four hours to hit him as best I can my way," I say, my hands clenching. "Then... unleash hell."

Chapter 26
Kat

The converted office I'm using as a hiding space is unfamiliar, and the computer I'm using is barely better than what I could have gotten if I'd just gone down to an electronics shop, but it was all Darcy had available to give me quickly, and for a laptop, it works okay.

"So he's on board now?" I ask, and on the screen, Darcy nods. In the background, Bo is wagging his tail and setting his chin on her shoulder, she's let him up on the couch.

"He is. He made me promise not to wide band the direct stuff on his father until tomorrow, but Samuel... the Miami-Dade cops and FBI are going to be getting the stuff in about ten minutes."

I nod, and rub at the back of my head, where the shaved patch on the back of my skull still itches. Darcy laughs, and I have to chuckle, too. "I don't know why it bothers me, it's just hair. It'll grow out."

"Well, next time you decide to fake getting your brains blown out, maybe remember to fall on the grass and not the sidewalk?" Darcy teases. "Besides, it's been a few weeks. I bet in another month nobody's going to be able to tell the difference, not with as short as you keep your 'do."

I smile and nod. "You're right. So Jackson is going to talk to Peter?"

"He's not going to do anything stupid, I made sure of

that. He knows that Andrea's on his side, and Nathan's going to make sure, too. Remember, Jackson still thinks he needs to walk on eggshells to even get close to Peter, so he won't have a gun or do anything stupid like that. I think he's going to just tell him off, maybe try to hurt him mentally, but I just don't see that having any effect."

I nod, reassured. "That's good. And he believes that you just tracked my computer this whole time?"

"Yeah. I hope you decide to tell him the whole truth someday soon."

"Me too. Okay. I'll confirm his actions with Andrea, he can't let himself get hurt."

"We'll do what we can. Listen Katrina, I don't want to doubt you, but are you sure this is the right way to go about it? I mean, he seems pretty much on our side."

I think about it for a second, while meanwhile on her end Bo licks her on the ear, causing Darcy to laugh and push her dog away, sending him off the couch and into the backyard. "I see you like getting ear kisses, too," I joke.

"Not from him, the big baby," Darcy laughs, then raises an eyebrow. "Well?"

"You and that dog, both of you never let go of something once you sink your teeth into it," I grumble, then nod. "I know it hurts, but I had to be sure, Darcy. I had to know we could take them down, even if Jackson backed out. And the plan's too far advanced now to change it."

"Well, you've broke that boy's heart," Darcy continues, and I wince. Still, I deserve it. "When Andrea called me up telling me what he's been up to the past few weeks, I nearly broke with the plan early. He was about to put himself in the damn hospital he's so broken up."

"I know, Darcy. I know. I regret it, but things are moving now. When the dam breaks, and the cops have both Samuel and Peter... I'll talk to him. I've already made arrangements with Nathan."

"And afterward?" Darcy asks, and I know what she means. Once the information hits the media, in addition to taking down the DeLaCoeur empire, there's going to be a lot of other people looking for blood. New Orleans isn't going to be safe for me anymore, even as a ghost. Too many ghosts get exorcised in New Orleans, and voodoo only works so well.

"Afterward, maybe Katrina Grammercy needs to go away," I say quietly. "But I'm pretty sure Coup De Grace will still be hanging around online."

Darcy nods, and I see a tear come to her eye. She wipes it away, and forces a smile. "I can live with that. It'll be good to see you out there. It'll be good to know... to know you do have a future."

"With luck, we'll all have futures," I reply. "I love you, Darcy."

"I love you too, Katrina. Take care, Baby Girl."

She hangs up, and I can feel in my heart the meaning behind Darcy's farewell. We know the truth, that she won't be able to go with me, and that the next time we see each other may be the last. If there is a next time.

I sit back, waiting the few minutes before turning on the Miami local stations. I'm tapped into the satellite feed each station has with their national desks, and I see that it's the Fox affiliate who gets the feed up first.

"Breaking news from our crime desk. The FBI and Miami-Dade police have found within our city a man who, for the past ten years, everyone thought was dead. Fox's Billie Wagner is on the scene with more."

The scene cuts from the studio to a news van outside the apartment complex where my parents live. The on-site reporter, a kind of young guy maybe a few years older than me, looks like he's halfway scared out of his mind, probably because until this point he's only done human interest stories, kissed puppies, and played with children for the morning show. Billie just strikes me as that sort of guy.

"Yes guys, I'm outside this apartment just south of the University, where an amazing story has come to light. It seems that this man..." the screen cuts to an ID photo of my father, "who for the past ten years has lived and worked in the Miami area under the name Michael Ball, is in fact not who he seems to be."

It continues, but I've seen enough. I turn off the feed and pull out my phone. Tapping quickly, I send a text to Nathan.

Has Jackson come home yet?

No, but I think he'll be here soon, maybe within a half hour. I've prepared the way as best I can. Why?

It just went down in Miami. He doesn't have a lot of time before Peter knows something's up.

I understand. I'll inform him, make it seem like I got a call. He'll let the gates open here.

Thanks. Take care of him, Nathan. And deliver my message.

I will. Thank you for your mercy.

You have more accounts to balance than just ours. Consider it a gift if Jackson comes out safe. If he doesn't...

I understand. I'll text you when it's done.

I hang up the messages with Nathan and sit back. There's nothing I can do now, except hope that whatever powers have watched over me the past ten years can watch over Jackson now.

Another idea comes to mind, and I make another call, this one to Andrea.

"Hello?"

"It's me. I know voice communication is dangerous, but I don't have a lot of time. It just went down in Miami, and I have one more idea I just had. This one... this one's for Jackson."

Andrea sounds suspicious, but hums. "What do you need?"

"I want to get every cent I can from Peter DeLaCoeur. For Jackson. Can you help me?"

Andrea laughs, and I realize she and I have had similar mindsets all along. "You're a little late. I've already been doing it. Give me fifteen minutes and you'll have the number and passcode to a numbered account in the Bahamas. It's one of his smaller ones, but it's all I've been able to verify."

I smile, thinking about just how generous Andrea's being. "And you?"

"I've got my own plans in place. I don't think we'll be seeing each other again. It was nice to spend some time together, my friend."

I hum, thinking that I regret not taking the time to get to know her better. She's a remarkable young woman, but she has her own mission to complete. "I hope that someday, maybe after you've found your own completion... I hope we can see each other again."

"That'd be nice, but we'll see. I'll keep in touch with you electronically at least. Take care, Katrina."

"You too, Andrea."

So the die is cast. I just have to wait, and see how it finally falls.

Chapter 27
Jackson

It's been over a month since I've seen the plantation house, and as I walk up the long driveway from the street, I'm surprised at how unfamiliar it feels. I took a taxi and Nathan told me that if I needed, my Audi was at home for me to get away. A nice option, but I'm not sure if I agree with it.

A few of the staff react with surprise when I walk up, but Nathan is the first to greet me, coming down the wooden steps of the porch. "Your father is out back, near the pool, with a young lady as his company," Nathan says quietly. "And I got a call. The police arrested Sam Grammercy about a half hour ago."

I nod and pull out my phone. I dial Darcy, who picks up quickly. "Yes?"

"Open the gates," I tell her in a flat voice, my emotions so roiling that I'm not able to put any sort of inflection in my speech at all. "Open them wide."

I hang up before she can reply, and go inside to the foyer. I look around, but the place is pretty much deserted already. "My mother?"

"Upstairs, drunk and passed out. Andrea is in the library."

I nod. "Inform her what I just did, and then tell any staff who don't want to deal with the cops to get the hell outta here. I'm going to go have a chat with Peter."

Nathan nods, but doesn't move. "What?"

He looks like he's about to say something, but instead pats me on the shoulder. "*De Oppresso Liber*. Free the oppressed. For too long, I betrayed that motto," he says instead. "Thank you for reminding me what right and wrong are." I nod and pat him in return.

"Thank you, Nathan. Now let's go do what we need to do."

I leave the foyer and cut through the dining room out to the pool area, where I see Peter sitting in a lounge chair next to a picnic table, his gut hanging out over the waistband of his ridiculous Speedos. It's definitely swimwear that might look appropriate on me, but not on a man over fifty and carrying the extra weight he is.

In the pool, a young woman is swimming, most likely his newest girlfriend judging by the thong string bikini and long blonde hair streaming behind her as she kicks under the water. He's so absorbed by the sight of her ass flexing that he doesn't hear me until I'm nearly on top of him. When he does, he has the balls to just give me a cocky smile. "Ah, so you finally got over your little temper tantrum. Good to have you back, Jackson."

"Little temper tantrum," I repeat softly, musing. I go around and sit in the other chair at the table, surprised I'm not in a total rage, but instead icy calm and focused. I've changed so much since that night in the limo with Katrina. "After all that you've done, including having the woman I love killed in front of me, you have the stupidity to call the past three weeks a temper tantrum?"

"Well, hasn't it been?" he asks, smirking. "I mean, the

bitch hurt our family. Nathan told me what happened, and I'm glad that you've finally come home. Now, how about you wait here, and you, me, and Kendra can have a nice dinner together."

"Bringing your girlfriends into the home now even," I say, shaking my head. "Well, enjoy it for another hour or two. It'll be the last."

"What do you mean?" Peter asks, suspicious. "What have you been up to?"

"Oh, not much. I just took all of Katrina's evidence, and there was a fuck-ton of it, and sent it to the cops, feds as well as the local news, and the blogosphere. I bet if you look right now, you'll find pictures of you with women, with gangsters, or maybe with a former governor of this state. Best of all, I've got the e-mails and files that you sent to coordinate the faking of Sam Grammercy's death. Did I mention he was arrested in Miami thirty minutes ago?"

Peter goes pale, and about that time Kendra comes up from another lap, and notices me for the first time. "Oh, hi! You must be Jackson!"

"Leave," I reply, not taking my eyes off Peter. "We have some family business to discuss. Go home, and don't come back."

Kendra stops, looking to Peter, who is staring back at me, and I'm not taking my eyes off him for a second. Kendra huffs, then gets out of the pool. In my periphery, her toned backside is the last thing I see of her as she disappears into the house.

"I don't think she'll be back."

"You inconsiderate little shit," Peter rasps, his voice

quaking in fury. "I gave you a house, raised you, let you do what you wanted, and all I asked for was your loyalty. And you couldn't even do that."

"No, what you did was give me money, nothing else. You never loved me, you never raised me, and the only example you gave me was how not to be a man. You wanted me to just spend your money and stay out of your way while you acted like a pig. Well, I found something more important than money, and you took it from me. So now I've got nothing to lose, and for the first time in my life, I'm doing the right thing. So fuck your money, and fuck you. I should kill you, but I won't. Enjoy prison."

It's cathartic, saying what has been burning in my heart for years, and I feel strong as I stand up, walking past him. He stands up, and tries to grab my arm, but I turn and kick, my foot planting directly in his stomach and sending him stumbling backward onto the lawn, where he lies, groaning and holding his belly. "You broke my ribs, you little shit!"

"For twenty-two years, you broke my heart. I guess that makes us even," I say calmly before I go to the door. Inside, I hear chaos breaking out as the remaining staff passes along Nathan's warning. I can hear the sirens in the distance, and I know we've only got a few minutes, five or six at most.

I see motion off to my right, near Peter's office, and I go over, finding Andrea inside. "What are you doing?"

"What should be done," she says, opening the combination safe that has rested behind a painting on the wall for years. I didn't know she had the combination, but I'm not surprised. Andrea's known so much for so long.

Inside the safe, I see that there's two guns, a white baggie that is most likely coke, and four stacks of cash, along with a black bag. Andrea looks at me, and gestures in invitation. "What do you want?"

I reach in and take the guns, tucking them in the waistband of my pants. "I'll keep you safe as you're getting out. You're ready, I hope?"

She points, and I see the backpack already sitting on the desk. "I've been packed for a while, figuring you'd be moving quick."

I nod and step back. "Leave the drugs."

Andrea chuckles in agreement and reaches in, taking out the cash and the black bag, opening it. Inside are dozens, maybe hundreds of diamonds and other gems. Andrea pokes around a little, then reaches in and takes out a diamond and a sapphire, which I note is the same color as Katrina's eyes. She puts them in my hand, and folds my hand over them. "I hope you can give them to someone special someday."

"Will I ever see you after today, Andrea?" I ask, and she gives me a mysterious smile.

"If fate smiles on us, I hope so. I had so much fun getting to know you better the past few weeks. I'd like to someday see that you've made it the rest of the way."

Andrea puts the stacks of hundred dollar bills in her bag, and then tucks the bag of gems away. "I know some places this can be turned into cash," she says, giving me a smile. "You ready?"

The sirens are getting closer, and I nod. "I love you, Andrea."

"I love you too, *oniichan*."

We leave the library, and in the foyer I see Nathan waiting for us. "The police are at the front of the driveway, waiting on the search warrant. I closed the gate to slow them down, but it won't stop them for long. I'd recommend not taking the streets to get out. There's some ATVs in the stable area, that'd be better."

"Lead on," I instruct, and Nathan's moving, his pistol out just in case, taking us out the side entrance, the three of us running over to the two quad runners and jumping on. We fire them up, Andrea hanging onto me as we haul ass out the back and up the fire road that leads deeper into the woods. "Where's Maverick?"

"A safe place," Nathan yells back, the wind tearing the words from his mouth almost before I can hear them, pointing to the right as we reach a fork in the trail. We take it, roaring at top speed as the sun rises. We're approaching noon, but here, on the edge of the swamps, the mists are still rising from the ground and the visibility is diminishing.

Nathan holds up his hand, slowing his ATV as we reach another split in the trail. "Here's where we split up. The cops shouldn't be looking for us, but still... better safe than sorry."

"Where are we?" I ask, and Nathan points to our right. "What's that way?"

"Two miles that direction is the Jean Lafitte Golf Course. I'd suggest walking in order to avoid attention. My path goes the other way."

I look at the trail he's going to go, wondering where life is going to take him, and give him an appreciative look. "Thank you, Nathan. For everything."

Nathan nods, and offers Andrea his hand, and they shake.

Andrea nods, and they share an unspoken appreciation. Nathan starts his ATV again, twists the throttle, then stops before he can put the vehicle in motion. Reaching into his suit pocket, he takes out a small envelope, like the kind you'd find a kid's Valentine's card in. "I promised someone that I'd give this to you after you spoke with Peter. I hope it brings you happiness, Jackson."

I take the envelope, and see that inside there's a slip of paper. "Where will you go, Nathan?"

He considers for a moment, then gives me a half-smile that's slightly sad. "To go see Aisha. I've got some more debts to balance before then though. Take care of yourself, Jackson DeLaCoeur."

He offers his hand and we shake, and I'm left wondering as the old warrior puts his ATV in gear and rides off toward the bayou. Andrea and I watch him for a minute, then I turn to her, and I see she's already pulled her backpack onto her shoulders. "You ready?"

"Just a minute," I say, tearing open the envelope and looking inside. There's a single piece of paper, an address in Federal City written on it. "Federal City. What's there?"

"Only way to find out is to go," Andrea says, cinching the straps on her backpack tight. I put the paper back in the envelope and tuck the whole thing in my pocket. "Come on. Walk with me one more time?"

I take her hand, and we start down the trail. I've got a

hundred dollars in my wallet, and as we walk, I toss one of the handguns into a nearby pond, where it barely makes a plop as it sinks below the murky, greenish water. So as the golf course comes into view, I've got a hundred dollars, one handgun, and the clothes on my back. The rest of it is useless junk, now probably frozen or soon to be frozen credit cards, a driver's license, and other assorted crap, but I've never felt freer, or richer, in my entire life.

Katrina was right. Without the money, or I guess the strings that come with the DeLaCoeur money, I've got a lot more freedom. It's more valuable than anything else.

Chapter 28
Kat

The local news is buzzing as the sun sets, and I sit on the floor of my hideout, but it's not as bad as I thought it would be. Darcy surprised me about forty-five minutes ago, showing up with a chocolate cake. "Happy Birthday," she says, handing it over. "It's only from the supermarket, but I thought you'd like it anyway."

"Thanks, but it isn't my birthday," I say, confused. "You know that isn't until October."

"No, today's your real birthday. You're born again today," Darcy says. "I left Henry with Jeff. He understands, and he's just grateful that he's not on-duty today. Tomorrow, though, he's not looking forward to work for the short-term. It's gonna hit the fan."

"I bet. Thanks for coming by. Have you heard from Andrea or Jackson?"

"Nope. You heard from Nathan, I take it?"

I nod, taking the cake and leading her into the loft. It's small, but for the past three weeks, it's been a good enough place to crash. I sit down on the couch, and Darcy pauses before sitting down, looking at the small box on the table. She does a double take and points once she recognizes the name that's upside down on the box. "Is that?"

"Yep. I'm late, and wanted to be sure."

Darcy picks it up, and sees that it's empty. "You took the

test."

I nod. "I did."

She gives me a sideways glance, and half a smile. "I've known you for six years, Katrina. You wouldn't be playing coy with me unless the results were something I'd like. Congratulations."

"Thanks," I say, still not sure how I feel about it. This was certainly not in my plans, but I have to admit I feel a little thrill about it. "Maybe now I'll get some decent-sized boobs."

"Either that or you're going to get really good at making formula," Darcy chuckles. "So you're going to keep it, no matter what?"

I nod, and look at the cake. Hey, I'm hungry, and stress makes chocolate look damn good. "I am. Even if he never comes, I want to keep it."

"You sound like he may not come."

I sit back, and turn on the television, where the local news should be starting soon. "Nathan gave him the address, but there's no promise he'll come."

Darcy gets up and goes to the kitchen area, getting two forks. We've been friends for a very long time, we don't need to worry about plates between us. I start on the right, she starts on the left, and we'll work our way toward the middle. "So are you going to take a chance with him?"

I think about what Nathan told me, about how Jackson had told off Peter, kicking him down when he tried to grab him, and more importantly, how Jackson passed up the money and jewels, taking with him only the handguns to protect his sister while they made their getaway. That's not the Jackson from the limo... hell it's not even the same Jackson who flew with me to Miami and thought that a seventy-five dollar a night hotel was slumming it.

Before I can answer, Darcy sets her fork down, and takes my hand. "You know I love you, right?"

"I know, Darce. You've been my big sister for a long time now," I reply, letting her speak. "I love you, too."

She swallows and smiles. "Well, for six years we've known each other, and there's been only one hope that I've had that I haven't been able to see. I've watched as you grew into an intelligent, beautiful young woman and into a hacker even better than me. And we're going to sit here and watch as you get your vengeance, your mission complete. So that leaves only one hope that I've kept inside myself for so long. I want you to find happiness, to find a future. Now, I've only talked with Jackson a little bit face to face. But I saw the way he cares for you, that boy is head over heels for you. Give him a chance. Andrea told me that he's trying to become something, even when it was just the memory of you. Imagine what he can be, what you both can be, together."

I think, then nod. "Well, first, let's watch the news."

The six o'clock news comes on, and Peter DeLaCoeur's arrest is top news. We watch silently as the video feed shows him being loaded into an ambulance, his wrist cuffed to the gurney, holding his ribs and groaning. "Damn, Jackson must have really gotten a shot in," Darcy says. "Wonder how the cops will spin that one."

The story continues as the lead anchor continues the story. Darcy and I had gone through at my lead and released only about half of my files, the ones that most damaged Peter while sparing Margaret DeLaCoeur and Nathan Black what I could. I spared Margaret because I feel at least a little bit of pity for the woman, who's lived in her own version of hell for the past twenty-five years. She's sick more than anything else, and part of me hopes that she'll get treatment for her sickness, although as I watch the police lead a broken, sobbing Margaret out of the DeLaCoeur plantation mansion, I doubt it.

I spared Nathan what little I could because, despite the evil acts he's done, he's trying to repent, to do the right thing. Maybe I've grown a little weak, or maybe I just think the man deserves a second chance, but none of the files that Darcy released have his voice or likeness, and most of the text files don't refer to him by full name. If Nathan moves quickly and uses the contacts I'm sure he has, he'll have a chance to redeem himself.

I couldn't do much for Andrea, but she's told me she wanted her mother's story told. She's got her own mission anyway, and the case of Aiko Mori's death is one of the more dramatic ones, even if it is smaller in terms of scandal compared to the other information the cops and FBI received. A tearjerker for sure, but since it is nearly twenty years old and doesn't have any political sizzle, it doesn't make the broadcast.

"The story of the downfall of what could be the most powerful man in New Orleans, the Don of the Delta, as some people are already calling him, is going to be even more intriguing as the days progress. With multiple sources receiving what is potentially thousands of pages of information along with dozens of hours of audio and video, it will take a long time for the full impact of today's events to be revealed."

I sit back and feel a great weight lift off my shoulders. I close my eyes and bow my head, resting my forehead in my hands as I start to cry, tears of relief and farewell to the pain that I've carried for a whole decade. I feel a hole inside me finally close, and Darcy rests her hands on my shoulders, letting me do what I need to do.

When the tears are done, I wipe at my eyes and look over at Darcy. "Thanks. I guess there's only one thing left for me to see now."

There's a buzz at the security system, and Darcy looks at me. "Ask, and you shall receive. Good luck."

Darcy hurries over to the fire escape and slips out, giving me a thumbs up and a smile as she does. Kneeling once she's out the window, she looks back. "I love you, Katrina. Goodbye."

There's a finality to it, and I nod, blowing her a kiss. "Goodbye, Darcy. I love you, too."

Darcy goes up instead of down, probably to take the second fire escape on the far side of the building, and I hurry over to the security system, where the monitor shows Jackson standing outside the building, looking at the buzzer. He's dressed differently than I've ever seen him, but the hair's the same, and my heart leaps in my chest. He hits the call button again, glancing between the slip of paper in his hand and the numbers on the box. "Hello? I was given this address. Can someone inside help me?"

I look back over my shoulder, to the bathroom area of the loft where I have the last piece of my tests for Jackson and hit the door lock release. I watch just long enough to see that he's pulled the door open and is going to come up the three mini-flights of stairs before I turn and hit the circuit breaker that controls all the lights in the loft and run for the bathroom. The dim light still filtering in through the fire escape window gives me enough light, and I pull on the oversized cloak with padded shoulders and Mardi Gras mask with the built-in electronic voice changer, waiting.

I don't have to wait long, Jackson reaches the door quickly and rings the bell. I come out of the bathroom, and flip the switch that unlocks the loft door, standing with my back against the fire escape, waiting.

I'm surprised, my heart is nearly in my throat as the door opens, and I see Jackson standing there. "Hello?"

"Enter, Jackson DeLaCoeur. You have come to the right place."

Chapter 29
Jackson

It was harder than I thought it would be, saying goodbye to Andrea, but in the end, there was no dramatic embrace or tears. Instead, she gives me a kiss on the cheek, and a smile. "E-mail me when you get a chance. I promise, I'll check it from time to time, although I don't know how often I can reply."

"Good luck, Andrea. I will," I say, watching her climb into the cab. She actually slipped me another hundred bucks from her pile to pay for my cab, which is waiting for me behind hers. I watch her cab pull away, and I get into mine, where the driver is waiting relatively patiently, especially after seeing the Benjamin that Andrea gave me.

"Hey man, that's one fine lady. Your girl?" the driver, a guy with a non-New Orleans accent, asks. He sounds like maybe he's from up north some, not all the way to 'Yankee land', but maybe Arkansas or Tennessee.

"No, she's my sister," I say, my tone clearly showing I don't want conversation. "Federal City."

"You the boss. Mind if I play some music, since you don't sound like you up for talking?" the driver asks, putting his cab into gear. "Federal City's a hell of a drive from here."

"Go ahead," I say, leaning back and closing my eyes. I'm not sleepy, but I still semi-doze as the cabby drives me to Federal City, lulled by the sound of the RnB. I come back to full awareness when he pulls over and turns around. "I'm good, I wasn't sleeping."

"All right man, but you need to give me more directions than Federal City. This is a pretty big place, you know what I mean?"

"Yeah, go along General Meyer here a bit," I say, recalling what I know about Federal City, "I need some clothes and stuff. Let's find a mini-mall or something, you can drop me there."

The cabby shrugs and we drive for about a mile before he finds a strip mall with a hardware store, a dollar store, and a pizza joint. Pulling over, the cabby looks at his meter. "That's forty-five dollars, my friend."

I pass him three twenties out of my wallet, keeping Andrea's hundred for later. "Keep the change, man. Thanks for the ride."

"Have yourself a good afternoon," he says, and I get out of the cab, watching him pull out. I look down at the clothes I'm wearing and realize I need to get rid of it. The name brands, the custom tailored gear... that was the old Jackson DeLaCoeur. The new Jackson... he's not that sort of guy.

My first stop is the hardware store, where I find a pair of carpenter's jeans that's way too baggy, but as I change in the bathroom, transferring my wallet and phone to them, I feel somewhat comforted. They remind me of jeans that Katrina would wear, the same sort of functional bagginess, even down to the fact that I cinch the waist tight with a friction buckle web belt. I chuck my pants in the dumpster outside, and toss my button-down shirt behind it, leaving me in just my tank top undershirt. Going down the mall's sidewalk, I stop in the dollar store and buy a two pack of plain black v-neck t-shirts which ironically costs seven dollars, strange for a place calling itself a dollar store, along with a cheap mesh backpack for ten bucks. I peel off my tank top and pull on one of my new t-shirts, but keep the shirt, tucking it into my backpack. I'm down to sixty dollars, and I don't care.

Content that I won't be recognized as Jackson DeLaCoeur any longer if someone's looking for me, I take out the address from my wallet along with my phone, and do a quick GPS search. My phone still works at least, and I see that I'm about a half mile away, the address being next to the river, in a line of warehouses it looks like. As I walk, I feel myself walking faster and faster, hoping that whoever or whatever is there, maybe there's a future for me.

The building is like I expected, although it looks like the former warehouse has undergone some renovations since the BRACing of Federal City a few years ago. The main door's got a security system along with a line of mailboxes, like a lot of office buildings, or maybe artists' flats. I hit the button for the second floor. "Hello?"

There's no answer, and I start feeling panicked. What if Nathan was fucking with me? What if whoever gave him the address was fucking with him to fuck with me? I take a deep breath and hit the button again. "Hello? I was given this address. Can someone inside help me?"

There's a click on the intercom and then the door buzzes, and I yank at the handle, pulling it open before whoever's inside can change their mind. I step inside and take a deep breath, looking up the narrow, steep staircase. It switches back before reaching the second floor, and I start up, my steps echoing off the painted concrete walls. Ten steps, and then a mini-landing, where I turn and go up another ten, and then another five to reach the landing for the second floor. There's a single steel door with a pane of security glass in it. The glass has been painted over though, clearly a leftover from the days of the building being used by the military.

I see another intercom button and hit it, finding out that it's a buzzer as well. There's a click in the door and I try the handle, finding that it opens easily. Inside, the room is dark, and near the far wall, which has a window that looks like it leads to a fire escape and overlooks the river, is a tall, dark figure. "Hello?"

"Enter, Jackson DeLaCoeur. You have come to the right place," the figure says, and I can tell right away that whoever it is, they're using some sort of voice distorter, there's a clear electronic hum to their voice.

"Who are you?" I ask, stepping in closer. It's so dark I can barely see anything, but there's enough light coming in that I can at least avoid running into anything. "I was given your address by... a friend."

"Nathan Black is a friend, is he?" the figure asks, circling around to the side. I circle with it, and as we move, the light from the window illuminates the person a little more. They're wearing a floor length robe, or maybe some type of cloak with a hood, the kind that looks like it's definitely straight out of a Halloween getup. They're also wearing a Mardi Gras mask, one of the type that covers your entire face and has painted decorations over the eyes, the type normally worn by women. But, if this person is a woman, she's a very tall woman, with shoulders bringing her up to definitely a man's size. "I didn't think Nathan had many friends."

"I don't know if he calls me a friend, but it's a convenient word to use," I reply, not getting rattled. Less than seven hours ago I kicked my father in the stomach and unleashed enough hell to put him in jail for life. Somebody using some parlor tricks and lighting to try and hide themselves isn't going to rattle me, even if it is confusing. "I trusted him enough to come here when he gave me this address, if that's a better definition."

"Better," the figure says. "Have a seat. I have some questions."

I look behind me and see a couch, although it's not much. It's probably been sitting here since this was a military building, and I sit down, carefully avoiding the small coffee table in front of it. I see there's some stuff on the table, but the light's too dim now in the early evening to figure out what it is. "Okay, I'm sitting. What are your questions?"

"First, are you going to use that gun?"

I reach into the waistband of my jeans and take the pistol out and set it on the table. "I don't think I'm going to need that here. I assume Nathan told you I had it?"

"He and I have talked. What brought you here?"

The figure's question stops me, and I think for a moment before answering. "Hope, I guess. Hope that there is a future for me."

"You're Jackson DeLaCoeur. Even with your father in police custody, you should have plenty of money and the ability to get in with the right society people. What do you mean, hope for a future?"

I laugh harshly and roll my eyes. "Money? I've got sixty-three dollars in my pocket, a cell phone that I might be able to hock for twenty bucks, and that's it. To hell with those society people with their connections. And to hell with any money I could scrounge from Peter DeLaCoeur. It's blood money. I can't spend it anymore."

"Who could? Hypothetically, who would be clean enough to spend it?"

"Who?" I ask with a laugh, shaking my head. "Well, I can think of two people. Andrea, my half-sister, and she got herself a share before we left that place... and if she were alive, Katrina. She deserved the whole damn pile."

The figure nods, barely moving. "Tell me about Katrina Grammercy."

I sit back, shaking my head in disbelief. "Are you nuts?"

"It's important to your future," the figure says, the voice emphatic even if it is distorted. "Tell me about Katrina Grammercy."

"What can I say? She was tall, deadly, smart... and so beautiful. I miss her so much. For six years as children, she was my best friend, and in just over a few weeks as adults, I realized she was the one for me."

"Do you love her?"

I stop, and nod, looking down. I reach into the pocket of my jeans and take out the two stones that Andrea gave me, and set them on the table. "If I regret anything about the time I spent with Katrina, it's not that she died. It's not that I'm still living, because as long as I do, there's a part of her that won't die. My only regret... my only regrets are that I didn't have a chance to apologize to her for letting money come between us... and I regret not telling her that I love her. I'll always love her. As we were leaving the plantation, Andrea gave me these two stones, saying that I should give them to someone special someday. I've carried them for the past seven hours in my pocket... and I don't want them anymore. Because the only woman I want to give them to is Katrina."

"How?"

I look at the figure, who's stepped closer, kneeling down on the other side of the coffee table. "If I could, the diamond would be in her engagement ring... and the sapphire would be in a necklace that I'd give her on our wedding day. The blue is the same shade as her eyes were. So yeah, I guess your answer to your question is, yes. I love Katrina, even if she's gone."

The figure reaches for the chin of its mask, pushing it up, and my jaw comes unhinged, dropping into my chest.

"I'm not gone," Katrina says, pushing the mask off and the hood back. "I'm right here, Jackson. And I love you, too."

Chapter 30
Kat

At first, Jackson stares at me, and I can see the thoughts running through his head. The first thought is that he's gone insane, that he's hallucinating, that somehow, the stress and maybe a bit of dehydration have pushed him over the edge for a little while. Next, he thinks that this is some sort of trick, maybe someone in an elaborate makeup job.

But then the truth comes through, and a complex brew of emotions boils inside him. "K... Katrina?" he stutters, and I nod, unzipping my cloak and pulling it off my shoulders. "But how?"

"After our fight, I had to be sure," I say, staying right where I am. It feels appropriate to be on my knees, penitent before him. "I had to make sure that I could complete my mission without you warning or trying to save your dad. Nathan helped me fake the shooting, and Andrea faked the text message from Peter."

Jackson sits back, hurt and angry, and I understand. "You didn't trust me enough to do it?"

"When Nathan and Andrea approached me, no. I loved you, but I knew that you hadn't grown enough at that point. I had to make sure that I could take down Peter. If I didn't, he'd haunt us for the rest of our lives. Hell, I'd be haunted by dedicating so much of my life to it and not succeeding."

Jackson gets up, trying to control his emotions, and walks

around the table, pacing back and forth in front of the window, wringing his hands. "You let Nathan and Andrea know—you obviously had their help in all of this—and you couldn't tell me? Was I just some pawn in your little game? Some puppet to be controlled, like the way Peter controlled other people?"

I lower my head, his words stinging, piercing to my very heart. "Jackson... I'm sorry. To get a monster, I became a monster, and nothing was more monstrous than what I did to you. If it means anything, after Darcy and Andrea talked with me, I did put it all in your hands. That was no lie. You had full control of when to take down Peter. The only thing I did was edit the information released to make sure that it was as tightly focused on Peter as I could make it, to limit the collateral damage."

Jackson stops and turns, looking at me carefully. "Why?"

"Because the first thing I thought of after Andrea woke me up was the look I saw on your face when the fake drive-by happened. Because I realized I'd made a mistake and rushed too quickly. I was too concerned about trying to get it done fast so that you and I could move on, and not doing it the right way. But it was too late. I couldn't take it back. I had to sit here, waiting for the whole thing to come to a head. I put you through hell, and all I could do was sit here and hope that you'd follow Nathan's paper. All I could do was hope that... that you're better than me."

I look down, resting my hands in my lap, ashamed to even look at Jackson any longer. What the hell was I thinking, setting up this elaborate scheme, and all to do what? Test his mental strength? What the hell is wrong with me? What was the purpose of this? I love him, and he loves me. Isn't that supposed to be more important than anything else?

I'm still looking down when I see Jackson's shadow fall over me, and I don't move, closing my eyes instead. I deserve to have him walk out on me and never come back. Instead, I hear Jackson shift around, and I open my eyes to see him kneeling down in front of me and take my hands in his. "You have nothing to apologize for," he says softly, squeezing my fingers. "You had every logical reason to doubt me, and it was only after the past weeks of living in your loft, living the way you have for ten years, that I really understood in my gut what you've put yourself through. You opened your heart to me, wanting me to show you that there's a future between us, and I took the most precious gift you could have given me, and I was worried about money, of all things. Can you forgive me?"

I nod, looking up into his eyes. "I love you, Jackson."

Jackson lifts my chin with his fingers and we kiss, his lips a cool balm on the searing pain that's been eating away at my heart since Miami. He cups my cheek, and I wrap my arms around his waist, tears still flowing, but these tears are of happiness and relief, not of sadness.

"I love you, Katrina," Jackson whispers in my ear. "I want to be with you forever."

I nod and hug him. "I want that, too."

He hums and pulls me close. "Then let's get out of here. I have only two things on my mind right now."

"What's that?" I ask, laying my head on his chest, listening to the heartbeat that I've missed and the heartbeat that I want to build my future around.

"One... I want to get some food. I haven't eaten today, and I'm going to need energy for later."

"Why?" I ask, giving him a smile, knowing exactly what he wants. It's what I want, and it's the right thing to do.

Jackson notices me smile and returns his own. "I think you know exactly why. Let's just keep it cheap, okay? Like I said, I've only got sixty bucks."

"No you don't," I inform him, getting to my feet and helping him up. "Andrea gave you a going away present. Besides the stones."

"Oh?" he asks, raising an eyebrow. "What?"

"A numbered account in the Bahamas. I checked it this afternoon... you've got three hundred and fifteen thousand dollars."

Jackson considers it, then nods. "Okay then. I guess we can get extra cheese on the pizza."

Chapter 31
Kat

The bed is actually more comfortable than my old loft bed. It's a simple queen-size mattress thrown on the floor, and as Jackson lies down next to me, he hums. "So is this what life in the underground is going to be like?"

"Maybe," I tell him, smiling. "But before we do this... I have to tell you something."

"What?" he asks, and I take his hand, placing it on my stomach.

"Jackson, I'm pregnant. I took the test yesterday." I'm a bit nervous saying this, but Jackson takes the news wonderfully, smiling. "You're happy?"

"To create a life with you?" he asks, his smile growing even wider. "Yes, of course! So... I guess I have a question for you, too. I was going to wait, but why wait any longer?"

"Yes and no," I tell him before he can ask. When he raises an eyebrow, I smirk. "Yes, I'll be your wife. No, I won't marry you. I want to keep living off the grid. We can set up fake IDs with a shared last name if you want, but for me... this right here is our wedding."

Jackson gets off the bed and goes over to the table, where the sapphire and diamond have been sitting since he took them out of his pocket and showed them to me. "Then can we get these set in gold at least?"

"Platinum," I counter, watching the lamplight sparkle in

each of them. They're beautiful, and I have to remember to send a thank you to Andrea for them. "Goes better with my skin tone. And no ring, pendants only. That way I never have to take them off when I want to do some martial arts practice."

Jackson laughs and sets the gems aside, letting them clatter lightly onto the small table next to the bed. "I can agree with that. So do you want to make any promises or vows?"

I sit up, and take his hand, placing it on my heart. Jackson takes my hand and places it on his heart, and we look into each other's eyes, his face so serious it's moving. "I promise, Katrina. Forever and always, I will love you and try to be the man you deserve to have."

I blink and take a deep breath, letting his words soak in a moment before replying, wanting every syllable to be the right ones. "I promise to love you, Jackson, forever and always. And I will always strive to be the best wife and woman I can be for you."

Jackson smirks, and leans in. "May I kiss the bride?"

"You better do more than that," I tease, my laugh becoming a moan when Jackson's hand brushes over my nipple. He kisses me tenderly, then with more strength, his arms coming around to pull me tight against him. His kisses move to my neck, nipping and thrilling my skin. "Mmm, that's amazing."

"Good," Jackson says with a light growl, "because now that you're mine, I'm going to punish you for making me go through hell for three weeks."

"Oh?" I ask, thrilled when Jackson pushes me to the side, not too hard, and I look up to see a naughty twinkle in his eye. "Like that, huh?"

Jackson nods and pulls his t-shirt off. He's lost a little bit of mass, but he's more ripped than ever, and I remember that he's spent weeks working himself as hard as I do with his workouts. The bodybuilder puff muscle is gone, and now he's more lean, real muscle. "Turn over, or I turn you over."

I've never been ordered around by a man like this before, and it's with a little thrill that I get on my hands and knees, my ass up in the air. "Take what's yours…"

Jackson leans down and kisses the exposed skin on my back in between the waistband of my pants and my top, and trails his tongue all the way up to my neck before whispering in my ear. "Now, undo your pants and let me see you."

I reach down and undo my belt, a gasp escaping me when Jackson takes my pants in his grip and pulls them down over my hips to my knees. I'm left in just my panties, and Jackson runs his hand over my left ass cheek, stretching out next to me as he does. "I want to look you in the eyes as I do this," he says, and I turn my face to look at him directly. "Three smacks, for three weeks. Fair?"

"Very fair," I agree, then purr. "Sir."

Jackson smirks and leans in. Our lips meet and we kiss, his tongue wrapping around mine. I'm so lost in the kiss that when his hand smacks down, cracking into my ass, the pain is lost in the pleasure and surprise, a warmth spreading from where his hand is rubbing now, massaging and squeezing my ass slowly. "One."

His hand lifts again, pausing for a moment before smacking down again, just on the edge where the warmth and sting become painful, and again he rubs my ass, this time slipping his hand inside my panties and making me moan in desire. My pussy is throbbing, and I can't believe that it feels this good. "Two."

Jackson gets behind me and eases my panties down, lifting my legs one at a time to pull my pants all the way off, leaving me naked from the waist down. I tremble in anticipation as the scent of my arousal hits my nose, and I know he can smell how turned on I am. "Ready, sir."

His hand descends again, smacking against my right cheek this time, a firework of heat that shoots straight through me, and I cry out softly. "Oh, Jackson... my husband..."

Jackson hums happily at my words, and I hear his belt release, but before he can do anything, I turn on the bed, grabbing his hands. "No... please, let me."

He takes his hands away and I unbutton his jeans, not even needing to do the zipper the waist is so baggy. We'd laughed and joked about it as we walked to the pizza parlor, how our fashion sense would be matching more from now on. Now I see another advantage as his cock surges from his boxers, and I wrap my hand around it, licking the head before Jackson can even react. He groans deeply, and I suck him in, running my tongue all around the underside and head of his cock lovingly, worshiping him and trying to show him just how sexy and powerful I know he is.

"Katrina..." he groans, resting his hands on my head. I pause and let him hold my head still as he begins to pump in and out slowly, fucking my face slowly and thoroughly. His cock is thick, sliding deep into my mouth and tickling the back of my throat with each thrust, and I reach under him to cup his balls and roll them between my fingers. "Oh my perfect Katrina."

He pulls out, and I smile softly. "Is that what you like?"

"Fuck yeah," Jackson replies, caressing my face. "Is this what you like?"

"This time," I growl, turning around and wiggling my ass at him. "And this is what I want most."

"Mmm, I like that idea," he says, grabbing my hips and pulling me back. "Just a little rough, but not too much?"

"I can take it pretty rough," I challenge him. "But remember that if you get too rough, I fight back."

Jackson pushes me down, stretching me out on the mattress, with just my ass sticking up a little bit. I feel his cock against the lips of my pussy and he drives forward, stretching me open in one long stroke until he's all the way inside me. Lightning shoots from his cock to my brain as he pulls back and thrusts again, and I give myself to him, wanting Jackson to take me, to make me his forever.

With unrelenting, powerful hammering thrusts, Jackson fills me again and again, his hips smashing into my ass each time. He stretches out on top of me, kissing and sucking hard on my neck, and when he bites, I'm moaning, lost in the pleasure of his cock filling me and his skin pressed against my back. I can feel the pain of his teeth on my skin, and I know he's leaving a mark, maybe a bruise, and I only hope that he actually breaks the skin, scarring me and marking me as his forever.

I'm crushed under him, but I push my hips back, begging for more, and Jackson groans, pleased. He lifts up, and pulls me back onto my knees as he settles behind me. "You are perfect," he says as he starts thrusting again, hard and fast, so fast I'm constantly being lit up with fireworks from another punishing stroke. "Nobody has ever pushed back and wanted more."

"Is that all you got?" I encourage him, looking back. He's covered in sweat, his eyes burning with intensity, and he grabs my waist, his grip almost painfully tight as he stares into my eyes at my challenge. His hips speed up, pounding at me even harder. I'm nearing coming, but I can see in his face, he is too. I urge him on with my most seductive look even as my mouth drops open and I can't say anymore.

My insides tighten, and I'm on the edge, trembling with the need to come. Jackson sees it and thrusts in one more time, burying himself deep inside me, and I'm coming, crying out breathlessly as my body rides the amazing feeling. He thrusts again, adding an exclamation point on my orgasm and sending me higher before he comes, both of us collapsing onto the mattress, temporarily exhausted.

I feel Jackson gather me into his arms again, and I hum softly. "You did this the last time. Are you planning on cuddling with me every time we have sex?"

"I was thinking every night, regardless of if we have sex or not," Jackson says, kissing the sore spot on my neck. "I'm sorry if I was too rough."

"It was perfect," I tell him, wrapping his arms deeper around me. "Absolutely perfect."

"I'm glad."

I chuckle, and kiss his knuckle. The skin is still pink and raw, and I remember the story Andrea told me about how he'd gone off on the tires at my old loft. Apparently, he hasn't let it heal fully before going off on the tires again. "That doesn't mean

I'm not going to give it right back to you tomorrow, though."

"Oh?"

I smile and stroke his forearm. "I've got Touches you haven't even imagined yet, and tomorrow morning, I'm using them all on you."

Jackson laughs softly and kisses my neck. "I can't wait."

Chapter 32
Jackson

I wake up to the sensation of gentle Touches on my forearms, and I smile, even as I keep my eyes closed. "When you said you wanted to give it back to me, I didn't think you were going to be so quick with it."

"After as amazing as last night was? I could barely wait, and you should be glad that you physically wore me out," Katrina throatily purrs in my ear. "Or else you wouldn't have gotten any sleep at all."

I feel her trace along my jaw, and my eyes open, my cock surging as fresh desire fills my body. Katrina... my wife, I think with amazement, is kneeling next to me, her body gloriously naked. I smile at the sight, her nipples already hard. "You know you don't need to Touch me to arouse me. A simple kiss and a smile from you is all I need."

Katrina smiles, and trails a finger down my left side between two of my ribs, electricity shooting throughout my body, concentrating in my cock, which is harder than it's ever been.

I pull her down on top of me, finding her throat and kissing the soft skin. Katrina's groaning from my hands running up and down her back, stroking her skin with tenderness. I kiss down to her collarbone and lift her body up until I can suck on her nipples. They're small, rock-hard treasures that I want to feast on forever, it's so wonderful to hear the sounds she makes as I lick around the edge of her left nipple. I roll her and me together, and kiss my way down her body to her pussy, teasing apart the light covering of dark hair that dusts her labia. "Oh Jackson, I've fantasized of this."

"Then let me fulfill our dreams," I say, dipping my tongue between her lips and tasting the sweetness that lies within. I lick slowly, savoring each inch and listening to the beautiful sounds she makes as I explore her nerve endings with my tongue. "Delicious."

She sighs happily as I lick again, dipping deep inside her and finding the tangy center, scooping out the wetness inside and feasting on it before licking again all the way to the top, where I find the precious shiny jewel nested at the top and just barely caressing it with the tip of my tongue. Her hips lift off the bed like I've just galvanized her entire body.

"Jackson... please," Katrina groans deeply as she wraps her fingers in my hair. "Don't stop."

I don't answer and instead lick, letting my tongue dance around her clit and exploring every nook and fold. I make love to my wife with my lips, tongue and a little bit of my teeth, showing her just how much I love her and will for the rest of my life. I'd die for Katrina... but even more importantly, I'm going to live for her, and make myself into a man that can be her partner as well as her husband and lover.

I pour myself into my licks and oral caresses, my tongue moving faster and lighter, flicking over the precious nub of her clit. Katrina's moaning, grinding her pussy up into my mouth, losing control until with a harsh, ecstatic scream, she comes, covering my face in her juices and clamping her thighs around my head, her muscles unable to relax as she squeezes, cutting off all sound except the sound of my own heart and the sound of her cries from her own body.

Katrina's legs relax, and her hips slowly fall back to the mattress, a long, shuddering breath escaping from her lips. I crawl up from between her legs and rest my left hand on the middle of her chest, looking into her eyes. "I love you, Katrina."

"I love you, my amazing Jackson," she answers, putting her hand over mine. She shifts her hips, then chuckles, feeling the head of my cock bump against her hips. "I may have created a monster."

I nod and raise an eyebrow. "Are you ready?"

She bites her lip and nods, her breath catching as I reach down with my right hand and slip the head of my cock in between her lips. I slide in slowly, knowing she's sensitive and tender, and besides, I want to savor this feeling. I want to savor it forever.

* * *

"Are you sure you don't need some ice?"

I chuckle and look down at my cock, which while limp is still slightly sore and aching after one hell of a time.

"No, I'm fine. Actually, I was thinking in a little bit that I'd like to put on some clothes."

"You don't have any, other than those jeans," she notes, coming over with a glass of juice. Katrina's gotten at least slightly dressed, a pair of boy-short panties and one of her ever-present sports bras. "Oh, and two t-shirts. Just what were you thinking not packing anything?"

"I didn't care about anything else at the moment," I tell

her, taking the juice and sipping gratefully. "I knew that I could make it without the money. Besides, I'm free now, which is better than all the designer clothing in the world."

"Well, tomorrow then, we'll get you outfitted. Until then, I guess you're just going to have to lie around mostly naked and let me pamper you."

I laugh lightly and reach up, taking her hand, pulling her down next to me on the couch. "You know, the first two times we were together, you embarrassed me, then nearly broke my arm while sticking a gun in my face. And now you're pampering me, as you put it. Don't tell me the sexy seductive ass kicker's gone?"

"Not at all," Katrina says, giving me a knowing smile. "But I have a soft side too, you know. I was thinking actually that I'd like to spend a few months exploring that softer side."

"What'd you have in mind?" I ask, sitting up. "I mean, besides maybe a honeymoon?"

"A honeymoon for sure," Katrina replies, smiling, "but only after we get you a fake ID. I know a guy who does good work."

"Then what?"

Katrina strokes my face and kisses me on the cheek. "Then we let you finish your education, with me being your guide. I can't help you on the business courses, but I can help us make a comfortable living below the radar for as long as we want."

I nod, knowing exactly why. Katrina's blast of information may have taken care of Peter and Samuel, but there will be friends, allies, and others affected who will be looking for revenge. It's going to be dangerous, but I think it's worth it. "Okay. Well, you said we've got what, three hundred thousand or so?"

"Something like that. More importantly, we've got connections."

"Then let's tag a quarter million for building our future, and the rest we can use for taking the time to figure out what that future is going to be," I tell her, taking her hand. "As long as that future is next to you and our daughter, I'll be happy."

"Daughter?" Katrina asks, giving me a little smile. "So you want a daughter and not a son?"

"Oh, I'm sure we'll have a son together eventually, but I've got a feeling," I tell her, and then kiss her softly. "Just a feeling, that's all."

"Careful, unless you're ready for what your lips are starting," Katrina purrs, then lays her head on my shoulder.

I kiss her and pull her closer. "Any ideas for the honeymoon?"

Katrina thinks for a moment, then nods. "Catalina Island, off the coast of California. I read about there when I was training... I've always wanted to go."

"That sounds perfect to me. Then we can plan the rest of our future."

Katrina hums and snuggles against me. "Our future. I like the sound of that."

Epilogue
An Online Chat Room

Kat- So did you guys get the files I sent you?

Andrea- Yes. She's beautiful.

Darcy- I agree. She's got your face and his eyes.

Kat- Which I am very grateful for. Although I guess I should worry when she gets old enough to attract boys.

Andrea- Are you kidding? The boys are going to be scared of pissing off her mother and father.

Darcy- LOL. True. By the way, you like her name I bet.

Andrea- Of course I do. I think Andrea's a beautiful name for a little girl.

Kat- As soon as she came out with those blue eyes, we both knew exactly what to name her. How's it going by the way?

Andrea- It's going. If I need help, I know who to call.

Kat- Damn right.

Darcy- Ditto. Hey guys, Jeff just got home, and Henry's hungry, so I'm going to take off.

Kat- OK. Hey, tell him congrats on the promotion. Detective now. Movin' on up.

Darcy- Deluxe apartment in the sky, Baby Girl. Take care, TTYL.

Kat- LU, Darce.

Andrea- Take care, Darce.

System- *BlakDhal1A has logged off*

Andrea- So is the gym going well?

Kat- We're doing the grand underground opening next week, but the privates and seminars are already netting us a good student base. Between him teaching the men, me the women, and us splitting the kid's classes, we're going to do well for a place that technically doesn't exist.

Andrea- What about your other investments?

Kat- Doing well. Your advice was dead on. Thanks.

Andrea- Don't thank me. I just verified what oniichan picked out. He's a smart one.

Kat- You sound proud of him.

Andrea- I am. Aren't you?

Kat- I'm proud of both of you. Hey, Andrea just woke up, she wants some Mommy time. I'm gonna take off myself. Give her some milk, then Jackson and I are going to work together on that '67 Corvette model that we picked up last week. I thought it'd be juvenile, but we're both loving it.

Andrea- OK. I love you, Katrina.

Kat- Not Katrina anymore, remember?

Andrea- Oh yeah. Sorry. I love you, Mercy. BTW, I like the sound of that. Mercy Hart.

Kat- Thanks. I like it, too. I love you too, Andrea. TTYL.

Andrea- TTYL

System- *CD Grace has logged off*

System- *Blue Sakura has logged off*

Thank you for reading. If you enjoyed this book, please take a moment to leave a review. Be sure to check out the next books in this series.

**Revenge is Book 1.
Retaliation, Book 2.
Retribution, Book 3.

Manufactured by Amazon.ca
Bolton, ON